A Penny for 'em

L.W.KING

ISBN:9798808285927

For my Mum, forever in my thoughts….

CONTENTS

A Penny for 'em……

Chapter 1

The door knocked breaking her chain of thought. "Come in." She called out. As the door opened, she sighed as she looked at her granddaughter. She hardly knew her, yet here she was, this thin, undernourished girl who, was now taking care of her every need, never complaining, and always smiling. Peggy placed the tray in front of her and gently wrapped the napkin around her neck, then took the cover from her steaming lunch of fish with bread and butter. Peggy smiled her wide smile and walked towards the door.

"Thank you." Carrie called out and smiled to herself, while Peggy nearly collapsed with shock. That was the first time her grandmother had spoken to her without wanting something, and it was the first time, since her sad arrival, that she had thanked her for anything. Peggy walked out to the kitchen shaking her head in disbelief!

Peggy filled the big sink with water, singing away to herself when she heard Carrie's bell ring. She dried her hands as she sighed and hurried to Carrie's room. She knocked on the door and flushed with relief when she heard Carrie tell her to come in. Since Doctor Clarke had visited a few days before, he told Peggy very quietly that Carrie may not have much longer, Peggy had been a bag of nerves. She walked in and Carrie gestured for her to take the tray, waving her hands as she coughed. Peggy took the tray and smiled.

"Is there anything I can get you?" She asked timidly, she didn't mind admitting that Carrie scared her. Carrie waved her hands at her and then gestured for her to leave. Peggy left the room and walked back to the small cottage kitchen. She scraped the majority of Carrie's lunch into the bin and washed the dishes.

She was putting the dried dishes away when there was a knock on the back door. Peggy hurried and opened it. There was a thick set, stern looking, middle aged woman with her arms folded in front of her. "Can I help you?" Peggy asked.

"And whom might you be?" The woman boomed.

"I am Peggy." She replied confidently to the sour faced woman. The woman shook her head and huffed.

"I wish to speak to Mrs Wells." She snorted. Peggy smiled and shook her head.

"I am sorry, but Ms. Wells is not accepting visitors at the moment. Is there something that I could help you with?" Peggy asked and smiled again, watching as the woman was becoming increasingly agitated.

"And when will she be accepting visitors again?" The woman

shouted. Peggy shrugged her small shoulders.

"I have no idea." She replied. The woman huffed.

"Well tell her that Mrs Baldwin was here, and I shall return in two days to collect what she owes me, six months is too long to wait!" The woman boomed and stormed up the path. Peggy chuckled as she watched the large woman struggle to get through the gate! Peggy closed the door and walked towards Carrie's door. She tapped gently, no reply. She knocked a little louder.

"What is it?" Carrie shouted. Peggy was worried that she had woken her. Peggy opened the door and peered around. To her astonishment Carrie was not in her usual position in bed, she was fumbling around at her dressing table. Peggy slowly walked into the room towards the dressing table.

"Sorry to trouble you Ma'am ,but there was a woman here to see you. She seemed very insistent. I told her that you were not accepting visitors at the moment. I hope I did the right thing Ma'am." Peggy said nervously.

"For goodness sake child, how many times do I have to tell you not to call me Ma'am!" Carrie said and frowned.

"Sorry" Peggy muttered quietly.

"Was she a big woman, with a hard face?" Carrie asked. Peggy nodded.

"Aye, she told me to tell you that Mrs Baldwin was here…."

"And she came for what she is owed. Yes?" Carrie interrupted.

"Aye. She will return in two days." Peggy replied.

"Oh why don't they all just leave me alone. Well, let her tell the authorities. What are they going to do to a dying witch!" Carrie shouted as she slammed her ornate hairbrush onto the dressing table.

Peggy wasn't sure what to say or how to react, she stood looking at Carrie as she now made her way across the bedroom towards the closet. Carrie opened the closet door and was struggling to pull something out. Peggy ran over to her.

"Let me?" She said and smiled. Carrie sighed and then smiled back. Peggy pulled out a big wooden chest and placed it at Carrie's feet.

"Thank you." Carrie smiled.

"You're welcome." Peggy replied as she walked towards the door.

"Peggy" Carrie called after her. Peggy turned and walked back to her. "Have you ever had visions, or anything strange happen to you?" Carrie asked. Peggy pondered for a moment.

"Aye, I knew that my Ma was going to die when I was young, I knew that I would come here to you. I saw you in my dreams." Peggy said. Carrie smiled and nodded.

"Mrs Baldwin is the wife of the local police sergeant. She has been visiting me for the last twenty years. She told me that if I didn't do as she asked she would tell her husband that I was a witch, and that I was cursing the folk in the village." Carrie said. Peggy frowned.

"What does she ask you for?" She asked. Carrie chuckled.

"Well between you and me, her husband has, how can I put it, a wondering eye. She wanted me to create a spell that would stop him from straying from the marital bed." Carrie said and laughed.

"Is there such a spell?" Peggy asked. Again Carrie laughed.

"If there were, I am fairly sure that my door would never stop knocking! No I found a harmless cake recipe in my old grimoire that was passed down to me, so for the last twenty years, once a month,

Mrs Baldwin has come to collect her magical cake." Carrie said and winked. Peggy chuckled.

"So what does the spell actually do?" She asked.

"It improves virility!" Carrie said and laughed, forcing herself into a fit of coughing. Peggy grabbed her hanky and handed it to her and then helped her back to the bed. She made sure that Carrie was comfortable, she could see that she was becoming fatigued.

"I could make the cake if you like." Peggy said. Carrie tapped her hand and nodded just as she fell asleep.

Peggy walked out to the garden to bring in the clean laundry, it was a surprisingly lovely day, which was unusual for Melrose, she was thinking to herself as she hummed. She looked into the bordering fields and saw William, he was putting in fence posts. He waved to her, she blushed and waved back. He walked towards the garden, Peggy's heart was beating fast. She was so lonely and seeing William, made her day.

"Hello Peggy." He said as he took his cap off and wiped his brow. He had a mop of beautiful dark hair.

"Hello William." She replied as she blushed.

"There's a dance in the village on Friday night, I was wondering, if you would like to come with me, you know, get to know the folk around here?" He asked and smiled a warm smile at her.

"I would like that very much, but…."

"But… I knew that there would be a but. Sorry forget that I asked." William said.

"No wait William. I really would like to come with you, it's just my grandmother, she's not too well at the moment." Peggy said as she began to panic. William frowned.

"It will only be for a couple of hours, I'm sure that she'll be fine." He said, looking almost disappointed.

"I'll see what I can do." She replied and smiled.

"Great I'll pick you up at seven then!" He grinned and walked back to the field.

Peggy walked back into to the cottage and looked at the clock. She placed the washing basket onto the table and walked to the pantry. She needed to start preparing the evening meal. She walked back through to the kitchen, laden with vegetables and meat, when she heard Carrie cry out. She dropped what she was holding and ran to Carrie's room. She flew through the door, to find Carrie lying on the floor beside the chest.

"Oh my goodness!" Peggy cried as she ran over to her. She tried to help her up, but she was only small, and couldn't do it. "Wait there, I'll go and get help." Peggy said, panicking as she ran out of the door, as she reached the garden she called William. He ran over to her and then followed her into the cottage. Together they lifted Carrie and put her back into bed.

"What on earth were you doing?" Peggy asked as she checked her over. Carrie looked at William who was standing beside the bed. "Oh sorry, this is William, he works at the farm next door." Peggy said and smiled at him.

"Does he now! Well thank you William, I feel embarrassed, I don't usually make a habit of falling over." Carrie said.

"That's ok Ma'am, it was no problem, I was happy to help." He said tipped his cap, winked at Peggy, and left.

"Now then what were you doing to make you fall?" Peggy asked

"I was trying to pull the chest closer to the bed. I wanted to give you the recipe for the cake." Carrie said and winced when she moved.

"Where does it hurt?" She asked anxiously.

"It's just my thigh, I must have bruised it that's all, stop worrying." Carrie said. "Now open the chest and look for a very old book." She added. Peggy nodded and opened the chest. She took out all manner of things until she reached the book. As she held it in her hands, it felt as though it was buzzing. Peggy passed it to Carrie. Carrie smiled.

"Did you feel the energy?" She asked. Peggy smiled.

"Aye" She replied. Carrie opened the book and smiled, the biggest smile. She stroked the pages lovingly, as she seemed to be lost in her thoughts. To Peggy's utter astonishment the pages began to flick back and forth on their own. Then they stopped.

"Ah here it is!" Carrie said and passed the book to Peggy. "What isn't in the pantry, you will find in the shed in the garden." She added.

"I'll start work on it tomorrow. Are you ok, do I need to call Dr Clarke?" Peggy asked. Carrie shook her head.

"No, no, no. I'm fine." Carrie said as she laid her head down on her pillow. Peggy walked back to the kitchen to start preparing the meal.

Peggy had made a scotch broth for tea. She had spent two years of her young life caring for her sick mother before she died and all that she could get her to eat was scotch broth. She prepared the tray and dished up a small bowl for Carrie. She sliced some bread and put it on the tray. She walked to Carrie's room and gently tapped on the door.

"Come in" Carrie called out in an unusually cheery voice. Peggy raised her eyebrows and opened the door. Carrie was sitting up in bed, she looked as though she had a new lease of life. Peggy placed the tray of food on Carrie's lap and was about to place the napkin around her neck, exactly as she had done three times a day, ever since Carrie had become bedridden. Carrie raised her hand to stop her.

"I'll do it." She said gently and smiled. Peggy smiled and walked over to the fire, she added some more coal. "Peggy, why don't you eat your supper in here with me? You must be sick of the sight of that kitchen." Carrie said and sipped the broth from the spoon. "Mmm, this broth is delicious." She said as she savoured her mouthful. Peggy flushed with embarrassment, she didn't know what to say. She smiled at Carrie.

"I'll go and fetch mine." She said still blushing, as she walked back to the kitchen. She dished herself a small bowlful and took some of the bread, then walked back to Carrie's room.

"Pull up a chair beside the fire." Carrie said. Peggy did just that. She sipped at the broth and could feel Carrie watching her. She turned slowly and noticed that Carrie had finished. She placed her bowl on the floor and jumped up. "What are you doing? Eat your food young lady, is it any wonder that you are all skin and bones!" Carrie said and tutted. Peggy blushed and continued eating.

"You must have felt incredibly lonely these last few years, I haven't exactly been the greatest companion have I ?" Carrie said sadly and shook her head. Peggy smiled.

"I cared for my Ma for two years before she died, so I'm pretty used to solitude." Peggy replied. She stood up and walked to the bed to take Carrie's tray.

"That was delicious! Why don't you make us both some tea, and maybe we can spend some time getting to know one another." Carrie said as Peggy took the tray.

"Ok" Peggy chirped. She smiled as she placed the tray down onto the table. She put the kettle on the stove and began to warm the teapot. For the first time in years, Peggy actually felt warm inside. She began to hum as she washed the dishes whilst waiting for the kettle. She cleaned the tray and placed the cups, milk, and sugar on, and then eventually the teapot.

She moved a small table in Carrie's room between the bed and the chair and placed the tray on it.

"Shall I be mother?" Peggy asked and chuckled. Carrie chuckled. Peggy handed Carrie a cup of tea and then poured herself one.

"Be a dear and pull the chest over here will you?" Carrie asked. Peggy did as she asked and dragged the heavy chest to the bed. Carrie threw back the covers and spun her legs around. Slowly she stood and bent over the chest. She passed Peggy a photo. In the photo was Carrie and a beautiful black and white dog. Peggy smiled and looked at Carrie.

"How long ago was this?" Peggy asked as she handed it back to Carrie. Carrie studied the photo.

"That was when I first moved here, so it must be about twenty-two years ago." Carrie sighed.

"Who was the dog?" Peggy asked.

"That was Merlin, my border collie. The farmer next door, you know the same farm where young William works, they were the parents of your Mum. When their dog had puppies they gave him to me to keep me company!" Carrie said and smiled. "Merlin was the best friend that I have ever had" Carrie said sadly as she looked at the dog.

"He was beautiful." Peggy said and smiled. Carrie smiled and then looked back inside the chest. She pulled something wrapped in black cloth out, and then sat on the edge of the bed and unwrapped it. It was a photo album. Carrie patted the bed beside her gesturing for Peggy to sit beside her. Peggy sat down and Carrie began to turn the first page of the photo album. The photo's looked really old.

"That was me as a baby. My father knew a student of photography who took it." Carrie said as she ran her hand over the decaying photo. Peggy smiled.

"You were a beautiful baby." She said. Carrie tapped her hand. Again she turned the page. It was a photo of three small children. Two boys and one girl.

"These are my children." Carrie said. Peggy looked. "The boy in the middle is your father." Carrie said and smiled at the cheeky faced boy. Peggy grinned. "Do you have memories of him?" Carrie asked. Peggy shook her head.

"No I was six when he died. I remember the day, as I had to care for Robert, while the undertakers were at the house." Peggy said sadly, when she thought about her little brother, it always made her feel sad. Carrie smiled a sad smile and nodded.

"So the eldest one, that one there was called George, the one in the middle, your father was called Albert, and the little girl on the end was called Polly." Carrie said, tears began to sting her eyes. Carrie wiped her eyes and turned the page. There was a photo of the three children with a man in uniform.

"Who is that?" Peggy asked as she looked at the handsome man.

"That is my husband Abraham." Carrie said, this time showing no emotion. Peggy wasn't sure whether she should say something.

"Did… did he die?" Peggy asked reluctantly, she thought that she had a right to know considering that he was her grandfather. Carrie looked at Peggy, and eventually shook her head.

"No… no he didn't die." Carrie said and closed the book. Then she yawned.

"Well enough of this I am absolutely exhausted!" She said as she yawned again and placed the book back inside the chest. Peggy stood up and moved the chest, so that it sat beside Carrie's bed, then gathered the teacups and placed them on the tray.

"Well I'll help you into bed and then I'll bid you a goodnight." Peggy said as she swung Carrie's legs around and pulled the covers over her.

"Peggy, do you think that tomorrow, you may be able to do something with my hair?" Carrie asked.

"Of course! I could curl it for you." Peggy replied.

"That would be wonderful!" Carrie said as she laid back and closed her eyes.

"Ok, well goodnight." Peggy said as she grabbed the tray and walked to the door.

"Goodnight dearest Peggy." Carrie mumbled half asleep.

Chapter 2

Peggy opened her eyes. The cockerel was in full song and the light was streaming through the thin curtains. She put on her glasses and looked at her watch. It was five thirty. She slid her legs out of her warm bed and winced when her feet touched the cold vinyl flooring. She put on her gown and slippers and walked down the stairs. She lit the aga in the kitchen and placed the kettle on top of the stove. The sun was shining, it looked as though it was going to be another beautiful day.

She crept along the small hallway until she reached Carrie's door. It was the dining room, but when Carrie became bedridden it was decided that she would be better down the stairs. Very quietly Peggy opened the door and looked around. Carrie was sleeping peacefully so Peggy went back into the kitchen and poured herself a cup of tea. She opened the back door and stood in the doorway drinking her tea and enjoying the fresh air.

She heard whistling and instinctively knew that William was nearby. She quickly patted her wild curls down and leant against the door frame. A shadow passed and then he appeared.

"Good morning!" He said cheerfully. Peggy's legs turned to jelly as her heart began to beat faster.

"Good morning" She replied and blushed.

"I have just finished milking so I thought that I would pop by and see how your grandmother is this morning?" He said in his husky voice, as he passed her a jug of milk. Every time he spoke it made every part of her tingle.

"She is doing ok. Would you like a cup of tea?" Peggy asked. William looked all around and then smiled and nodded. He sat at the table, while Peggy poured him a cup. He was gazing at her. She looked down and realised that her gown had opened, and he could see her nightdress. She quickly wrapped herself up and could feel her skin redden.

"So what about Friday? Are we still on?" He asked as he finished his tea and placed the empty cup in the sink. Peggy nodded.

"Aye, I don't see why not." She said and smiled. William walked over to her, towering above her. He leant down and pushed his soft lips against hers.

"Terrific!" He said and walked out of the back door whistling.

Peggy was so happy. She grabbed the broom and danced around the kitchen pretending that it was her and William. Then Carrie's bell rang. She straightened herself up and glided to Carrie's door.

"Good morning!" She almost sang as she opened the curtains. Carrie yelped as the light hit her tender eyes.

"Good morning. Did I hear voices?" Carrie asked.

"Oh it was just the young boy delivering the milk." Peggy said as she blushed, helping Carrie to sit up.

"Really? I thought that it sounded like William." She added and grinned.

"What would you like for your breakfast?" Peggy asked as she straightened the sheet. "How about porridge?" She added. Carrie screwed her face up.

"Urrgh, no thank you, absolutely detest the stuff. I would rather have some bread and jam." Carrie replied.

So after breakfast once all of the chores were done Peggy washed Carrie's hair and then sat her at the dressing table. She ran the comb through her long white hair. It was beautiful.

"So are you going to tell me about yourself then?" Peggy asked as she wrapped the first section of hair around the roller.

Carrie's story.....

Life was hard, so very hard. London was filthy and their tiny house was falling apart. She was born around 1890 and they lived in a pig keepers cottage in Notting Hill. Her father, Ambrose a man from Kent, was a kind man and he thought that he would provide better for his family if he moved them to London. Her mother Kate was Irish, she was a harsh stern woman with a violent temper.

She could remember back to the time when she must have only been about three or four years old. She was going through a bout of sleepwalking. One night she had left the cottage. When she returned her mother demanded to know where she had been. She had no recollection, so her mother tried to beat it out of her. She remembered being huddled up on the hessian mat crying and sobbing until her father came home. He hugged her and told her that he was sorry, sorry for the shit life that she had, and he made a promise that things would change. She loved her Dad so much, he was such a kind soul, and always tried his hardest to put food in their mouths.

She shared a tiny room with her sister Hester who was three years older than her, and her Mum and Dad. One night, when Carrie was about seven, she and Hester were in the bedroom, having been sent there by their mother. She had been drinking and was demanding money from their father to go back to the alehouse.

She was screaming and shouting at him. He was exhausted, out at dawn until sunset, trying to scrimp a living from selling fish. Then they heard it. Their mother began a violent attack on their father, and him being the good soul that he was would not retaliate. Carrie could stand it no longer. She ran down the stairs and jumped onto her mother's back as she repeatedly punched their father. She threw Carrie off, who landed in a heap on the floor. *Get up and stop her!* She heard the voice say. She jumped back up and pulled her arm back. She went to punch her mother, but before her hand even touched her, her mother flew through the air and landed by the door unconscious.

"What the bloody hell?" Her father said as she stood next to the unconscious woman.

"I'm sorry Dad, I didn't want her to keep hurting you!" Carrie sobbed, holding onto her Dad's leg. He bent down, cradling the sobbing child in his arms.

"Hey, I'm not cross with you. I only shouted at the way you packed that punch" He said and smiled. He wiped Carrie's tears away as she chuckled. Her mother started to regain consciousness and Carrie looked at her dad. She was scared. Her mother pulled herself up and wiped the blood from her mouth. She looked at the blood and then at Carrie.

"You defiant little bastard!" Her mother screamed as she headed towards Carrie with her fist clenched. Hester jumped on her mother's back, her mother threw her off. She raised her hand to strike, when Carrie pulled her fist back and threw a punch, again without even touching her it sent her mother hurtling through the air.

Carrie's father walked over to the dazed woman, put his hand in his trouser pocket and threw whatever coins he had at her.

"Go on, piss off to the alehouse, drink yourself into a bloody stupor, see if we care." He growled. She grabbed the money and headed out of the door.

Later that night their dad was snoring so loudly that it was keeping both the girls awake.

“Carrie, how did you do that?” Hester asked.

“I don’t know. My hand felt all tingly. Do you think that she’s going to beat me when she gets home?” Carrie asked anxiously.

“I think she’s probably too scared to!” Hester laughed, Carrie laughed too, even though deep down she was petrified at the repercussions that may happen. Eventually they both fell asleep.

Carrie woke the following morning to shouting on the street. She got up and moved the hessian that was covering the small hole, which was supposed to be a window. Two men were shouting at one another. Carrie moved away from the window and looked around the room. Her dad had left already, Hester was asleep as too was her mother, who reeked of alcohol. Carrie quietly crept down the stairs and out of the broken door.

She wasn’t sure which stench was worse, the stench of sewage outside or the stench of her mother inside. She walked to the nearest standpipe with her jug. She wanted to wash her face. There was quite a queue when she arrived, and at least two fights broke out while she was waiting. She stood quietly taking it all in, speaking to no-one and not making eye contact. It was finally her turn to fill her jug. Once filled she turned and a filthy looking man who was stood beside her sneering at her. He walked towards her and grabbed the jug. She held onto it, water spilling everywhere. He pulled his hand back and smacked her across the face. She yelped out in pain. Without thinking she pulled her fist back, as she lunged to hit the man, he flew through the air to the gasps of all the onlookers. Carrie dropped the jug and ran as fast as her small legs would carry her.

She ran into their tiny cottage, trying to catch her breath as she closed the door behind her. She was met with her mother's angry gaze.

"Where's the water?" Her mother yelled.

"I filled the jug, but a man attacked me and stole it." Carrie said fearfully. Her mother walked towards her, and back handed Carrie across the face. Carrie defiantly showed no emotion, even though her cheek was throbbing.

"Go on cry you little bastard!" Her mother said and pulled her hand back to strike again. Carrie pulled her hand back and sent a punch towards her mother. Exactly the same thing happened again. Her mother was sent through the air, landing in a heap on the floor beside the door. Carrie opened the door and ran, as fast as her small spindly legs would carry her. She had to dodge through the legs of the many people on the streets. She ran down a dark alleyway and stopped so as to catch her breath.

She looked all around her and apart from the alehouse delivery cart, she was alone. She looked towards the end of the alley and noticed a strange mist, which was making its way towards her. She gulped and cowered backwards. The mist stopped at her feet and vanished. There stood a woman, dressed in strange looking clothes. She smiled at Carrie and from that moment, Carrie knew that she had nothing to fear. The woman said not a word but held her hand out for Carrie to take.

Carrie gripped hold of her hand, she felt the same tingling sensation, that she felt when she first lashed out at her mother. They walked to the end of the alley and turned the corner. To her complete astonishment they were now in a meadow, the wildest, most beautiful meadow, it was just as she had seen in her dreams. The woman beckoned for her to sit on the grass, which she did. She sat down beside her.

"My name is Abagail." The woman said gently. Carrie instantly recognised the voice. It was the same voice that she had heard many times before. It was the same voice that had spoken only the night before, telling her to get up and stop her mother. "I am your ancestor. I watch you young Carrie, I see the pain and torment that you go through, and I am aware of your gift." Abagail said and smiled.

"What gift?" Carrie replied in almost a whisper.

"What happened with your mother and the man at the standpipe. You have so much powerful energy, that when you are threatened or afraid, you do not even have to strike a person to stop them." She said and brushed Carrie's dirty hair out of her eyes. Carrie nodded, being but a child she didn't really understand what the stranger was saying to her.

"You will suffer greatly through this life Carrie, because you have a good soul and a kind nature. Whatever comes your way, always bear that in mind and continue to be the best that you can. I will always stand beside you." Abagail said, then vanished. Carrie looked around and she was sat in the middle of the alleyway, where Abagail had appeared to her. She jumped up and ran back towards the cottage hoping that her vile mother had gone to the alehouse.

As she approached the cottage she walked slowly towards the door. The door flew open, and she hid behind a cart. Her mother walked out, looking up and down the street, mumbling to herself. She stumbled out onto the filthy street and headed towards the alehouse. Carrie ran into the cottage and closed the door.

Ambrose had finished his fourteen-hour day selling fish to local businesses and was walking back towards the cottage with his horse. He couldn't afford a cart. He was dreaming to himself of how he would so much love to take his girls away from this filth ridden hole and that monster that he married. Take them to the countryside, where the three of them could live happily.

"Your young un can pack a punch." George the meat seller said from across the lane. Ambrose looked at him and frowned.

"What you on about?" Ambrose replied, as he tied the horse up.

"Caused quite a stir she did at the standpipe this morning." George replied. Ambrose shook his head, he didn't have a clue what he was talking about. "Some geezer tried to take her jug, sent him flying she did!" George coughed and laughed at the same time. Ambrose chuckled and raised his hand as he took the fish from the saddlebag and walked into the cottage.

Hester was sitting looking out of the small hole at the world going by. "Where's your mother?" Ambrose asked as he threw the fish onto the dirty cabinet. Hester shrugged. "Where's young Carrie?" He then asked, again Hester shrugged. "What? You don't know, you should be looking out for her!" He said angrily.

"She said sumink about getting water." Hester huffed and then smiled as she saw young John walk past the cottage, he whistled to her, and she jumped up.

"Where do you think you're going?" Ambrose asked as Hester walked to the door.

"Out!" She said and slammed the door behind her. Ambrose shook his head.

"Bloody charming!" He muttered as he searched for a pan to cook the fish in.

A while later Carrie skipped through the door with a jug of water. She placed it on the cabinet and kissed her Dad's cheek as he slept on the chair.

"There's some fish in the pan if you want it." He said sleepily. Carrie walked over to the pan and looked. It did not look in the least bit appetising. She screwed her face up. "Go on girl, you gotta eat." He added when he saw that she wasn't eating.

"I did some chores for Mrs B, she gave me some bread and an apple." Carrie said and smiled.

"Alright, do you know where your mother is?" He asked.

"Alehouse" Carrie replied and yawned. She walked to the bedroom and laid on the hessian mat, she was exhausted and hungry. She drifted off to sleep.

There was a loud rap on the door causing Carrie to jump out of her sleep. She walked to the doorway. Ambrose answered the door. He was talking to a man. He closed the door, rubbed his tired eyes, and sighed.

"What is it Dad?" Carrie asked. Ambrose shook his head.

"It's your mother. She has just dropped down dead in the alehouse." He said calmly, showing no emotion. He walked to the jug, poured some water into the washbowl, and splashed his face. He dried it on a dirty rag. "I have to go to the mortuary, tell your sister, whenever she gets back." He said rubbed the top of her head and walked out of the door.

Carrie sat at the hole. There was so much noise from the street and Hester still wasn't back. She felt so lonely, so hungry, so tired. She thought about her mother and as much as tried to feel sad, she just couldn't. Although she was scared to admit it, deep down she was glad. She would never have to take another beating. Never have to watch that woman beat her Dad or Hester.

"Good riddance" She whispered. The door opened and Hester

walked in.

"Where have you been?" Carrie asked. Hester looked around the tiny cottage and then at the pan of rotten smelly fish.

"Out" Hester replied.

"Where's Dad?" She asked as she looked at his empty chair.

"Mortuary." Carrie replied still looking out of the hole in the wall.

"Eh?" Hester asked.

"Mum, she dropped down dead in the alehouse." Carrie added. Hester just stared into space. She reached into her pocket pulling something out and handed it to Carrie.

"Can you look after that for me?" She asked. Carrie looked at the crystal ball with wide eyes.

"Where did you get this?" She asked.

"Me and John, we see this old Gypsy woman down the lane. We do jobs for her. She gave this to me today." Hester said suspiciously.

"So why do I have to look after it?" Carrie asked, not believing a word her sister said.

"Because I am going out and I don't want it to get pinched do I?" Hester said turned and left the cottage.

The following morning Carrie woke and looked at the empty mats scattered around. No Dad and no Hester. She looked out of the hole, everything was still the same. The same stench, the same noises. She got up and poured a small amount of ale into a dirty cup and drank. It tasted disgusting and made her shudder. She splashed the last of the water over her face and then left the cottage.

Chapter 3

"Right, that's all the rollers in now. Should I help you back to bed, while I prepare your lunch." Peggy said as she put the remaining pins back into the box. Carrie sighed.

"It's such a beautiful day, I think that I would rather sit and look out at the garden." Carrie said and smiled. Peggy wasted no time. She moved the armchair so that it sat beside the window overlooking the pretty garden. She helped Carrie to get off of the dressing table stool and sat her in the chair. She grabbed a blanket and pillow, ensuring that she was comfortable before she left her.

Peggy went out to the kitchen, straight to the cold store. She grabbed some ham and took it into the kitchen. It wasn't until she looked she realised that they were low on bread. She walked back up the hallway and quietly opened Carrie's bedroom door, popping her head around, Carrie was fast asleep in the chair.

Peggy walked to the large mirror and put her head scarf on. Although the sun was shining the wind was brisk and if she didn't cover her already wild hair it would be a complete mess! She grabbed the basket from the kitchen and quietly closed the back door.

She walked through the lanes, enjoying the peace, listening to the bird song. She soon came to the village. She knew that the bread would be fresh, she could smell a fresh batch baking as she walked into the bakers shop. She paid for the small tin loaf and two cream buns and left the shop. She walked straight into the path of a young woman, forcing Peggy to drop her basket.

"Oh I am so sorry!" The woman said sarcastically and smirked. Peggy slowly looked up and took an instant dislike to the pretty face looking back at her.

"No problem." Peggy said as she stood up, forcing a smile. The woman chuckled and walked into the bakers.

"Cow!" Peggy muttered under her breath and walked with her head held high back towards the lanes. She was close to the cottage when she heard a whistle. William leapt over the wall and walked along beside her.

"How has your day been?" He asked as he grabbed the basket and carried it for her. Peggy sighed.

"It's been ok, we had run out of bread." She said as she moved the scarf away from her face.

"What are your plans for the rest of the day?" He asked.

"I am curling my Grandmother's hair. I just want her to be happy." Peggy replied and smiled.

"What about you?" Peggy asked. William took his cap off before the wind took it.

"Oh we have some more fences to put in before I do the evening milking." He replied as they reached the gate to the cottage. He handed the basket back to Peggy and smiled a wide smile.

"Thank you." She said and blushed.

"Well if I don't get to see you before, I will see you on Friday." He said and winked. Peggy chuckled and nodded.

She emptied the basket and then prepared the lunch. She placed it all on the tray and carried it through to Carrie's room. Carrie was awake, just looking out at the garden. She turned to Peggy and smiled.

"He's taken to you hasn't he?" Carrie said and smiled. Peggy could feel her face redden.

"Who?" She asked pretending to be ignorant. Carrie laughed.

"You know who." She said as she chuckled.

"Aye well I had better make the cake. I'll finish your hair afterwards." Peggy said as she placed the tray on Carrie's lap. Carrie grabbed Peggy's hand.

"Thank you Peggy." She said in a most heartfelt way. Peggy felt warm inside and smiled the biggest smile.

"You are more than welcome." Peggy replied and headed back to the kitchen.

She found most of the ingredients in the pantry, there were just two items that she needed from the shed. She skipped down the path and unlocked the large lock on the door. She walked in and gasped. It was a real workshop. The shelves were all filled with jars containing herbs and things. She slowly looked through all the jars and finally found the two things that she needed. She placed them into the basket, locked the door and walked back to the cottage.

She went to collect Carrie's tray. To her surprise she had eaten it all.

"That was delicious!" She said and grinned. Peggy smiled. "And the cake smells wonderful!" She said as she sniffed hard.

"It has another ten minutes, as soon as it's done, I'll be back to finish your hair. Would you like some tea?" Peggy asked.

"Please" Carrie replied.

Peggy washed the dishes while she waited for the cake to finish cooking. All the time thinking about Carrie. Peggy thought that her life was hard, but that was nothing compared to Carrie's non-existent childhood. She emptied the sink, shook her head, and growled angrily. She placed the now cooked cake on the cooling rack and walked to Carrie's room carrying a tray of tea. She poured Carrie and herself a cup and then helped Carrie back to the stool. Peggy placed her cup in front of her.

She began to unravel the hair from the first roller. "So, where did your sister go?" She asked.....

She was walking through the busy streets, not really knowing where she was going, she just let her feet take the lead. She was standing in the same alleyway. It was deserted. She walked further down into the darkness.

"Pssst" She heard. Then she heard laughing. She recognised it. Hester!

"Where are you?" Carrie called out.

"Over here" She heard Hester whisper. Carrie looked towards the sound of the voice. She saw her. Hester ran behind a mound of rubbish. Carrie ran to find her. No-one there.

"Carrie, I'm here." She said again. Carrie looked and now Hester was standing at the top of the alleyway. Carrie ran as fast as she could, but by the time she reached the top, Hester had gone. Carrie huffed, and then began to walk back onto the street.

She was so hungry and thirsty. She walked to Mrs B's cottage. She had eight children and not a minute to herself. She tapped on the door, Mrs B opened it.

"Do you have any jobs for me today?" Carrie asked, desperately hoping that she would say yes.

"Yeah, you can watch the littlun's while I goes to the butchers." Mrs B said. Carrie smiled and nodded.

Carrie sat and played with the two- and three-year-old while the baby slept, and the six-year-old boy threw things at her. "Stop it!" She shouted as a large stone hit her on the back of the head. The boy laughed. Carrie was growing increasingly angry. Thankfully, Mrs B then walked in. She handed Carrie a chunk of bread, two apples and some apple juice. She gulped it all down in seconds.

"Ere don't your Mum and Dad feed ya?" Mrs B asked as she watched the starving girl eat. Carrie shook her head.

"Me Mum died yesterday and me Dad's always out working." Carrie replied with her mouthful. Mrs B shook her head and looked at the young girl with such pity.

Carrie walked out of Mrs B's house smiling. Her tummy was full, this made her happy. She felt something hit her on the back of the head hard. She winced and turned to see Mrs B's six-year-old standing behind her laughing.

"GO AWAY!" She shouted. He threw another stone, this time hitting her on the cheek. She lost all self-control and ran at him. She ran to push him. Before her hands touched him, he went flying through the air landing in the biggest pile of horse dung. Carrie burst out laughing and skipped away. She was yet again dodging through the many people when she spied her dad talking to The Bobby. She skipped over and listened.

"I'm so sorry Ambrose. Lady luck is not on your side at the moment is it?" The Bobby said. Ambrose wiped the tears from his eyes.

"When can I see her?" He asked.

"Anytime you like, just pop down to the mortuary." The Bobby replied and walked away. Carrie looked up at her distraught dad.

"Are you going to see mum again?" She asked him. He bent down and scooped her into his skinny arms and sobbed. He grabbed her hand and led her back to the cottage. After he had tied the horse up he took her inside and sat her on his chair. She was confused.

"Carrie I need you to be brave now." He said as his eyes filled with tears again. Carrie frowned.

"They found Hester and young John's bodies in the Thames this morning." Her dad said and sobbed again. Carrie shook her head.

"No dad that's not true. I saw Hester today, she kept hiding from me." Carrie said. Ambrose frowned.

"Darling she is most definitely dead." He said. Carrie shook her head.

"I don't believe you. I saw her today!" Carrie insisted.

"Look I don't want to get cross with you, but I'm telling you that she is dead Carrie, dead do you hear me!" her dad bellowed. She jumped from the chair and ran out of the door. She ran and ran until she tripped on a stone falling straight on her face.

She opened her eyes and looked around. She smiled when she realised that she was back in the meadow. She stood up, brushed herself off and walked through the mixture of lush long grass and beautiful wild flowers. She picked a blue flower and put it to her nose. The smell was amazing and for the first time in forever she couldn't smell the stench of the city. She sat down and saw a person walking towards her, all the time she was wondering if it was the same lady as yesterday. She gulped when the person approached her.

"He's not lying Carrie. I am dead." Hester said. Carrie rubbed her eyes, shook her head, and then looked back in Hester's direction.

"If you're dead how come I can see you?" Carrie asked. The woman appeared behind Hester, making Carrie jump.

"Your gift child." Abagail said and smiled.

"What? You mean I can see ghosts?" Carrie asked anxiously. Abagail chuckled and nodded. "Oh no, but I don't want to!" Carrie said looking absolutely horrified at Hester. Abagail put her hand on the girls shoulder.

"I am sorry, but it is not a choice that you have. You should see it as a gift. You may be able to help spirits that have lost their way." Abagail said trying to reassure the small girl. Carrie shook her head. Everything began to spin. She closed her eyes and then opened them. She was back in the filthy streets of London!. A crowd had begun to gather around her.

"What are you all looking at?" She asked as she climbed to her feet.

"Well blow me! I could have sworn she was dead not two minutes ago!" A woman said. The woman walked over to Carrie and began to pull at her bottom eyelids.

"Get off of me!" Carrie shouted and pushed the woman, who went hurtling down the street crashing into a horse. The crowd gasped.

"That's the work of the devil if I'm not mistaken!" An old preacher in the crowd said. They all started to shout and call her names, so she took to her heels and ran.

She made her way back to the cottage ran inside and slammed the door closed. Breathlessly she walked to the hole and looked out, making sure that she hadn't been followed. Much to her relief she hadn't. She looked at the floor and noticed a strange light shining up through the rotten floorboards. She shuffled over and removed the loose one. The crystal ball that Hester had given her to hide, had a bright light emanating from it. With a shaky hand she leant in and grabbed the ball. It was vibrating.

She held the ball in her hand and watched as visions began to appear inside. She watched as Hester and John were standing on a bridge. A huge gust of wind picked them both up, dropping them both into the river. She grabbed a dirty piece of rag and wrapped the ball inside. Her heart was beating so fast. She needed to find the gypsy and give her back the ball, she was thinking to herself when the door opened, and her dad walked in. Carrie could tell that he had been drinking, he smelt the same as her mum when she had spent all evening in the alehouse.

"Come and give your old dad a cuddle" He slurred and lunged towards her. She dodged him, grabbed the ball, and ran out of the door. It was getting dark, which meant that the streets would turn meaner, meaner than they already were. She shivered from the icy wind and headed in the direction of the first gypsy camp.

She could smell the fires and the food cooking, so she knew that she was nearby. She turned the corner and hid behind a bush, she watched as the gypsy folk sat around their fires eating, drinking, and laughing. A hand went over her mouth, and she was then carried to a group of people around a fire.

"Look what I have just found." The man said and laughed as he put Carrie on the ground. She pulled herself away and scowled. A woman stood up.

"What's a young un like you doin round here at this time o night?" The woman asked and lifted Carrie's chin to get a good look at her. Again Carrie pulled away.

"Feisty!" The man said and laughed.

"Leave me alone!" Carrie cried out. They both laughed. The man grabbed her again as the woman leant down to be face to face with her.

"Have you been sent by the beak to spy on us?" The woman scowled. Carrie frantically shook her head. "Well if you don't tell us we aint gonna know are we?" She added.

"I need to find who this belongs to." Carrie said and reached into her pocket and pulled out the bright crystal ball. The woman gasped. The man began to snigger.

"If I aint mistaken, that there belongs to Bloody Mary." He sneered.

"Yeah!" the woman replied as her eyes lit up.

"How did you get your hands on that?" The man asked and went to snatch it away from Carrie. She pulled the ball in close to her body as the man struggled with her to take it.

Then the flames of the fire grew to about ten feet tall and turned blue. A woman was stood at the side.

"Put her down now!" She demanded. The man did as she asked. The woman walked over to Carrie and held out her hand. Carrie slipped her hand inside the woman's and walked with her towards a bow top caravan. There was a small fire lit outside and a beautiful black and white horse grazing. The woman sat Carrie on a hay bale.

"You need not fear me child. My name is Mary and I believe that you have something of mine." The woman said gently. Carrie nodded and handed Mary the crystal ball.

"Tell me why you brought it back?" She asked. Carrie was frozen with fear.

"My sister told me that you had given it to her, but I didn't believe her, so I brought it back." Carrie said nervously. Mary smiled and nodded.

"And where is your sister now?" Mary asked.

"Dead" Carrie replied. Again Mary nodded.

"There is a valuable lesson to learnt here young one. Never steal from a gypsy!" Mary said. Carrie nodded.

"Can I go home now?" Carrie asked.

"And where is home?" She replied.

"Notting Dale" Carrie replied.

"Tell me, are you hungry child? You don't look like you have had a decent meal in your life?" Mary asked.

Carrie nodded, she could smell the food and it smelt like nothing she had smelt before.

"Right then. I'll do you some of my broth, pour you a drink and then I'll take you home. Will that do?" Mary asked in her strong Irish accent, which reminded Carrie of her own mother. Carrie nodded.

Carrie was enjoying the warmth from the fire when Mary handed her a steaming bowl of broth, with a large chunk of bread. Carrie ate it. It was the nicest food she had ever tasted and as she ate she smiled. This made Mary smile too.

Mary walked her back to the cottage, and on the way Carrie told her about her life. Mary looked so sad. As they reached the cottage door, Mary crouched down and beckoned to Carrie. She handed her the crystal ball.

"Now you know where to find me. If you are ever hungry, sad, in trouble, lonely or anything and I am not here, look into the ball, call my name and I'll hear you." She said kindly. Carrie threw her arms around Mary's neck.

"Thank you" She whispered.

"My pleasure" Mary whispered back. Carrie walked into the cottage. Her dad was asleep in front of the tiny fire. He still stank of ale. His face had lines of fresh tears staining his cheeks when Carrie kissed his cheek and whispered goodnight. She walked into the cold lonely bedroom and laid on the mat, pulling the blanket up tight, she was so cold. She looked around and then cried herself to sleep.

Chapter 4

There was a loud rap on the door making both Carrie and Peggy jump, Peggy was so engrossed in Carrie's story. She tapped Carrie on the shoulder and walked to the front door. Mrs Baldwin was standing at the door with her arms folded across her heavy frame.

"Is *she* taking visitors now?" The woman asked impatiently as she looked at her watch.

"Did you mean is *Carrie* taking visitors now?" Peggy corrected her. Mrs Baldwin huffed. "No she isn't but she has given me what you asked for. Give me a tick and I'll fetch it for you." Peggy said, scowling.

"Well hurry, I haven't got all day." She fumed. Peggy closed the door and walked into the kitchen muttering under her breath about the rudeness of people. She grabbed the carefully wrapped cake from the side and gave it to Mrs Baldwin, who snatched it from her hands. Peggy shook her head in disbelief.

"I will be back in a months' time. Tell her not to make me wait!" Mrs Baldwin said, turned and walked up the path.

"Tell her thank you!" Peggy shouted after her. She turned and glared at Peggy. She walked back to the door.

"Were you talking to me?" She bellowed. Peggy nodded.

"Yes I was. Manners do not cost anything!" She said with her hands on her hips.

"It is now apparent that you are a relative of the witch, you are just like her!" Mrs Baldwin scoffed her face now bright red.

"I would rather have a million of my grandmother than one of you.!" Peggy raised her voice. "Now go on! Be off with you!" She shouted.

"Well!" Mrs Baldwin said and hurried back up the path, making Peggy laugh. Two women appeared at the gate just as Mrs Baldwin struggled to get through the gate.

"I would stay well away from here. Pure evil!" Mrs Baldwin said, her voice now quivering. The older of the two women looked at her and shook her head. They both headed towards Peggy.

"Hello, does Carrie still live here?" The older woman asked. She had a kind face, the younger woman did too. She smiled at Peggy.

"Aye she does but she is not taking visitors at the moment." Peggy replied. The woman sighed.

"That is a shame. We have travelled many miles to see her. I understand that she is unwell." The woman said sadly. Peggy frowned.

"How do you know?" Peggy asked.

"Peggy, my name is Molly and your grandmother, and I have been good friends for many years. I had a vision that she was unwell and made it a priority to see her." Molly replied.

"I'll just go and speak to her." Peggy said and pulled the door to.

Carrie smiled as Peggy entered the room, then she clapped. "Well done you! It's about time that someone put that old cow in her place!" Carrie said and laughed sending her into a fit of coughing. Peggy handed her a clean hanky. "There is someone at the door that would like to see you." Peggy said and smiled. Once Carrie had finished coughing and wiped the tears from her cheeks she took in a deep breath.

"Would you be a dear and serve them tea in the lounge? I would like to make myself presentable." Carrie asked. Peggy nodded and smiled.

"Aye, I'll make the tea and then I'll come back and finish your hair." Peggy smiled.

She showed Molly and the young lady into the lounge. She stoked the fire and told them both to make themselves comfortable. She took in the tray of tea and placed it on the table.

"Carrie is just making herself presentable, she shouldn't be too long." Peggy said and smiled.

"Thank you Peggy, oh this is my niece Joanna by the way." Molly said. Peggy smiled and held her hand out to shake Joanna's hand.

"Pleased to meet you Peggy" Joanna said quietly. Peggy could feel energy running through her hand.

Peggy finished brushing Carrie's hair through. She looked beautiful. Carrie smiled when she looked in the mirror.

"Thank you Peggy!" She said gratefully. "Now what should I wear I wonder?" Carrie muttered under her breath.

"I think that you look beautiful just as you are. Molly has been your friend for years, I'm sure she is not expecting you to dress formally!" Peggy said and chuckled. Carrie sighed.

"Yes I suppose you're right." She chuckled. She looped her arm through Peggy's as she helped her to walk to the lounge. Peggy helped as Carrie lowered herself into the armchair. She draped the blanket that she was carrying over Carrie's legs and then poured her a cup of tea. Molly jumped up from the sofa and walked to Carrie. She threw her arms around her as they both sobbed. Peggy looked at Joanna, neither of them knew what to do or say.

They both sat beside one another on the sofa, and after a few minutes Molly stood and walked back to where she had been sitting, wiping her eyes as she did. Peggy looked at Carrie who was also wiping the remnants of tears from her face.

"Oh dear, you girls must be thinking that we are both potty!" Molly said and smiled. Peggy grinned. She liked her. They all sat chatting for a while. Peggy looked at the clock and realised that she should be preparing the dinner.

"I don't wish to be rude, but I really should go and prepare the dinner." Peggy said awkwardly.

"Will you stay for dinner?" Carrie asked Molly.

"Oh that would be wonderful, only if it's not too much trouble." Molly smiled.

"No trouble at all!" Peggy chirped. Carrie looked at her and smiled widely.

"I'm sure that Joanna would love to help." Molly said and looked at the pretty young woman. Joanna was nodding. She got up and followed Peggy into the kitchen.

Peggy was making a corned beef pie, so thankfully there was enough to go around. As they both worked together in the kitchen Molly walked out.

"I am popping out for a while. Carrie is resting. I shouldn't be long." She said as she put her coat on and walked out of the back door.

"Where's she going?" Peggy asked Joanna. Joanna shrugged her shoulders.

"No idea." She replied.

"Well it's a long walk into the village." Peggy said as she rolled out the pastry. Joanna chuckled.

"We have a car." She said still chuckling.

"Ooh! How posh!" Peggy said in a posh voice, making Joanna burst out laughing.

A while later Molly returned. She came through the back door with a wheelchair. Peggy frowned. "The weather is kind at the moment, and I thought that it might be nice to take Carrie outside. I'm sure that the fresh air would do her the world of good!" Molly beamed. Peggy smiled. She was a lovely woman and Peggy could see why Carrie held her in such high regard.

Molly took the wheelchair into the lounge and within minutes she was pushing Carrie around the garden, looking at the unblemished flowers that had just began to bud and bloom.

"Oh Molly it's so lovely to see you!" Carrie sighed. Molly tapped her shoulder.

"The moment that I had the vision, I just knew that I had to come. I must say that young Peggy is wonderful." Molly smiled. Carrie nodded.

"Yes, yes she is. I feel terrible though, I was really quite mean to her for the first few years that she was here." Carrie said, her voice full of regret.

"It's hardly surprising Carrie, if I were you I would struggle to trust a single soul." Molly said trying to ease Carrie's conscience. Carrie tapped Molly's hand.

"I know that it is nearly time, I need to pass over everything necessary to Peggy. I just hope that I have enough time Molly." Carrie said.

"I'm sure that you have my dear. Anyway, let's not get morbid, tell me about that awful woman that was leaving when we arrived." Molly said and smiled. Carrie chuckled and went on to tell Molly all about the awful Mrs Baldwin!

"So do you have anyone special in your life Peggy?" Joanna asked as she mashed the potatoes. Peggy blushed with embarrassment.

"No. How about you?" She replied. Joanna reached into her purse and passed a photograph to Peggy. It was a handsome man in uniform.

"Very handsome chap!" Peggy said and smiled.

"Hmm, his name is Benjamin. We are engaged to be married." Joanna said. She had an air of sadness about her.

"You could sound a little more enthusiastic." Peggy said trying to cheer her up. Joanna sighed.

"I'm not sure that we are right for each other. You see there is a guardian that I see every day. He always asks me if I would like to go out on a date with him, and if I am totally honest Peggy I would love to." Joanna replied deep in thought.

"What is a guardian?" Peggy asked. Joanna chuckled.

"Sorry I thought that you knew about the Guardians of Albion." She replied. Peggy shook her head. Joanna stared into space.

"Well.... who are they?" Peggy pressed her for an answer. She sighed.

"They protect the sacred sites and people of this land. They are an ancient society that pledge their lives to protect Albion." Joanna replied. Peggy smiled.

"Well he sounds like a good chap. Why don't you be honest with Benjamin, tell him how you feel. I couldn't imagine spending my life with someone when I cared for someone else." Peggy said. Joanna nodded.

"I know that you're right, but I don't want to hurt his feelings." She replied.

Peggy and Joanna opened up the drop leaf table in the lounge and laid it ready for dinner. Over the meal the four of them chatted. Peggy was watching Carrie, she looked exhausted. Molly noticed it too, so as soon as they had finished eating, Molly and Joanna washed the dishes and left to go to their hotel.

"Wheelchair or walk?" Peggy asked Carrie. Carrie chuckled.

"Definitely walk!" Carrie replied as she held onto Peggy's arm.

Peggy ensured that Carrie was comfortable and tucked the blankets in. Carrie tapped the bed beckoning for Peggy to sit.

"There is much to tell Peggy." She said quietly.

"Aye but you look exhausted." She replied. "You can always tell me tomorrow." She added.

"But what if there is not tomorrow for me?" Carrie said.

"Don't be daft!" Peggy said and gently nudged her. "Ok shall I make some tea and you can tell me more." Peggy said. Carrie nodded.

So the next couple of years were hard for Carrie. Her dad had turned to drink, so when he wasn't working he was in the alehouse. Most of the money that he made also went to the alehouse. Carrie had to make do with scraps and the kindness of Mrs B to survive. One night there was a knock on the door. It woke Carrie. She opened the door to George the meat seller.

"Sorry to bother you Carrie love but I think that you should come." He said. Carrie rubbed her tired eyes and nodded. She followed George up the road and stopped when they approached a crowd of people. George pushed his way through the crowd and Carrie gasped when she saw her dad face down in the mud.

"He's just drunk love." George said as he could see that she was beginning to panic. He called to two of the men in the crowd, they picked him up and dragged him back to the cottage. Once inside they threw him onto the mat and walked to the door.

"Thank you." Carrie said to George as he and the other two men walked outside.

"It's not right you know. He should be taking care of you, not spending all his time in there." George replied as he nodded to the alehouse. Carrie closed the door and placed a blanket over her smelly, snoring dad. She was looking out of the hole, she was wide awake now, when she saw one of the men that had helped her dad earlier. He was walking towards the cottage. Carrie ran to the door and opened it before he had the chance to knock.

"Hello darling. I've come for me reward." He said as he leered towards her. She ran out onto the street thinking that it was the safest option. He grabbed her smock and started to drag her back inside the cottage. She let out a scream. She turned ready to hit him, when her Dad jumped on his back and began punching his head. The man threw her dad off sending him crashing to the ground, hitting his head on a rock. Blood poured from his mouth, he gargled then stopped, stopped moving, stopped breathing. Carrie screamed as she realised that he was dead. She lost control. She lunged at the man, sending him hurtling through the cottage door. Again she lunged at him, he hit the wall. He slid down and landed in a heap. *Get out of there* she heard. She ran to the floorboard, grabbed the crystal ball, and ran.

She found herself at the gypsy camp. It was dark and hard to see. She was looking for Mary's caravan. She felt relief flush through her when she saw Mary's horse. She ran over, landing in a heap on the ground beside the horse.

"O my goodness. What has happened to you child?" Carrie heard Mary say. She opened her eyes. The sun was shining. Mary picked Carrie up and walked her to the caravan. She sat her on the rug, wrapping a warm blanket around her shoulders, she was shaking violently. Mary gave her a mug and told her to drink. Carrie almost spat it out. It was the most disgusting thing she had ever tasted, and it burnt her mouth.

"Urgh! What is that?" Carrie said as she shuddered. Mary laughed.

"It's gin child, drink it, it's good for shock." Mary said. Carrie then went on to tell Mary everything that had happened.

"I think that we should move from here. Just in case. You can't work on the streets here someone might spot you." Mary said, thinking about where to move on to.

So for the next six years Mary taught Carrie how to make a fair living on the streets. They stayed in Surrey for a year or so, enough time to let the dust settle, then they returned to Notting Hill. Mary taught Carrie how to read Tarot cards and the crystal ball and that is how they made their money. Josie an old gypsy woman from the camp would draw people to them especially the middle-class folk who went there in disguise just to see how they lived. Josie could spot them a mile off.

Carrie was sixteen, well that's what she thought. She didn't even know when her birthday was! She was working Portobello road. Josie had drawn in a few punters, and she was doing ok. A couple of times she spied a man on the corner watching her. She kept her eye on him and noticed that every time she had a new customer, he was watching, she wasn't sure if he was the beak.

She had a quick count up, and happy with her days earnings she walked to meet Mary. All of a sudden she was being dragged towards an alley. She dug her heels in and managed to turn. It was the man that had been watching her. She began to kick out, her head spun, and she lost all control. She began to attack the man, throwing him everywhere. He landed in a heap on the ground, so she straightened her clothes and walked back to the street.

Someone grabbed her from behind, thinking it was the police she turned to see a man in military uniform. Not that it was unusual,. "Sorry, you dropped this, I just wanted to return it." The man said.

Carrie blushed when he placed her money pouch into her hand.

"Thank you." She said quietly, turned and walked away.

"Hey, wait!" he called out. Her heart was beating fast, he was the most handsome man she had ever seen, and she did not have a clue what to say to him or how to speak to him. He ran to catch her up. "That was quite a fight you put up there. Where did you learn to fight like that?" He asked. Carrie shrugged her shoulders.

"Life" Was her only reply. He smiled. It made her heart melt just a tiny bit. He had the darkest hair, with a small silver streak running through. His eyes were blue and beautiful.

"So are you local?" He asked and smiled. Carrie just laughed. She saw Mary waiting for her on the corner.

"Right, thanks again but I have to go." She said and walked in the direction of Mary.

"Wait, what's your name?" He shouted.

"Carrie" She shouted back. He blew her a kiss, she grinned like a Cheshire cat.

Mary raised her eyebrows at Carrie as she stood beside her. "What?" Carrie said.

"Who was that beauty?" Mary asked. Carrie shrugged.

"Some bloke tried to steal me takings. I fought with him, not realising that I had dropped me money pouch. That bloke picked it up and gave it to me." Carrie said and smiled.

"Bit of alright he is." Mary said and nudged Carrie as they walked to the horse.

Chapter 5

So, Peggy knew that she had to speak to Carrie about the dance, but she didn't know how to. She walked into Carrie's room and opened the curtains. It was a dull cloudy day, there was not much light coming through the cottage windows. Carrie turned and moaned. Peggy walked over to the bed and helped her to sit up. Peggy could see that Carrie was clearly in pain.

"Would you like me to call on Dr Clarke, see if he can't give you something for the pain?" Peggy asked. Carrie shook her head and attempted a smile.

"No need, Molly is going to try some healing on me this afternoon." Carrie said and coughed. Peggy smiled. She walked back to the kitchen to fetch Carrie's breakfast tray. She returned with the tray and placed it on Carrie's lap. Carrie had already fastened her napkin around her neck.

"Er, you know tomorrow…" Peggy began.

"Yes it's Friday." Carrie said with a mouthful of bread and jam.

"Aye …well I was er wondering…."

"If you could go to the village dance with William." Carrie finished Peggy's sentence. Peggy wore a look of shock on her face.

"How did you know?" She gasped. Carrie chuckled.

"They don't call me the old witch for no reason!" Carrie chuckled. Peggy stood wide eyed.

"Yes of course you can go! Molly is coming to play cards tomorrow evening anyway." Carrie smiled. Peggy grinned and then gently hugged her grandmother.

"Is Joanna coming with her?" Peggy asked. Carrie shook her head.

"No she has gone to Salisbury to see her fiancé, well actually between you and me she has gone to break off the engagement." Carrie said, her eyes wide.

"Oh really why?" Peggy asked as she blushed. Carrie laughed.

"You damned well know why. You advised her to do it!" Carrie said and laughed.

"Aye I did, but I never thought that she would take my advice. I was only telling her what I would do." Peggy said defensively. Carrie nodded and then gestured for Peggy to take the tray.

"Molly is coming over at 2 this afternoon. If you write a list, she said that she would drive and fetch the groceries." Carrie said. Peggy smiled, she was relieved that she wouldn't have to carry the heavy basket all the way home from the village. "So come back soon and we can continue with our chat." Carrie continued. Peggy grabbed the tray, smiled, and nodded as she whistled along the hallway back to the kitchen.

She finished the chores that needed to be done, then returned to Carrie's room. "Could I sit in the chair by the window?" Carrie asked.

"Of course!" Peggy replied as she helped her over to the chair and made her comfortable.

"So did you ever see him again?" Peggy asked as she passed Carrie a steaming cup of tea.

"Who?" Carrie replied. Peggy grinned.

"You know who… Mr beautiful of course!" Carrie chuckled.

"As it happens I did!" She smirked.

They were back at the camp counting out their takings. Mary passed Carrie her share. "Don't spend it all at once!" Mary said and winked. Carrie smiled. No-one knew about her stash. Every day that she worked she hid two thirds of her takings. She had dug a deep hole and stashed it in there. She was desperate to get out of London, she detested the place. As soon as she had saved enough money, in the middle of the night she would leave the city for good. She would go to the coast and live a quiet life there. She had thought about it every day for years.

A few weeks later it was Carrie's turn to work Portobello road. She hadn't been there since the attack, Mary thought it was better for her to work Lambeth instead. Carrie preferred Portobello. Josie had sent at least fifteen people to her and that was just the morning shift. There had been an influx of rich people 'slumming it' that morning.

She was sitting on her crate looking at the ground when a shadow was cast, and someone stood over her. She looked up, her heart skipped as she realised that it was him. She hoped every morning since that day that she would see him again and secretly that is why she wanted to work Portobello.

"Carrie, I thought you had gone and left me!" He said and smiled. She chuckled and shook her head.

"Such a silver tongue!" She said not even looking at him. He crouched down and looked at her.

"No really, every day I have walked up and down this street hoping to catch a glimpse of you. When your friend Mary told me that you had moved away, I stopped for a while, but this morning something told me that you would be here." He said smiling.

"Well here I am!" Carrie said with a hint of sarcasm in her tone.

"Listen, tomorrow I have to return to my base. I was wondering if you would do me the honour of dining with me this evening?" He asked.

"No can do" She replied, again avoiding eye contact. His beautiful smile turned to a frown.

"Ok, understood, I'll leave you to your work." He sulked, turned, and began to walk away.

"Wait!" she called out. He turned. "What's your name?" She asked. He walked back.

"I am Abraham, Abe to my friends." He replied and held his hand out. She slowly put her hand in his. The energy was amazing. His entire hand was buzzing.

"Pleased to meet you Abe." She said shyly. He stood back and looked at her. Then sighed.

"Ok, obviously dinner is too much. How about a fish and chips in the park?" He asked. Carrie grinned and nodded.

"Wonderful, should I meet you back here at 6.30?" He suggested.

"Look forward to it!" Carrie said and watched him as he walked up the road. She could feel eyes on her, she slowly turned to see a young woman staring at her from across the street. *Not again* she was thinking to herself. The woman then walked towards her. She was about Carrie's age maybe a little older. She was wearing posh clothes, but Carrie noticed what a kind face she had.

"That my dear is clearly meant to be!" The young woman said.

"Sorry?" Carrie looked at her in complete confusion.

"You and that man, you are clearly meant for one another." She said again.

"I'm sorry can I get you something. A tarot reading, crystal ball?" Carrie asked. The woman chuckled and shook her head. She handed Carrie a piece of paper. Carrie looked at it and then back at the woman.

"It's my name and address" The woman said. Carrie shook her head.

"I can't read or write. Never been to school." She said feeling slightly humiliated. The woman looked at her in shock and covered her mouth as she gasped.

"Oh, I am so very sorry, I should have realised. My name is Molly, at the moment I am living just beside Hyde park. Do you know it?" Molly asked. Carrie nodded.

"What about it?" She replied. Molly sighed and crouched down so that she could look her in the eye.

"I know who you are." She said. Carrie stood up and prepared herself to run. How did she know her. Was she going to be sent to prison for killing the man that killed her father! All these thoughts and many more were swirling around in her mind. Molly held Carrie's arm and stopped her from moving.

"Please, just hear me out." Molly said gently. "Your ancestor Abagail told me where to find you. I am a guardian of Albion, we protect the sacred sites and magical people of this land. Carrie you come from an incredibly magical blood line, and this alone puts you in great danger. There are people out there who wish to take your power. I am here to help you. To show the old ways." Molly said. Carrie burst out laughing, she had never heard anything so ridiculous in all her life!

"You must have me mixed up with someone else. I come from a poor family, both my parents cared more for alcohol than they did me!" She scoffed. Molly smiled a sad smile and nodded.

"I am aware of the awful things that have happened to you and your family. Tomorrow, meet me at the gates of Hyde park at 4.30." Molly said quickly. Carrie felt someone behind her, she jumped as she turned and was nose to nose with Mary. She then turned back to speak to Molly. She was gone!

Carrie frowned when she looked at Mary, thinking about what Abe had said to her earlier. She always thought that she could trust her, but now she was beginning to doubt that.

"Goodness it's almost twelve. I need to go and prepare the lunch!" Peggy said as she looked at her watch. She hurried out to the kitchen and placed the smoked haddock into the steamer. There was a tap on the back door. Peggy opened it and jumped back when she was faced with William, who had blood dripping down his hand.

"Can you help me?" he asked. Peggy pulled him into the kitchen. She turned on the tap and placed his hand under the running water. He had a deep gash running across the top of his hand. She grabbed a sheet and tore it up, she wrapped it tight around the open wound.

"Wait there!" She said and hurried to Carrie. She quickly told Carrie.

"Grab the wheelchair, I need to look at it." Carrie said anxiously.

In the kitchen Carrie unwrapped the wound and winced when she saw how deep the cut was.

"How on earth did you do this?" She asked the pale young man.

"I was sawing wood. The saw slipped and went through my hand." He said shakily.

"Close your eyes." Carrie said calmly. He did as she asked. She placed both hands over the wound and inhaled deeply. Peggy gasped as she watched the wound closing. "Ok, you can open them now" She smiled and winked at Peggy. William reluctantly looked at the wound and gasped.

"Where's it gone?" He asked in bewilderment. Carrie and Peggy both laughed. "Thank you so much Ma'am" He said and grinned.

"My pleasure." Carrie said and then began coughing. Peggy quickly handed her a hanky and wheeled her back to her room. She settled her in bed and then went back to William in the kitchen.

"Your grandmother is brilliant!" He exclaimed, smiling. Peggy nodded.

"Aye but you're best not telling folk around here what she did. Some of them already think badly of her." Peggy said sadly. She poured William a cup of tea then took the fish from the steamer.

"That smells grand." William said as he sniffed in, making Peggy laugh.

"Would you like some, there's plenty?" She asked.

"Aye, so long as there is enough, please." William smiled making Peggy's tummy do somersaults. She handed him his plate, then took Carrie's tray into her. She was sitting up in bed, she looked bright as a button.

"You look so much better than you did this morning!" Peggy said as she gave her the tray. Carrie smiled.

"I feel full of vitality. I haven't healed anyone in such a long time!" Carrie said and took a bite of fish from her fork. "Hmmm, delicious!" She said.

They had all just finished their lunch when Molly walked through the back door. She smiled at Peggy and William and made her way to Carrie's room. Peggy began to clear the plates. William stood up. "I had better get back to work. Old McGregor will be wondering where I am." He smiled at Peggy. She smiled back. He walked over to her and pulled her in close. He kissed her, making her head spin.

"I'll see you tomorrow night beautiful" he said as he walked out of the door whistling.

Molly walked out to the kitchen. "Do you have a list?" She asked and smiled. Peggy smiled and passed the list to her.

"I hope that there is not too much on there." Peggy winced. Molly chuckled.

"Of course not!" Molly replied and walked out of the back door. Peggy walked into Carrie's room and sat on the chair beside her.

"So what about Mary?" Peggy asked.

"Who was that?" Mary asked aggressively. Carrie shrugged.

"She wanted a tarot reading, but I told her to come back later." Carrie said matter-of-factly. Mary looked at Carrie suspiciously.

"What you doing now then?" Mary asked. Carrie looked at the large clock hanging outside the jewellers.

"I'm gonna get something to eat and then carry on." She replied.

"I'll come with you." Mary grabbed Carries' arm. They both walked up to the pie man and grabbed a mutton pie each. Carrie wasn't even hungry, but she had to make her story look convincing.

"I thought that you were working Lambeth today?" Carrie said as she picked at the pie.

"It's dead there." Mary replied shaking her head.

"Josie told me that a load of the 'slummers' were heading that way this afternoon. I have done fifteen tarot readings this morning." Carrie said as she discreetly threw the pie to two small children that were begging on the street. Mary's eyes lit up.

"Really! I'll head back over there now. I haven't shifted a single elixir this morning." She tutted and walked off in the opposite direction. She turned "I'll see you a bit later." She called out. Carrie nodded and walked back to her spot.

All afternoon she was thinking how she could get out of meeting Mary without being seen with Abe.

She was in the middle of a tarot reading when one of the lookouts shout "BEAK!" at the top of his lungs. Carrie quickly threw her things into her sack and knocked the crate over. She looked at the man for whom she was reading. "Gotta go!" She said and ran down a nearby alleyway. She hid in a doorway for a few minutes when she heard cries. She looked down the dark alley and saw two men roughing up a woman, she was obviously a 'slummer', any local woman who couldn't look after herself would not be down any dark alley. Carrie was thinking.

The men were getting rougher, and the woman's cries were becoming louder. Carrie took to her heels and ran towards them.

"OI" Carrie shouted as she approached the spot where they were. One of the men turned and sneered.

"Piss off and mind your own." He said and turned back to continue assaulting the woman. Carrie grabbed hold of his shirt and pulled him backwards, sending him flying into the opposite wall. The other man watched and pulled his fist back to punch her, while the one she had thrown off, got back on his feet had now jumped on her back. She took a punch on her left jawline, she saw stars. Then she lost control. She lunged at the man throwing punches, as the one on her back, was thrown off. The man was pinned against the wall as she continued to hit out. There was blood everywhere.

Enough she heard, it was that same voice again. She let go of the man who slid down the wall, landing in a heap. The other man watched in horror, then ran as fast as he could, back towards the street. The woman was hysterically sobbing.

"It's alright, I'm not gonna hurt you." Carrie said and held her hand out. As she stepped out into the light, Carrie was taken aback. She had the reddest hair that Carrie had ever seen. Once the woman had calmed down she looked at Carrie.

"Thank you so much!" She gasped. Carrie smiled.

"This is no place for a lady like you. I'll walk you back to the street." She said and held her arm out gesturing for the woman to take it. She did and slowly they walked towards the end of the alley.

"Where on earth did you learn to fight like that?" The woman asked. Carrie chuckled.

"If I had a penny for every time someone asked me that question." She replied and shook her head. "Well here we are. If I were you I would get as far away from here as possible." Carrie said and beckoned to a carriage.

"I will and thank you once again." The woman said as she reached into a money pouch and handed Carrie a wad of notes.

"Don't be daft. I never did it for money." Carrie said and passed the money back.

"What's your name?" The woman asked.

"Carrie." She replied.

"Lovely name. I am Katarina and I must insist that you take this as a gift for your kindness." She said and pushed the money at Carrie. Carrie reluctantly took the wad of money and slipped it inside her shoe. "Carrie I wish you good fortune and I hope that we meet again under better circumstances." Katarina said as she climbed into the carriage.

Carrie watched as the carriage pulled away and then hurried towards the river. She ran down the slope and under the bridge, to quickly count the money. There was more money there than she had earned in the past six years. She rolled it up and put it in her underwear. And then ran back to Portobello. She looked at the clock. It was six fifteen. She hid in a doorway when she spied Mary out of the corner of her eye. Mary walked to Carrie's pitch and asked Old Sal, who worked the pitch beside her, if she had seen Carrie.

"Nah the beak was 'ere. I have only just come back to grab me gear. I'm guessing young Carrie is hiding." Old Sal said. Mary walked away in the direction of the camp. Carrie sighed and once Mary was out of sight she stepped out, directly into the path of Abraham.

Chapter 6

"Well, hello again!" He smiled, together they walked down to the fish and chip shop. "Carrie what will you have?" He asked as he was being served by Mrs Turner.

"She'll just have chips. Tis all she ever 'as!" Mrs turner said as she wrapped Abe's haddock and chips in newspaper. Carrie nodded, she couldn't eat fish, just the smell reminded her of the times her Dad would bring back the rotten fish that he couldn't sell.

They both walked to Italian Park and sat on the grass beneath a huge tree. Carrie picked at the chips while Abe tucked into his haddock. "So Carrie tell me about yourself." He said with a mouthful of fish.

"Not much to say really. I was born in Kent, but my Dad moved us here, thought life would be better for us. What a joke!" Carrie replied and wrapped the remainder of her chips into the newspaper. Abe looked down at his own food and screwed his nose up.

"Not the best fish and chips that I have eaten." He said. Carrie chuckled. "So, do you still live with your parents?" He asked. Carrie shook her head.

"No they are both dead, died years ago." She replied. Sadness washed over Abe's face.

"Oh, I am sorry" He said remorsefully.

"No need, we weren't close. They preferred ale to me!" She said and shrugged. "So, where you off to next then?" She asked. Abe smiled.

"Hmm, ,top secret information I'm afraid.." He replied.

"So you're a pilot then?" Abe nodded. "Where are you based?"

"Salisbury" He replied. Carrie shivered, the sun had gone down making the temperature drop rapidly.

"Well I suppose I had better head home." She said as she wrapped her arms around herself, trying to conserve any heat that she did have.

"So soon!" Abe said, taking off his thick coat and draping over her shoulders. It was so warm and smelt of him. She inhaled deeply. "Where is home?" He asked.

"Gypsy camp not far from Notting Dale."

"Ok, so how about, we take a stroll along the riverside and then I'll walk you back?" Please?" He asked. She thought for a moment. "Please, I don't know when I'll be back this way, and seeing your pretty face in my mind will keep me going." He added. Carrie chuckled.

"Alright then!" She sighed.

Peggy placed her hand over her mouth. "Why didnee you say that you hate fish?" Peggy asked as she blushed. Carrie chuckled.

"I do like it now, especially the way that you cook it." Carrie replied and smiled.

"Thank goodness!" Peggy exhaled with relief. After Carrie had told her about the fish thing she kept thinking about all the times she had served Carrie fish for lunch. "Well, I need to go and stew the steak for dinner, shall I bring you in some tea?" Peggy asked as she smiled.

"I'm sure Molly will be back soon, you can wait until she returns." Carrie said as she yawned.

"Shall I help you into bed?" Peggy asked. Carrie smiled and nodded.

Peggy was chopping the vegetables when the back door opened, and Molly came in with the groceries. "Thank you Molly, it's really kind of you." Peggy said as she relieved her of potatoes.

"It's no trouble." Molly replied.

"I helped Carrie back into bed. I'll bring in some tea." Peggy said smiling. Molly walked in the direction of Carrie's room.

Peggy took in a tray of tea and some cakes. Molly had already begun with the healing. Not saying a word, Peggy put the tray on the table and crept out of the room.

Peggy was sitting at the table scrubbing potatoes, she was lost in thought. She remembered the day as if it were yesterday. Mother had put Robert in his best clothes and at 7am the squire knocked on the door. Peggy's heart sank. Her mother looked at her and scowled, seeing the tears building in Peggy's eyes. "You must be strong, for his sake!" her mother whispered sternly. Peggy choked back the tears. The squire grabbed Roberts hand and pulled him out of the door towards the waiting carriage. As the carriage door opened Robert looked at Peggy and her mother, tears rolling down his cheeks, as the squire pushed him forcibly into the carriage and rode away at high speed.

"What will happen to him?" The frightened six-year-old girl asked. Her mother's face was like stone, she glared at the little girl.

"It's best not thinking about it. I had no choice but to send him away. If not the three of us would have nowhere to live." Her mother scorned and ushered her back inside. She ran to her tiny room and sobbed into her pillow.

"Peggy, Peggy are you alright?" Molly broke her thoughts. Peggy wiped the tears away and smiled.

"Aye, I was just thinking about my wee brother. I miss him so much Molly." Peggy sniffed. Molly put her arms around Peggy and held her tightly, Peggy sobbed. It was the first time she had been hugged since her Robert was taken by the squire all those many years ago.

Molly put the kettle on the stove and washed the tea things up. She made a fresh pot of tea and sat beside Peggy at the table and joined in, scrubbing the potatoes.

"Would you like me to heal some of the heartbreak?" Molly smiled. Peggy smiled and then sighed.

"No thanks. I'm afraid that I might forget him." She replied. Molly shook her head.

"Bonds like that rarely sever Peggy and I'm sure that one day you will be reunited." Molly placed her hand over Peggy's.

"You really think so Molly?" She asked. Molly smiled and nodded.

"Carrie was exhausted from the healing session, so I have left her to rest. I had better go back now." Molly said looking at her watch.

"Are you sure that you won't stop for dinner?" Peggy asked.

"That's very kind of you, but I am having dinner with the head guardian this evening." She said. She wore a smile that told Peggy that Molly must be very fond of the person with which she was dining! Peggy nodded. Molly kissed Peggy on the top of her head and walked out of the back door.

Carrie was dreaming. It was that awful dream again. There were five of them, all tied to wooden stakes. Wood and straw piled high below them. Carrie looked to her left and saw the two young girls that were beside her. They looked petrified. She turned to her right, the other two were staring into the baying crowd that had now gathered, who were shouting obscenities at the five of them. She looked at the two girls again. "Fear not, we will find peace soon" She said as the crowd jeered.

She woke with a jump when Peggy entered her room with the dinner. Sweat was running down her face.

"Are you alright?" Peggy asked anxiously. "Do you have a fever?" She added as she felt Carrie's forehead with the back of her hand. Carrie smiled and shook her head.

"No it was just a nightmare." Carrie said and smiled. "Will you dine with me?" She asked. Peggy gave her a wide grin and nodded.

"Aye, I'll go and fetch mine!" She said as she hurried back to the kitchen.

As they sat eating the beef casserole with dumplings, Peggy looked at Carrie. She somehow looked different, younger perhaps, Peggy was thinking to herself. She caught Carrie gaze and smiled.

"Molly seemed excited about dinner with the head guardian this evening." Peggy said as she filled her mouth with the delicious casserole. Carrie nodded and finished chewing her food.

"Of course she is. It's Michael, Molly has had feelings for him for such a long time." Carrie said and smiled.

"So why haven't they ever got together then?" Peggy asked. Carrie's smile turned to a frown, she shook her head.

"Unfortunately, Michael does not feel the same. He loves Molly but on a purely platonic basis." Carrie replied.

"That's sad." Peggy said and automatically thought about William. "So going back to our conversation earlier, did you go and meet Molly at Hyde park?" Peggy asked. Carrie smiled and nodded.

She finished work early and made her way to Hyde Park, double checking throughout the entire journey that she wasn't being followed. She had a feeling that Mary was on to her. She was relieved when she spied Molly waiting at the gates. She didn't know why but Molly had a sense of safety surrounding her, that for the first time in her life, made Carrie feel at ease.

"I'm so happy that you came!" Molly said as she linked Carrie's arm and led her towards a large house. They walked up the stone steps, Molly pulled the doorbell. The door opened and a kind faced man let them in. He took Molly's coat and hat, then looked at Carrie. She had neither.

"Would you serve us coffee in the parlour Douglas?" Molly asked the man.

"Of course!" He said and bowed. Carrie looked in complete shock. She followed Molly into a huge room, it was like nothing that Carrie had ever seen before. She was gob smacked.

"Please sit down." Molly said and pointed to a pretty ornate sofa. Carrie was slightly apprehensive. She didn't want to mark the pretty material with her dirty clothes. "Please" Molly insisted. Carrie blushed and then sat. The large door opened, and Douglas walked in with a tray. It had a large silver pot, small jug and two pretty cups and saucers. He placed it on the occasional table and left the room.

"How do you take your coffee?" Molly asked. Carrie shrugged.

"I don't know, I've never had it before." She replied. Molly smiled.

"Ok, so do you drink tea?" She asked. Carrie nodded. "And do you like it sweet?" She added. Again Carrie nodded. Molly smiled placed some sugar in the cup and poured in the coffee and cream. She handed it to Carrie, who curiously breathed in the aroma and then took a sip. It was the most wonderful thing that she had ever tasted. She grinned a huge grin and nodded her head. She desperately wanted it to cool down so that she could drink more.

"You like?" Molly asked. Carrie nodded frantically. "Now then, let's get to business." Molly added. Carrie frowned.

"Wait! You never said anything about business." Carrie scowled. Molly chuckled.

"It's simply a turn of phrase." Molly chuckled. "Your bloodline goes way back Carrie, and within that bloodline there is powerful magic. Some it skips, but some it remains high. You have powerful magical blood flowing through your veins Carrie. Unfortunately, there are dark ones that are aware of the power, and they have watched for many years, waiting for the next to be born. They are aware of you, and I believe that they have now tracked your whereabouts." Molly said seriously. Carrie gulped the remainder of the delicious coffee and looked at Molly.

"So, what?" Carrie replied.

"I don't think that you quite understand Carrie. These revenants are evil, pure evil and they will stop at nothing to get their hands on what they want." Molly replied. "There are two in particular that are the vilest, and it is those that have sought you out. You must remain vigilant at all times Carrie." Molly said anxiously. Carrie wasn't really taking any of it seriously, I mean why would these revenants or whatever they are called take the trouble to track someone like her down. She was thinking to herself.

"What are revenants?" Carrie asked.

"They are the undead. They feed from human blood to remain human-like, and they are evil!" Molly said. Carrie burst out laughing.

"You don't expect me to believe that do you!" She howled. Molly shook her head in despair.

"Yes Carrie, yes I do." Molly said seriously. After Carrie had stopped laughing she looked at Molly and how serious she looked.

"So what do I have to do?" Carrie asked, still chuckling.

"Take this seriously, to begin with." Molly said sternly. Carrie's smile left her face. "The two that I spoke about take the appearance of two women, they will approach you separately." Molly said. Carrie gulped. "We believe that one will make contact soon. She will appear to be friendly, she is most definitely not!" Molly continued. Then Molly rang a small bell which was on the table. Douglas entered the room and handed something to Molly. Once he had left Molly passed it to Carrie. It was a pendant on a necklace. Carrie looked at Molly in confusion.

"Wear this at all times. If you feel as though you are in danger, rub the crystal in the centre. It will alert us of your whereabouts." Molly said and gestured for Carrie to put the necklace on. Molly helped Carrie to fasten it.

"So do you still have the pendant?" Peggy asked. Carrie nodded and pointed to the chest.

"Open it. It should be in a wooden box." Carrie said. Peggy opened the chest and began to look for the wooden box. She eventually found it close to the bottom. She opened the box and gasped. It was beautiful. It was a silver chain, the pendant was a purple crystal encased within silver. "Put it on, it's yours." Carrie said and smiled.

"No, I, I couldnee" Peggy said and blushed.

"Peggy I have no use for it now. I would like you to have it. At least I will be safe in the knowledge that you have the protection of the guardians." Carrie said smiling. Reluctantly Peggy put the necklace on. It was humming with energy.

"Thank you!" She beamed, making Carrie chuckle.

The following morning Peggy woke to bright sunshine bursting through the curtains. She smiled as she climbed out of bed, realising that tonight she was going to the dance with William. The entire morning was filled with Peggy getting on with her chores singing as she did. Carrie could hear her, and it made her smile. After lunch she rang the bell and within seconds Peggy appeared.

"Could you pass me my bag?" Carrie asked as Peggy took her tray. Peggy did as she asked and left Carrie to rummage. Again Carrie rang the bell. As Peggy entered the room, Carrie passed her a purse. Peggy looked confused. "Molly will be here in a few minutes she will drive you into town. I want you to buy the prettiest dress that you can find." Carrie said smiling.

"No really, you have given me the necklace, I can't possibly take this." Peggy said as she pushed the purse towards Carrie.

"Nonsense. You have been here for years and not a penny have I given you for yourself. You work so hard and it's about time, I gave you something for you. Now take it I insist!" Carrie said. Peggy smiled, took the purse, and nodded.

Carrie and Molly were in the lounge. Molly had treated them all to a fish and chip supper. Peggy was ready. She looked in the mirror. She was worried. What if there were other girls in prettier dresses. She was thinking to herself. She walked into the lounge to the gasps of Carrie and Molly.

"Oh Peggy you look beautiful!" Molly squealed. Carrie grinned.

"I love that dress!" Carrie said and they all smiled. The kitchen door knocked. Molly went to the kitchen. She walked back into the lounge followed by William. Peggy blushed.

"Wow! You look lovely!" He said bashfully as the two older women cooed.

"Now young William, I am trusting you to take good care of my Peggy." Carrie said wearing her sternest expression. He nodded.

"I will I promise." He said and held his arm out for Peggy to take.

The village hall was quite small, it was full of youngsters making merry. William went to the bar while Peggy sat at a table close to the back of the hall. He came back with two glasses, handing one to Peggy.

"Thank you. What is it?" She asked as she looked at the amber liquid.

"It's shandy." He smiled. Peggy took a sip and smiled.

"Mmm. That's lovely!" She said and took a big gulp.

"Go easy, I canee take you back drunk!" William said and laughed. They got up to dance. Peggy felt the happiest she had ever felt. William was charming! Handsome and charming, almost too good to be true! She thought to herself as he spun her around.

They were back at the table, William went back to the bar to fetch another drink. Peggy watched as the pretty girl that knocked the basket out of her hand in the bakers shop approached William at the bar. She put her arms around him, but he moved them. She did it again, and again he moved them. Then she slapped his face. Peggy saw red. She got up and confidently strolled up to her and tapped her on the shoulder. The girl turned around and stood back when she saw who she was.

"Not her! Surely you haven't turned me down for the ugly one!" She said and laughed. Two other girls that were close by started to laugh. "Go on, run back to granny you strange thing" She added. Peggy desperately wanted to hit out, but she was waiting for William to defend her, he said nothing. " I mean really Will, there's little old me, ready and waiting to give you what you want, but you settle for Miss ugly 1952. Does her grandmother witch have a secret stash of money that you are after!" She scoffed. Peggy felt the sting of tears.

"That's enough Jean!" William shouted. A large framed young man headed for the bar.

"Did you just shout at my sister?" He loomed over William.

"She was being rude to my friend." William said his voice quivering. The large man looked at Peggy.

"What that?" He shouted and pointed at her, making nearly everyone in the hall laugh. That was it, Peggy could take no more. She ran out of the hall and along the lane. The rain was pouring hard, and the wind was howling, but yet she ran.

When she reached the cottage she was soaked. She opened the back door, collapsing in a heap and sobbed!

Chapter 7

"Oh Peggy, you poor child! What on earth has happened?" Molly gasped when she found Peggy curled up in the corner of the kitchen. Peggy was still sobbing so much that she could not speak. Molly ran into the lounge to tell Carrie and seconds later Molly returned pushing Carrie in her wheelchair. Molly wrapped a blanket around Peggy's shoulders.

"Molly could you run upstairs and grab the child her clean nightclothes and a towel?" Carrie asked. Molly nodded and did as Carrie asked. Carrie looked at Peggy, tears formed in her eyes. "Peggy please, please talk to me, tell me what happened." Carrie asked. Peggy wiped her face and sniffed.

"They were all so nasty to me. They called me ugly and made me look like a fool!" She wept. Carrie shook her head as Molly returned with clean clothes for Peggy. She handed them to her.

"Go into the lounge and change into these dry clothes in front of the fire. I will put some milk on to boil." Molly said and helped Peggy to her feet. She left the kitchen, Molly looked at Carrie she could sense how angry she was.

"That boy had better not darken my door for a long time, I cannot be held responsible for what I might do!" Carrie said through gritted teeth.

"We haven't heard the full story yet!" Molly said as she made the cocoa and filled the cups. She placed them on a tray and tapped on the lounge door. "Are you decent Peggy love?" Molly asked gently.

"Aye" Peggy replied. Molly placed the tray on the table and then rushed back to push the wheelchair.

"Who were being nasty?" Carrie asked, trying her hardest to control her anger.

"There were three girls, you know pretty ones with their hair all fancy. The other day at the bakers shop, one walked right into me, knocking my basket out of my hand. I had a feeling that she was a cow then. Anyway she had her sights on William and when he turned her down she slapped him in the face. I walked over to them and then she began saying awful things about me." Peggy explained as tears refilled her eyes. Molly hugged her.

"So, what did William do?" Carrie asked angrily.

"He told her to stop and then her big oaf of a brother came over and started on him. He called me a *that* and everyone laughed, so I ran." Peggy cried. Molly looked at Carrie and nodded. She passed Peggy her cup of cocoa.

"Drink that, it will warm you up." Molly said, nodded at Carrie and left the room. Carrie stroked Peggy's hair while she warmed up in front of the fire.

"Anyway, tell me some more of your story. It will cheer me up." Peggy said and smiled.

Carrie was back at Portobello Road, she had done the last few days at Lambeth, which hadn't bothered her. She wasn't going to see Abe and even though business was slow, it didn't really matter after that 'slummer woman' had given her money. Portobello road was busy. Josie had so many punters lined up that Carrie was struggling to do all the readings.

"Do you want me to fetch Mary, maybe she could do some?" Josie asked. Carrie frowned and shook her head.

"No, I'll do 'em, I need the money." Carrie replied. She worked through the crowd and didn't even stop to eat when she was left with just one. Carrie looked up, she was shocked to see the woman with the red hair waiting.

"Hello again Carrie." The woman said.

"What do you want?" Carrie asked.

"Well I wanted a chat. I have a proposition for you." She replied. Carrie raised one eyebrow.

"Go on then, what is it?" Carrie asked. The woman looked all around her.

"Not here, maybe we could talk in my carriage." She said and gestured in the direction of the carriage. Carrie looked at her and then the carriage. She thought for a moment and then nodded. It would be safer that way in case Mary turned up. She never liked Carrie talking to anyone. They walked over and the woman's footman opened the carriage door, the woman climbed in followed by Carrie.

"Now then, I take it that you are aware of the slummers." She began.

Carrie nodded. "Well I have heard so many good things said about your readings." She continued. Carrie raised her eyebrow. "I have a shop in the West End. At the back is a room that is not in use. I wondered if you would like to work in the shop instead of on the street. You could charge so much more, it would most certainly be your ticket out of here?" She said. Carrie frowned.

"How did you know that I want to leave here?" Carrie asked suspiciously.

"Well it's hardly the best life here is it?" She said, her piercing green eyes felt as though they were boring a hole straight through Carrie.

"And what's in it for you?" Carrie asked.

"Well of course I would take a cut, you know to cover rent, food, and things, but you would still treble your daily earnings." She replied.

"Wait, rent and food. Why would I have to pay you for staying on the gypsy camp?" Carrie asked. The woman laughed.

"My dear girl, you couldn't possibly work in a high-end shop, and live like a gypsy. No. I have an apartment close to the shop. You could live there with me." She said and smiled. "I guarantee that you will have saved enough to set yourself up away from London in a matter of a few months." She continued. Carrie sighed. It all sounded too good to be true, but if it were true she could be out of London before the winter. In a cosy cottage somewhere, she might even get herself a cat.

"Ahem!" The woman said loudly breaking Carrie's daydream. "Well?" She asked now that she had her attention.

"Can I sleep on it?" Carrie replied. The woman shook her head.

"I will return tomorrow for your answer. There are plenty of others that would leap at the opportunity!" She said and opened the carriage door. Carrie climbed out and closed the door. The carriage pulled away.

Carrie walked back to her pitch to be met by Mary, who was stood with her hands on her hips. Carrie climbed up onto the cart, as too did Mary. She took the reins and headed in the direction of the camp.

"Where in God's name have you been?" She asked as Carrie grabbed her sack.

"I have been offered work in the West End." Carrie said and smiled.

"Have you really? By whom may I ask?" Mary scorned. She looked displeased to say the least.

"I take it that you turned it down!" She added. Carrie chuckled.

"I have to tell her tomorrow, I might go for it." Carrie replied.

"Who?" Mary asked.

"I dunno. She was a slummer that I stopped being attacked by two blokes. She came today and asked me if I wanted to work for her." Carrie replied as they walked towards the camp. Mary stopped and looked at Carrie.

"What does she look like?" Mary asked. Carrie shrugged.

"She's got the reddest hair that I've ever seen!" Carrie said wide eyed. Mary chuckled.

"Did she tell you her name?" Carrie nodded.

"Yeah, but it was a bit weird I can't really remember it. Er it was Katina or something like that." Mary nodded.

"I knew it! Katarina!"

"Yeah, that's it. Hang on, how do you know her?" Carrie asked.

"She does it all the time. She swans around here like lady muck, trying to poach all our good readers. Well you can tell her tomorrow, thanks but no!" Mary shouted.

"Why? I could be out of this place in months!!" Carrie argued.

"You really believe that don't you? Carrie don't be so naïve! You won't see a penny, and in any case, I didn't teach you the ways so that you could go and work for that harlot!" Mary shouted.

"I think that I am able to make my own choices Mary. I have paid my way, and now I am moving on!" Carrie shouted back.

"Right! Get your stuff and go then!" Mary yelled as she began to throw all of Carrie's belongings out of the bow top caravan.

The following morning Peggy woke with a banging headache. She opened the curtains and looked at her watch. "Oh no!" She gasped. It was 9.30 and Carrie hadn't had her breakfast. She threw on her robe and ran down the stairs. She could hear voices, and one was a man's voice, was it Dr Clarke? She was thinking as she ran into the kitchen.

Molly was stood at the sink washing the dishes, Joanna walked through with Carrie's tray. "I am so sorry. Is Carrie ok?" Peggy asked anxiously. Molly walked over to her and tapped her shoulder. "Carrie is fine Peggy. I stayed over last night, and she asked me to give you something to help you sleep. She is worried about you!" Molly said as she handed Peggy a cup of tea. Peggy took a sip of her tea and then walked to Carrie's room.

"Good morning." She said as she entered the room, she jumped when she saw a man sitting on the chair beside Carrie's bed.

"Here she is! Good morning Peggy. This is Michael, head guardian." Carrie said cheerfully. Michael stood and held his hand out to Peggy. She shook his hand and smiled. "Now today, Michael, Molly and myself have some things which we need to discuss, so Joanna is going to take you to Edinburgh!" Carrie smiled.

"Why are we going to the city?" Peggy asked.

"Joanna is going to take you shopping and for some lunch!" Carrie replied. "Well don't just stand there. Get yourself dressed!" She added and chuckled. Peggy nodded, smiled, and walked up to her bedroom.

They parked up and Joanna led the way. They went in and out of many dress shops, with Joanna picking out many different outfits, saying 'do you like this' or 'this would really suit you'. Peggy was exhausted. They found a nice café and went in for some lunch.

"So last night was a bit of a disaster." Joanna said. Peggy nodded, her mouth full of food.

"Aye, I felt such a fool. Those girls all had pretty hairdo's and faces full of makeup, and there was me, wild hair and not an ounce of make up to my name!" Peggy replied once she had finished eating. Joanna smiled.

"This afternoon we are going to buy you a whole new wardrobe, and some make-up, then next weekend, you and I will go to the dance and show them all how it's done!" She beamed. Peggy frowned.

"No way am I going near any of those people ever again!" She said and ate a mouthful of food. Joanna nodded.

"Yes Peggy, yes you are. You are far too beautiful to hide away!" Joanna said and smiled. "What about William?" She asked.

"I don't ever want to see him again!" Peggy said adamantly. "Anyway enough about me. How was your weekend?"

"Oh, well I broke off the engagement." Peggy looked at her wide eyed.

"And… was he heartbroken?" She asked. Joanna scoffed.

"Not at all! He has been seeing someone else for months!" She said and laughed. Peggy tutted and shook her head.

"Well at least it leaves the coast clear for you and the guardian." Peggy said. Joanna's face lit up.

"Yes he is coming up!" She beamed.

"Ooh, does that mean that I get to meet him?" Peggy asked. Joanna smiled and nodded.

They got back to the cottage at around 4pm. Peggy was fretting because she needed to prepare the dinner. They walked through the back door, laden down with bags full of new clothes and make up, to the sound of laughter. They both chuckled when they heard Carrie, Molly and Michael laughing so loudly.

Peggy took all her new things up the stairs and put them away neatly, she then hurried to the kitchen to start preparing the dinner. As she walked through the kitchen she could smell food cooking. She looked at the stove, it was full of pots bubbling away. Molly walked out and smiled.

"Did you do all of this?" Peggy asked. Molly smiled and nodded.

"Yes, I thought that I would give you a well earnt break Peggy, goodness knows, you deserve it!" Molly said. "Now I believe that Joanna is going to give you a makeover, so you need to wash your hair!" Molly said as she shooed Peggy back towards the stairs.

Joanna sat Peggy at the dressing table. "First, I'm going to show you how to apply makeup." She smiled. Slowly, step by step she showed her. Then she took out a scary looking contraption. "Now I'm going to Iron your hair." She said holding onto the monster like thing.

"What with that?" Peggy asked anxiously. Joanna laughed. Once she had finished the hair, Peggy took out one of her new outfits and got changed. They had people coming for dinner. Joanna had also got changed and together they walked down the stairs. It sounded busy!

The small lounge was full of people. Peggy walked in and looked for Carrie, who was chatting to an unfamiliar couple. She walked over to her. Carrie looked up. "Oh Peggy, you look beautiful!" She sighed as the couple smiled.

"Peggy, this is Mr and Mrs Hubbard." Carrie said.

"Pleased to meet you." Peggy said smiling.

"They are William's parents" She added. Peggy frowned, which grew deeper as she spied William walking in her direction.

"If you'll excuse me." She said and turned, heading for the kitchen. She walked past William, not making eye contact but brushing up against his arm. She was furious! What was Carrie thinking! Peggy thought to herself. He grabbed her arm in the hallway and turned her to face him.

"Peggy please!" He pleaded. She turned to look at him. His face was swollen, bruised, and cut, making Peggy gasp.

"What happened to you?" She whispered.

"I hit him, just as you walked out. I was just about to run after you when all his pals jumped me." He said. Peggy had never felt so ashamed. She put her hand gently on his swollen cheek.

"I'm so sorry William, I should never have run away. I should have stayed to help you." She whispered.

"No it's me that should be sorry. I should never have taken you there. They are all nasty, and I should have known that they would have turned on you" he replied as he grabbed Peggy's hand and kissed it. He looked around and then gently kissed her, again making her head spin with delight!

Everyone was sat around two tables eating the delicious meal that Molly had cooked. Carrie was in conversation with William's parents, Molly was gazing at Michael as he spoke to Joanna and Matthew, the guardian that Joanna liked. Peggy turned and watched as William struggled to chew the food. She grabbed his plate and cut the food into very small pieces and passed the plate back, without anyone noticing, well all except for Carrie, who smiled as she watched.

Peggy and Joanna cleared the plates after the meal and began to wash the dishes. Michael and Mr Hubbard walked out to the kitchen.

"I believe that the young men would like to take a stroll, so we will take care of these." Michael smiled. Peggy walked along the hallway to fetch her coat and scarf, Joanna did the same, then the four of them walked out onto the lane. Peggy linked William's arm as they walked slowly.

"I am sorry Peggy. You are the most beautiful girl that I have ever met. I canee stop thinking about you. Peggy will you be my girl?" He asked coyly. Peggy grinned the widest grin.

"William, I'd love to be your girl!" She said and chuckled. He picked her up in his strong arms and spun her around. As he lowered her down he kissed her! She blushed and looked to see if Joanna was watching. She gasped, putting her hand over her mouth when she looked. Joanna and Matthew had their lips locked and were more or less eating one another. Peggy had never witnessed anything like it!

She looked at William and they both began to laugh.

"Shall we try it?" He asked as he laughed. Peggy screwed her face up.

"I'd rather not!" She said as she roared with laughter, forcing Joanna and Matthew to stop and look at her.

As the four of them walked back towards the cottage they were chatting. "So next Friday, the four of us go to the dance together?" Matthew asked. Peggy and William looked at one another, they both frowned.

"I don't really want to." Peggy said. William nodded in agreement with her.

"Come on you two, it will be fun, and if anybody starts anything…." Joanna said as she hit her fist into her palm, Peggy roared with laughter.

"Ok then, we'll come won't we?" Peggy said looking at William for approval. He smiled and nodded.

As they got to the gate William put his arms around Peggy's waist. "Will I see you before next Friday then?" He asked hoping that she would say yes. Peggy smiled and nodded.

"Breakfast tomorrow?" She asked.

"Only if it's a fry up!" He said and winked. Peggy nudged him and laughed.

Chapter 8

Everyone had left, and now it was just Carrie and Peggy. Carrie sighed as Peggy tucked in the blankets of her comfortable bed, then looked at Peggy and smiled.

"Shall we share a pot of tea?" Carrie asked. Peggy smiled, nodded, and headed for the kitchen. She returned a few minutes later with the tray, which she placed on the table and poured into the cups. Once she had sat on the chair beside the bed Carrie looked at her. She had a look of concern about her.

"Everything ok?" Peggy asked anxiously. Carrie attempted a smile.

"You look so happy." She said and grinned.

"I have never been so happy. Well, not since Robert was taken away!" Peggy replied. Carrie nodded. "Yes I have been meaning to speak to you about that." She said.

"Oh?"

"Peggy, you must find Robert. You must go to London and track him down." Carrie said earnestly. Peggy frowned.

"Do you know something? Is he in danger?" Peggy asked as she began to panic. Carrie placed her hand on Peggy's to calm her. She smiled and shook her head.

"No, no nothing like that. Robert will have three children, one of which will carry the magical bloodline. She will be most powerful, and you must guide her." Carrie replied. Peggy looked confused.

"But, I don't have the power. How can I guide her?" Peggy asked.

"You do Peggy, just not as strong. I am telling you my story, so that when I'm gone, you can take over and teach her the ways of the earth." Carrie smiled.

"But I don't know the ways of the earth." Peggy replied.

"That's why Molly and Joanna are here. The things that I am no longer able to teach you, they can." Carrie said and sipped her tea. She yawned and Peggy chuckled as her eyes began to close. She took the cup from her, pulled up the blankets and turned out the light.

The following morning Peggy opened the curtains and groaned. It was pouring with rain, and she had laundry to do! She prepared Carrie's breakfast and put a pot of porridge on the stove. She opened Carrie's curtains and sat her up. She looked bright, she had a twinkle in her eye, Peggy smiled.

She placed the tray on Carrie's lap, then heard a tap on the back door. "That will be William!" Carrie said and smiled. Peggy nodded.

"Good morning!" He said as she opened the door. He walked in, he was soaked to the skin. Peggy helped him out of his wet coat and hung it next to the fire. She dished up two bowls of porridge and passed him his cup of tea.

"You are wonderful!" He said as he gulped a big spoonful of porridge. Peggy smiled. "So how did you end up here?" He asked as he wiped his mouth on the napkin. Peggy sighed.

"My mother died a few years ago, the squire sent me here." She replied.

"Do you have no other family then?"

"I have a younger brother, but he was taken away when he was three." She replied sadly. "One day soon, I have to go to London and track him down." She added. William nodded and smiled.

"I'll help you. Always thought of myself as a detective, you know a Sherlock Holmes type of guy!" He said and laughed. Peggy laughed.

"Seriously though. Would you help me find him?" She asked.

"Aye of course I will."

William went back to work on the promise that he could see her later that day. She promised that she would take him some lunch to the field where he was working. She managed to get some of the laundry done when the sun had finally made an appearance and she hung the wet washing on the line. She looked at her watch and smiled. In the kitchen she boiled the kettle and took the tray into Carrie, who was sitting in the chair next to the window. As she poured Carrie inhaled deeply.

"If I'm not mistaken, that very much smells like coffee!" Carrie smiled. Peggy grinned.

"There was a shop in Edinburgh, it sold coffee. I told Joanna that I had to get some for you!" Peggy smiled as she poured in the cream and passed a cup to Carrie.

"That smells wonderful!" Carrie exclaimed and then sipped. "mmm" she said and smiled. Slowly she continued to tell her story.

Carrie picked up her belongings and walked out of the gypsy camp. She hid around the corner. She watched the camp waiting for Mary to go out. After about three hours, Mary emerged from the bow top and walked towards Portobello road. Carrie quickly hurried around the back of the caravan to where her stash hole was. She took out her money and ran.

She was in the Piccadilly area when she finally ran out of energy and had to stop running. It was so busy! She slid inside a shop doorway, just to catch her breath and figure out where she was going to sleep. A man walked past and glared at her. She huffed and he walked away.

Another shadow appeared and stopped. Carrie looked up. "What on earth are you doing here?" Katarina asked as she looked at Carrie huddled up in the corner.

"I told Mary my friend that I was coming to work for you, so she threw me out!" Carrie said quietly. Katarina nodded.

"Yes, I know who she is. Awful Gypsy woman! Come on, my apartment isn't far from here." Katarina beckoned. Carrie got up and followed. They walked for a few minutes until they reached a large building. There was a footman outside who opened the door for Katarina, turning his nose up at Carrie. She pulled a face at him when she walked past.

They went into a lift. Katarina smiled at the attendant as he pulled the gates closed and the lift moved. Carrie was petrified, this made Katarina chuckle. Katarina led her to a door, which opened. Carrie gasped as she peered inside. It was the most beautiful place she had ever seen. There were so many paintings, pretty flowers on the walls, real flowers in vases everywhere. It was like a palace! A maid walked through. "Polly could you prepare a bath for Carrie please?" Katarina asked and gestured for Carrie to follow her. They walked up a long hallway. Katarina opened a door and walked in, Carrie followed. "This is your room, I hope you will find it comfortable." Katarina said. The maid began to fill a large copper bath with steaming water.

"When she's in, put her belongings in this and put it down the shute." Katarina said as she passed the maid a jute sack.

"Wait, what are you doing with my things?" Carrie asked as she frowned.

"They have to go! You cannot possibly walk around in those rags any longer!" Katarina replied. Carrie shook her head.

"Well it's better than walking around with no clothes on. There are all that I've got!" Carrie fumed. Katarina grinned, walked to a huge closet, and opened the door. It was full of clothes.

"They are yours!" She said excitedly. Carrie frowned.

"I don't understand?" She said shaking her head.

"Just get into the bath, wash your hair, then we can pick out an outfit ready for dinner. I have some friends coming to dine." Katarina said and left the room. The maid smiled at Carrie.

"Your bath is ready Ma'am" She said and curtseyed.

"Right, my name is Carrie not Ma'am, and please don't do that." Carrie said.

"As you wish Ma'am, whoops I mean Carrie." The maid said and covered her mouth with her hand.

"Thank you Polly" Carrie said and smiled as the maid left the room. Carrie looked around the room. She lifted a large rug and checked the floorboards. There was one loose. She pulled it up and placed her stash of money inside. She replaced the floorboard and removed her dirty rags. She dipped her toe in, the water was so warm. Slowly she lowered herself into the warm foamy water. It was the best feeling!

Polly walked back in carrying a jug. "I must wash your hair Miss." She said as she walked to the bath. Carrie hid her bits, trying to retain some dignity, as the maid poured warm water over Carrie's long, dark hair. She rubbed in some soap and then rinsed it. She placed a cloth over Carrie's head and began rubbing her hair dry. Carrie thought that her head might fall off.

Polly then held up a bath sheet. Carrie stood up and wrapped herself in the sheet and climbed out. On the bed Polly had laid out undergarments for her, which she quickly put on. Katarina returned. She opened the closet door and was shuffling through the many dresses inside. She took two out and held both of them in front of Carrie. "Try this one." Katarina said as she pushed the dress at Carrie.

Once dressed Katarina sat Carrie in front of a mirror at the dressing table. She ran a brush through Carrie's matted hair. Carrie yelped as the brush pulled chunks of her hair out. Katarina then put beautiful braids in Carrie's hair. Carrie stood up, Katarina stood back to take a look.

"What a transformation!" Katarina said and smiled. She walked Carrie to the mirror. She did look completely different, but the clothes felt so uncomfortable.

They were served dinner in a huge dining room. There were twelve people that Katarina said were her friends, Carrie thought that they were all just la-di-da snobs! The people left and Katarina handed Carrie a brandy while they were sitting in the drawing room. Carrie was looking at Katrina. "How did you know where to find me?" Carrie asked as she screwed her face up from taking a sip of brandy. It burnt!

"I just happened to be walking that way. Pure coincidence!" Katarina replied as she sipped her drink. Carrie didn't believe a word of it.

"What time do I start tomorrow?" Carrie asked. Katarina laughed.

"That's what I like, eagerness!" She scoffed. "No tomorrow, I thought that I could get you acquainted with the area, maybe visit a couple of museums and such." She added. Carrie frowned.

"But I don't want to be acquainted with the place, I just want to work." She replied.

"Oh, how unfortunate! Well if you insist, shall we say up and ready by ten?" Katarina said disappointingly.

"Ten! I usually start at six!" Carrie said and placed her glass on the table. She didn't want anymore, it made her head spin. She yawned. "Well if you don't mind, I am going to bed, I'm knackered!" Carrie said and stood up.

"The expression you use here is tired!" Katarina said and scowled.

"Goodnight then." Carrie said and walked her weary body to her room. It took her ages to get out of the dress that she was wearing. She found a nightdress, slipped it on and climbed into the bed. The sheets were so soft, before she knew it she was sound asleep.

Polly walked into the room and opened the huge floor length curtains. Carrie opened her bleary eyes. "What's the time?" She asked.

"It's half nine Miss" Polly replied.

"What!" Carrie jumped out of the bed and began rooting through the closet for practical clothing. She had pulled everything out. There was nothing unless you were planning a trip to the theatre or dining out! Carrie thought to herself as she grunted in frustration.

"Polly could you fetch Katarina for me?" Carrie asked. Polly nodded and left the room. A few moments later Katrina strolled in, with not so much as a knock!

"What is it?" She asked agitatedly.

"There is nothing practical for me to wear to work." Carrie replied. Katarina laughed an over exaggerated laugh.

"Are you joking? You have hundreds of pounds worth of clothing in that closet!" She shouted. Carrie frowned.

"Not that I can wear to work! What if I got into a spot of trouble. I would never be able to defend myself wearing any of that!" Carrie shouted back.

"What is it that you wish to wear?" Katarina bellowed. Carrie shrugged.

"Something that I can move in might be nice!" Carrie growled.

"Fine! Wait here!" Katarina stormed out of the bedroom.

Katarina returned a while later and threw a dress at Carrie. Carrie looked at it. It was a light material, all one colour and quite loose. She smiled. Katarina left the room and Carrie slipped into the dress.

They walked for around five minutes and then Katarina walked them down an alleyway. It was the cleanest alley that Carrie had ever seen. They walked into a small shop, which sold China teapots and cups. There was a large red curtain hanging behind the counter. Katarina pulled the curtain back and gestured to Carrie. The room was bare, except for a small circular table covered with a red velvet cloth.

"This is where you will work from." Katarina said. Carrie nodded. She threw the sack onto the table and began to take out her cards and crystal ball. Katarina was watching her with great intent. She walked over to the table and picked up the crystal ball. She gazed at it.

"Will you get rid of that dirty sack, before a customer comes in!" She said tensely. Carrie threw the sack beneath the table. "Where did you get this. It's rather unusual?" She asked. Carrie was looking through her tarot deck. She looked up.

"Oh, Mary gave it to me a long time ago." Carrie said.

"Would you mind if I took it next door to the jewellers. I believe it would be of great interest to him." Katarina asked in her sweetest voice. Carrie frowned, then nodded.

"I wouldn't steal it. The last person that did that ended up a gonna" Carrie muttered under her breath as Katarina left the shop.

Carrie heard the bell above the door shop ring, then the curtain pulled back. Carrie was taken aback when Josie walked through.

"I'm not going back. You can tell Mary that I am not going back!" Carrie said forcibly. Josie smiled and shook her head.

"No girl, you got it all wrong. I'm working with you now aint I" Josie said and smiled revealing the one tooth that she left. Carrie frowned.

"So where are you staying?" Carrie asked suspiciously.

"Same place you are. Not as fancy as you though, I'm in with the servants." She replied. Carrie still wasn't buying it. "Anyhow, I'm off to grab some punters" She coughed and left the shop.

Carrie had done at least seven tarot readings, Katarina had still not returned with the ball. She yawned and stood up to stretch. She walked over to the curtain and peered into the shop. It appeared to be closed. She walked through and tried the door. It was locked.

"Shit!" She whispered. She walked back through the curtain, earlier she had noticed a back entrance. She tried that, and again locked. "Urrgh!" She shouted and slumped onto the chair. She was thinking…. How could she get out. She walked back through to the shop door and tried it again. She started to push the handle hard… nothing. She went back to the other door and tried the same thing, again nothing. Then in a fit of rage she punched the door with both fists, taking the door clean off of its hinges. She ran back inside, grabbed her sack, threw the tarot cards into the sack, and ran, the entire time thanking herself for having the insight of taking her cash with her that morning. She ran out of the alleyway and onto a busy street. She had no idea where she was or where she was going. She darted in and out of the many people, then she spied Josie. She quickly ran down a side street. Something went over her head, covering her arms and she was being carried. She struggled as much as she could, then bam! Something hit her on the head.

Peggy prepared Carrie's lunch and wrapped William's in some paper. She took Carrie's tray through and placed it on the table in front of her, once she had moved the newspaper that she was reading. She looked over the top of her metal framed glasses and smiled.

"I promised William that I would pop to the field to see him. Is that ok?" Peggy asked. Carrie nodded and smiled.

"Don't be too long, Molly and Joanna are due to arrive at 2." Carrie said as she removed the cover of her lunch and began eating.

"Don't worry, I won't be long!" Peggy called out as she fastened her coat and tied on her head scarf.

She walked out of the back door and climbed over the wall into the first field. She knew that William was working on the second field. She climbed over the fence and saw him. He was digging. He looked up and waved. She waved back and almost ran to him. She passed him his lunch. He wiped his face on his sleeve, then kissed her. She smiled.

"Let's go and sit on the wall up there." He said as he pointed.

They were sitting on the wall chatting and laughing when they both spied a car driving towards them up the lane. "Oh no!" Peggy heard William whisper. She looked at him.

"What's wrong?" She asked. He gestured to the car.

"That's Jean's brother's car." He said and put his lunch on the wall. The car stopped where they were. Her brother glared at them both as Jean climbed out of the passenger seat. She walked around the car and stood with her hands on her hips.

"Aww how sweet. Has the good lady brought food for her master." She scoffed. Peggy shook her head and laughed. "What ya laughing at ugly?" Jean asked. Peggy saw red. She walked over to her, they were nose to nose.

"Why don't you piss off before you get hurt." Peggy growled through gritted teeth. Jean jumped back in horror.

As she ran back to the car she looked at her brother. "See I told you that they were witches. I'm telling the reverend!" She shouted as she jumped into the car, and they sped off. William sat on the wall laughing.

"You are amazing!" he said as still he laughed!

Chapter 9

Molly and Joanna were already there when Peggy returned. She panicked when she saw the car parked outside the cottage, thinking that she must be late. Molly was making the tea when Peggy walked in through the back door. "They are all in the lounge." She said and smiled. Peggy hung up her coat and went straight to the lounge. Carrie was in her wheelchair, Joanna and Michael were sitting on the sofa.

"Did you have fun?" Carrie asked as Peggy leant over and kissed her cheek.

"I'll tell you about it later!" She replied and rolled her eyes. Michael smiled. He had a kind face, he looked like a school master, Peggy thought to herself.

"Now Peggy, there are certain things which you need to learn, and that's why we are all here to teach you." Michael said. Peggy nodded. "Do you have any understanding of the spirit realm?" He asked. Peggy frowned.

"I don't quite know what you mean?" She said wearing a puzzled expression. She looked at Carrie who smiled and nodded towards Michael.

"Well, as guardians we work closely with the realm of spirit, our ancestors, ones that have left this mortal coil." He smiled. Still Peggy had no idea what he was talking about.

"What Michael is trying to say Peggy is, that we talk to our loved ones that have passed away. They go to the spirit realm, and we communicate with them." Molly said in a more simplified manner. Peggy smiled and nodded her head, now she understood, they talk to ghosts, she thought to herself.

"So I am here to teach you how to do that." Michael chirped. Peggy smiled. "If we finish our tea, then we can go out to the garden and begin!" He added.

"Why the garden, it's a wee bit chilly out there. Can we not do it here?" Peggy asked. Everyone chuckled. Michael shook his head.

"No dear, we really need to be outside, that way we are closer to nature and the earth itself!" He smiled and sipped his tea. Peggy nodded. She wasn't happy about this, she was going to freeze!

They were seated underneath a small oak tree in the garden. "Now Peggy I want you to become aware of your surroundings." Michael began, she nodded. "Feel the grass, feel the breeze and the teeniest warmth coming from the sun's small rays." He added. She nodded. "Now close your eyes" He said.

Later as Peggy was preparing the dinner Carrie wheeled herself out to the kitchen. "What are you doing? Why didn't you ring the bell?" Peggy asked as she wiped her hands on her pinny and was about to wheel Carrie back through.

"I'm alright Peggy, I wanted to come out here and keep you company while you cook. Besides, I am sick of looking at the same four walls!" Carrie said as she parked at the end of the table. "Anyway I thought that you were desperate to find out who had captured me?" Carrie said and grinned.

She was in some mode of transport, she could feel wheels beneath her she was being thrown all over the place. It finally stopped and the sack that she was contained in, was being dragged. Finally the sack was removed, and she could breathe again. She looked up and was not in the least bit surprised to see Mary glaring down at her. She was stood with her hands on her hips. "Where is it?" She shouted.

"What?" Carrie roared back.

"The fucking ball. Where is it Carrie?" Mary was close to screaming now.

"Katarina took it, she was showing it to a jeweller or something." Carrie replied.

"You idiot! She was never to get her hands on that! That was always meant for you." Mary shouted.

"Why? Why me?" Carrie asked quietly.

"I don't know why! I was just told when it was handed to me that it would be stolen, and that the young girl that returned it to me was the rightful owner and it should never leave her." She said still shouting. Her face red with rage.

"Yeah but when Hester stole it, she ended up dead. Surely the same will happen to her." Carrie said trying to calm the gypsy down.

"Idiot! I killed them!" She screamed. Carrie shook her head.

"No I saw it in the ball." Carrie said frowning.

"Yes, yes you did but only because I put that vision there!"

"Well, I'll go and get it back!" Carrie shouted. Mary laughed.

"Ok, you do that!" she replied. Carrie got to her feet and brushed the dirt from her dress. Mary laughed.

"Where the hell did you get that ugly thing?" She laughed. Carrie scowled. She went to walk away, Mary stopped her.

"Where the fuck do you think you're going?" She asked.

"To get the fucking ball back" Carrie bellowed. Mary grabbed hold of her as two large gypsy men tied her hands behind her back. Mary gestured to them, they dragged Carrie to a large rock, they moved a boulder that concealed an entrance and the threw her inside moving the boulder back across the opening.

She was thirsty and hungry, she hadn't eaten since breakfast and goodness only knows what time it was now. She kicked at the boulder, but it would not budge, she was angry and frustrated. She kicked and kicked until eventually she fell asleep.

She woke up, she will still inside the rock, it was pitch black. "Arrgghhh!!!" She screamed. She could see nothing nor hear anything. Then she remembered the crystal pendant. Shit her hands were tied. Molly said that if she rubbed the crystal in the centre that they would be able to find her. She put her head down and managed to catch the pendant under her chin. Frantically she began moving her chin, rubbing the crystal, all the time thinking Molly, please, please find me!

Soon the boulder began to move. Carrie was prepared for another showdown with Mary. The light stung her eyes as it shone through as the boulder was moved. When she could eventually see, she was full of relief. It was Molly with three men. They helped Carrie out of the rock and then put her in the carriage that was waiting. Two of the men climbed in with Carrie and Molly the other was driving the horses.

"Thank you!" Carrie said as she looked at Molly. She smiled.

"We have a long journey ahead of us, so you may be wise to get some rest. I don't suppose that you have eaten?" Molly asked. Carrie shook her head. Molly took out a basket and handed it to Carrie. It had pies, bread, and fruit inside, and a large jug of apple juice. Carrie drank the entire jug in one go, apple juice spilling down her chin then her dress. She ate everything inside the basket.

"Where are we going?" Carrie asked.

"We are going to a safe lodge, now that she has the crystal ball she can track you wherever you go." Molly replied.

"Yeah, but I need to get the ball back." Carrie said angrily. Molly shook her head.

"Not yet. It is too dangerous. Trust me, she will come looking for you." Molly said and smiled.

"Now try and rest." She added as she passed Carrie a warm blanket. Carrie wrapped herself up and soon fell fast asleep.

She woke to the carriage rocking from side to side and for a moment she wondered where she was. She then looked at Molly and smiled. She stretched her stiff body and yawned.

"Where are we?" She asked sleepily.

"Nearly there!" Molly replied. Carrie pulled the black velvet curtain across to reveal the tiny window in the carriage door. It was pitch black, she could see nothing!

Very soon the carriage ground to a halt. The two men climbed out and held the door open for Molly and Carrie. The house was grand to say the least.

"Cor!" Carrie said as she stood with her mouth gaped open. Molly gently took her by the arm and led her into the mansion. A large man stood at the door to greet them.

"Carrie this is Jensen, he will see to anything that you need." Molly said as she handed her coat to Jensen. Carrie smiled and he smiled back. They walked up the sweeping staircase and Molly opened a door. "This will be your room" Molly smiled. Carrie was again stood with her mouth gaped open. There was a lovely big bed, with the prettiest cover over it. There was a dressing table with a beautiful ornate mirror on it. Carrie looked at Molly and grinned. "Get yourself acquainted with your room, I'll send Jensen up with some tea, then you can have a lovely warm bath before bed." Molly said. Carrie grinned again, then frowned.

"But, but I have no clothes. That stupid woman binned 'em!" Carrie huffed. Molly chuckled.

"That's not a problem, you look the same size as me, I'll get one of the maids to fetch some night wear for you." She replied.

So she had a lovely cup of tea, a lovely hot soapy bath and now she was sat up in this beautiful comfortable bed. She sighed. It was the first time in her life that she had felt truly happy. She snuffed out the candle and snuggled down beneath the warm covers, listening to the gentle crackle of the fire.

"Now, where would you like to eat this evening?" Peggy asked as she drained the potatoes. There was a knock on the front door. Peggy looked at Carrie and frowned. She wiped her hands and walked through the hallway to the door. She gasped when she opened it. The Reverend was standing with a stern look on his face, behind him were half a dozen or so locals, Jean being one of them.

"Can I help you?" Peggy asked.

"Fetch your grandmother." The Reverend said abruptly.

"No need she is here" Carrie said from behind Peggy. They all looked at one another in complete horror. They could all hear her, but not one could see her! Peggy stood to the side to reveal Carrie in her wheelchair. The Reverend cleared his throat.

"It has been brought to my attention, that you and your granddaughter participate in the practice of witchcraft, which as you well know is illegal. Therefore if you insist upon conducting tasks for the devil, we must insist that you leave our community!" he snorted. Carrie laughed.

"Hang on, I'll just pop back inside and ask the Lord of Darkness, what we should do!" She shouted as she coughed.

"Do you have any evidence, to back up your ludicrous accusations!" Carrie shouted.

"Yes, well er, Miss Douglas, she said that you were placing curses on the local folk." The Reverend stammered.

"Did she? Well in that case, I suggest that you all take it up with the local constabulary. Now if you don't mind I would like you all to get off of my land. NOW!" Carrie roared. They all quickly shuffled out of the gate.

Carrie and Peggy went back to the kitchen, Peggy was anxiously chewing her fingernails.

"What a damned cheek!" Carrie fumed. "I mean, what on earth? I bet it was that bloody Mrs Baldwin!" Carrie added still seething. Peggy looked down at the floor.

"I had words with Jean earlier today." Peggy said quietly.

"What sort of words?" Carrie asked.

"I just said that she should piss off if she knew what was good for her. You did tell me not to allow her to bully me!" Peggy said, tears stinging her eyes as she fought to hold them back. Carrie touched Peggy's cheek.

"Yes I did, and you did the right thing Peggy, you mustn't let people like that walk all over you!" Carrie said.

"Aye but now, I've brought trouble to your door. I am so sorry!" Peggy said, releasing the tears to run down her cheeks.

"Nonsense! Trouble was always going to find me. It always did. Now come on, dry your eyes, we have a delicious dinner to eat, and I'm famished!" She replied. They sat at the table in front of the fire, eating their dinner.

"So what happened at the safe lodge?" Peggy asked. Carrie grinned.

She woke the following morning to the sweetest sound of birdsong. It was the one thing you could never hear in London! She climbed out of bed and walked to the window. She pulled back the long drapes and sighed with great contentment. The gardens were beautiful. The door knocked.

"Come in" Carrie called out from the window.

"Sorry Miss, I have brought you a robe and something to put on your feet. Miss Molly says to tell you that breakfast is served." Carrie turned and gasped, as Polly the maid from Katarina's apartment was placing the robe on the chair. She turned back to face the window.

"Thank you, tell Molly I will be down in a minute." Carrie said quietly, wondering what on earth Polly was doing there. Had Katarina sent her? She thought to herself as she slipped the robe and soft shoes on and opened the door.

Jensen was standing at the bottom of the huge staircase. "Good morning Carrie, I take it that you slept well?" He asked her as he led her towards the dining room.

"Yes I slept like a baby thank you!" She beamed. He nodded and opened the door. The dining room was huge, with long windows that overlooked the gardens. Molly was sitting at the huge table, and she gestured to the chair beside her. Carrie sat down and looked at her.

"Good morning, did you sleep well?" Molly asked as a maid poured Carrie some coffee and served her boiled eggs. Carrie nodded as she took a sip from her coffee cup. She smiled inside to herself. She loved coffee! "Is there something wrong?" Molly asked.

"Well, you sent a maid into my room this morning…" Carrie began. Molly smiled.

"Yes Polly." Molly replied.

"Well that Polly was the same maid at Katarina's apartment!" Carrie said and frowned. Again Molly smiled and nodded.

"Yes that's right." She replied. Carrie shook her head in disbelief.

"Well what the bloody hell is she doing here then?" Carrie asked anxiously. Molly chuckled.

"She is part of the guardianship. She was placed at Katarina's to keep an eye on you. How do you think that we found you so quickly, guardians were following your every move." Molly said.

"Oh! I thought it was because I rubbed the pendant with me chin!" Carrie said. Molly laughed.

"Well, yes it was that too, although I didn't realise that it was your chin!" She laughed. "After breakfast, Michael head of the guardians would like to speak to you in his office." Molly added.

"Am I in trouble?" Carrie asked as she swallowed the last mouthful of egg. Molly shook her head.

"No, he wants to explain, who we are and what we do, and your involvement in all of this is." Molly replied. "Polly has put clothing in the closet in your room. I am sorry if they are not to your taste. This afternoon we have an appointment at the dressmakers." Molly said as she excused herself and left the room. Carrie took her coffee over to the window and slowly sipped at it, savouring every mouthful.

She found a pretty dress and some shoes to match, luckily they all fit her. She tried her hardest to replicate the braids that Katarina had put in but failed badly. She ran a brush through her hair and pulled it back away from her face. She opened the door to be met with Polly.

"I was just about to ask you if you would like me to braid your hair Miss." She said and smiled. Carrie grinned.

"Yes please, and stop calling me Miss, me name is Carrie!" She smiled. Polly put some beautiful braids in Carrie's hair and showed her in the mirror.

"They are so good. I wish I could do 'em" Carrie said smiling.

"When you're not so busy, I could show you." Polly said and smiled.

Carrie walked down the stairs, wondering where Michael's office could be. She walked along the bottom hallway, she was wandering back and forth and looked completely lost.

"Ahem!" Jensen cleared his throat to get Carrie's attention. She looked and he gestured to Michael's office. She smiled and saluted him. She gently tapped on the door. She could hear more than one man's voice.

"Come!" She heard, looking at Jensen, who gestured for her to enter. She turned the door knob and pushed the door. She hadn't realised how hard she had pushed it and went flying into the room, crashing into the huge oak desk, and nearly landing on the lap of the man that was sitting there.

"Oh, I'm sorry!" Carrie said her face red with embarrassment. The man who was sitting behind the desk chuckled.

"That's absolutely fine! Carrie I take it. I am Michael." He said and held his hand out to shake. Carrie grabbed his hand and smiled. "Please take a seat." He added. Carrie sat on the empty seat opposite Michael and turned to see who was sitting in the seat that she almost landed in.

He grinned like a Cheshire cat! "What the bloody hell are you doing here?" She asked, completely baffled!

Chapter 10

"Well, who was it?" Peggy asked impatiently as Carrie paused. There was then a tap on the back door. She sighed and got up to answer the door. Molly and Joanna walked in smiling. Carrie chuckled.

"You must wait until tomorrow!" She said as she laughed.

"No, that's not fair. Just tell me who it was. Was it Abraham?" Peggy pleaded. Carrie shook her head.

"All in good time my dear!" She said and Molly laughed. Peggy cleared the dishes, Joanna made the tea, then the four of them sat in the lounge discussing what had happened earlier. Molly sighed.

"Maybe you should both come to the lodge." Molly suggested. Carrie shook her head, Peggy frowned.

"At my time of life I am most definitely not running away! I have been running for too long!" Carrie said wearily. Molly smiled a sad smile and tapped Carrie's leg.

"Of course! I will go and speak to the Reverend tomorrow." Molly said.

"Wouldn't it sound better coming from Michael?" Joanna asked. Molly looked at Carrie, who nodded, she agreed with Joanna. Those kind of people never took women seriously.

"Very well. I will go and speak to Michael now. Joanna are you coming?" Molly asked as she stood up. Joanna shook her head.

"Can you collect me once you have seen him?" She asked. Molly smiled.

"Of course!" She grinned. Joanna looked at Peggy, who was smiling. Carrie yawned.

"If you girls don't mind, I think I might go to bed now. I am absolutely exhausted." Carrie said as she yawned again. Peggy wheeled her to her room and helped her get ready for bed. She helped her into bed and tucked in the blankets.

"Would you like some cocoa?" Peggy asked. Carrie tapped her hand.

"No thank you Peggy, I just need to sleep." She said as she closed her eyes. Peggy turned out the light and pulled the door to.

Peggy walked to the kitchen, she could hear Joanna clattering about out there.

"I'm just making some cocoa." Joanna said and smiled. Peggy looked bemused.

"Why have you put four cups out?" Peggy asked. Joanna grinned.

"Because Peggy darling, we have guests!" Joanna replied as she picked up the tray and walked towards the living room.

William grinned at Peggy as she entered the room. She smiled and sat down on the sofa beside him. Joanna passed around the warm cocoa and then perched herself on Matthew's lap.

"What are you two doing here?" Peggy asked as she blew on the hot drink. William put his hand on her knee.

"Twice in one day isnee enough. I want to see you all the time" He said sincerely. Peggy blushed.

"Aww!" Joanna and Matthew said in unison. Peggy shook her head, then looked deep into William's eyes, and for a moment she was lost!

"Matthew and I are going for a stroll, while we wait for the drinks to cool down." Joanna said as she was pulling Matthew by the hand, heading towards the door.

"Just you and me then" William said as he took Peggy's hand in his. She smiled shyly. "I meant every word Peggy. I just want to be with you all of the time, and you are always in my thoughts." He said tenderly. Peggy's head was spinning. She had never been so happy as she was right at that very moment. She had never met anyone so sweet and gentle as William and if she was to be completely honest with herself, he was never out of her thoughts. He put his arm around her shoulder and pulled her towards him. He kissed her. "One day, we will have a cottage just like this, a couple of our own wee kiddies running around." He whispered and smiled.

"I can't go anywhere. I have to take care of Carrie." She said.

"Aye, I know that. I can wait." He said and kissed her again. Sadness washed over Peggy's face.

"Did I say something wrong?" He asked anxiously. Peggy smiled.

"No of course not! I was just thinking about Carrie. She has had such a hard life, and I only know a wee part of it. I have only just got to know her, and I want to make the remainder of her days as happy as I possibly can." Peggy said as she wiped the tears away from her eyes. William held her tightly.

"We'll do it together! We'll make these days the best she has ever had!" he said and kissed Peggy gently on the head.

"Thank you William, you are such a kind soul." She said as she looked deeply into his big brown eyes.

The back door closed, ending their precious moment. Joanna and Matthew walked in laughing and joking. Peggy looked at Joanna, she was truly stunning and so full of fun. Peggy wished that she had one ounce of her confidence! The boys drank their drinks and left just before Molly returned to collect Joanna.

"Will you be here tomorrow?" Peggy asked them both as they readied themselves to leave.

"Yes we most certainly will. We will be here for a long while, Michael wants to do some more meditation with you tomorrow once he has paid the Reverend a visit." Molly said as she kissed Peggy on the cheek.

"See you tomorrow Joanna" Peggy said smiling.

"Call me Jo" She said as she then kissed Peggy on the cheek and they both left. Peggy washed the cups through and dried them, then yawned. She felt absolutely shattered, she had never been around as many people as she had lately, and it was pretty exhausting. She poured herself a glass of water and made her way up the stairs to bed.

She took Carrie's breakfast tray in. It was a beautiful morning, the sun was shimmering through the trees and there was not a single cloud in the sky! She pulled back the small curtains, Carrie stretched and yawned. "Did you sleep well?" Peggy asked as she helped her to sit up. Carrie sighed.

"No not really, I had those awful nightmares again." She said and yawned again.

"Is there an elixir that I can make for you to help you sleep?" Peggy asked. Carrie grinned.

"Be a dear and grab the Grimoire out of the chest." Carrie winked. Peggy did as she asked and placed the heavy book on Carrie's lap. Carrie smiled and opened the book. "Sleeping elixir." She said quietly. The pages flicked back and forth, then stopped. Carrie read through and gestured for Peggy to take a look. She scrolled through the script and smiled.

"I could do that for you." She grinned. Carrie tapped her hand.

"Stay while I eat my breakfast, those nightmares have unnerved me a little." Carrie asked.

"Of course, but only if you tell me who was in the office with Michael. Carrie took a bite from a large chunk of bread and jam.

"Where was I....oh yes... Michael's office..."

"I was in the area, thought I would pop in!" He replied.

"Look I know that to some people I come across as a bit dim, but I am not entirely stupid!" Carrie said and frowned. Michael leant forward and smiled.

"Nobody here thinks that you are in any way stupid or dim Carrie, and I believe that Abraham should tell you the truth." He said and frowned at Abraham. Abraham cleared his throat, then sighed.

"When I first saw you, I was aware of who you are. I am part of the Guardianship, but from a different department. I am also a pilot. I was sent to track you down by the Elders, who had been made aware that the Dark Realm had located you through bloody Mary and were going to intercept." Abraham explained. Carrie shook her head and looked at Michael.

"So all the oh Carrie you have such a pretty face, and it may be a while until I see you again… well you only said it to lure me in!" She fumed as she screwed her eyes up at Abraham. "And who the bloody hell are the Dark Realm?" She continued, making Michael chuckle.

"No, that is not true. I think that you have a beautiful face, what I said, I meant, every single word!" Abraham said trying his best to defend himself. Carrie did not even look at him.

"The Dark realm are a group of revenants that work together. At present, it is Katarina that leads them although, how long that lasts remains to be seen!" Michael said and looked at Abraham.

"I'm sorry but you have both lost me. I don't have a clue what you are going on about! And what's Mary got to do with it?" Carrie asked.

"Katarina is a revenant. Do you know what that is?" Abe asked. Carrie nodded.

"Yeah, Molly told me. They are the undead that feed from humans." Carrie explained. Michael and Abe both nodded.

"Yes but it runs so much deeper than that. Katarina is a powerful sage. She has extraordinary magical power. Because of her extreme greed and vanity, she will only feed from the magically gifted. Not only does she get to retain her youth and beauty, but her power becomes even more enhanced." Michael said staring directly at Carrie.

"And Mary?" Carrie asked again.

"Mary, she has power, and once Katarina tried to take it. To stop her, Mary forged a pact with Katarina, that she would supply her with gifted people, so long as Katarina left her alone. Just before your father died, Katarina told Mary about you and asked her to track you down, which she did through your sister Hester." Abe said. Carrie frowned.

"What, so she used Hester to get to me?" She asked, both Abe and Michael nodded. "Then she killed her." Carrie continued, again both men nodded.

"Yeah, but now she has the crystal ball, she'll leave me alone won't she?" Carrie asked.

"Unfortunately not! She has tried to get her hands on the ball for many years. It was given to Mary to take care of until you were at an age to use it properly. The ball has been passed down by your ancestor Abagail Walcott. Have you ever heard of her?" Michael asked. Carrie nodded.

"Yes she appears to me and speaks to me. You know when I begin to lose control, she speaks to me, and I sort myself out." Carrie said. Abe chuckled.

"Indeed! Abagail was a incredibly powerful sage. She also wrote a Grimoire. Do you know what that is?" Michael asked. Carrie shook her head. Michael walked to the wall and moved a huge portrait that was hanging, to reveal a hole in the wall. He took out a big wooden chest, struggling to carry it to the desk. Abe stood and helped him eventually! They placed it on the desk with a thud. Michael wiped the dust off and opened it. He passed Carrie a huge leather book.

"That is Abagail's grimoire. All the knowledge and wisdom that she had, is held within those pages, and it is yours?" Michael exclaimed excitedly.

"Molly will teach you how to use it. Reading it is not as straight forward as you may think!" Abe said and smiled. Carrie frowned then felt her face grow hot as she blushed with embarrassment.

"I can't read." She said so quietly, it fell short of a whisper. Michael looked at Abe in horror.

"That's fine, you do not have to able to read. The grimoire will give you whatever you need." Abe said, smiled and tapped Carrie's knee. She exhaled and smiled at Abe.

"Carrie, you have an incredibly magical power. It flows through your veins. Our job is to teach you how to use it and protect you from those who wish to take it all from you. Katarina is desperate to get her hands on the grimoire." Michael said solemnly. "And she is desperate to take your power!" He added. Carrie gulped. Life on the streets of London was hard enough, but at least you were aware of the dangers. This was a different kettle of fish completely! She was thinking to herself as she gazed at the floor. The door knocked, breaking her daydream.

"Come" Michael called out. The door opened and Molly walked in.

"Sorry to interrupt, but we have an appointment at the dressmakers." She said and smiled longingly at Michael.

"Yes quite, that's absolutely fine. I believe that we have frazzled Carrie's mind enough for today!" He said and chuckled. Abe raised his eyebrow and looked at Carrie, making her stifle a laugh.

Carrie sighed as the dressmaker held up another dress and then began making adjustments. It must have been the twelfth one! Carrie thought to herself. Molly could see that she was becoming agitated. "Should we have some tea?" Molly asked the dressmaker. He sighed, shook his head, and called the assistant, giving her instructions to prepare tea. Carrie smiled and mouthed thank you to Molly.

In the carriage on the return journey back, Carrie looked at Molly, who was smiling as she looked at her. Carrie frowned.

"I was just thinking to myself, you have such spirit and confidence. I admire that from someone who has suffered so greatly." Molly said. Carrie smiled and shrugged.

"I never knew any better though, did I? Well not until now!" She said and grinned.

"No I suppose not. What are your thoughts on Abe?" Molly asked and grinned a cheeky grin.

"I think he's a rogue!" Carrie replied and laughed.

"A loveable rogue, wouldn't you say?" Molly said laughing.

"Hmm, maybe. I think he could be a heart breaker." Carrie said and laughed.

"Aren't they all!" Molly sighed and gazed out of the window.

"I take by that you mean Michael?" Carrie chuckled. Molly frowned.

"I don't know what you mean!" She huffed. Carrie laughed.

"Yes you do. I've seen the way that you look at him." She said and looked wide eyed at Molly, who burst out laughing.

"Do I really make it that obvious?"

"Yes!"

"Well it's a shame he doesn't see it. Isn't it?" Her voice was now tinged with frustration.

So for the next six months, Carrie stayed at the lodge being taught by Molly, the ways of the earth. Molly was amazingly gifted, she had such a powerful connection to the earth. Abraham throughout her time there tried his hardest to woo her, but Carrie needed to know that he was sincere. She was afraid that he may break her heart.

One morning at the breakfast table, Polly walked through. "Michael would like to see you in his office when you have finished." She whispered in Carrie's ear. Carrie nodded, Molly looked at her with a puzzled expression. Carrie shrugged her shoulders.

She tapped on Michael's door and walked in. "Good morning!" he said cheerfully.

"Morning" She replied suspiciously.

"I have been in discussions with the Elders, and we are all in agreement that you are now ready!" Michael said.

"For?"

"To reintegrate with society and start to live your life." He replied.

"Doing what?" She asked and frowned. Michael chuckled.

"Tomorrow you will travel back to London, you can stay in the apartment in Hyde Park." He said looking pleased with himself..

"And do what Michael?" She asked again.

"Things, things that ladies do, coffee mornings, afternoon tea's, lunches, bridge evenings." He said.

"Hmm, not really me is it? I would rather be working, that's what I'm used to. I can't sit around all day talking complete bollocks with women that I don't know and don't like!" She fumed.

"Carrie, let's not be difficult!" Michael said as he looked over the top of his glasses at her.

"Michael, I am NOT being difficult! I appreciate everything that you have all done, but I am not a high society lady, I am a working girl. I have savings, so I will leave here tomorrow and find my own way." She said angrily.

"Fine! Let's see just how far you get before Katarina storms into your life and takes everything that you have!" Michael said angrily. Carrie wanted to laugh. It was the first time that she had known Michael to be anything but pompous!

"Fine!" She turned, walked out, and slammed the door, taking the entire thing off of its hinges. As it landed with a crash on the ground Carrie cringed and ran to the kitchen.

She found a hessian sack, which she took up to her room. She threw her favourite clothes inside, found her secret stash and then looked around for anything else she might need. She tied the sack and hid it beneath her bed. The weather was awful, not the kind of day that you would want to walk for miles. Carrie was thinking to herself when there was a knock on her door.

"I hear that you are leaving us?" Abe said as she stood with his arms folded across his body.

"You heard right!" Carrie said and walked to the window. Abe followed her. Gently he turned her around, holding her arms. "Carrie please be reasonable. For your own safety, why don't you stay in London, just for a few weeks. You need to adapt back to city life." Abe said quietly.

"I'm going to Kent!" She said adamantly. Abe laughed. "What's so funny?" She asked.

"And what do you propose to do there? I had no idea that you came from a farming background?" He laughed.

"What's that supposed to mean? There's the seaside!" She fumed, making Abe laugh even more. "Abe, I'm being serious!" She now shouted angrily as Abe wiped the tears of laughter from his face.

Chapter 11

MICHAEL.....

He strolled up the path towards the rectory and gave the knocker a loud tap. A tall thin woman with a solemn looking face opened the door and frowned. "Yes!" She asked abruptly.

"Oh hello, would it be possible to speak with the Vicar?" Michael asked politely.

"No! He's not taking visitors today." The woman replied and began to close the door. Michael quickly placed his foot inside, stopping the door from closing.

"That is rather inconvenient, I need to speak to him as a matter of urgency." Michael said smiling his sweetest smile. The woman showed no reaction.

"Well there are these things called telephones!" She huffed.

"Yes but I'm er I'm afraid that the matter is rather delicate, and I would like to speak to him face to face." Michael smiled again. A shadow appeared behind the sour faced woman and the Vicar appeared. "My goodness, John Green! How are you old chap?" Michael asked excitedly.

"Michael! Goodness me, it must have twenty years since we last met!" The Vicar said as he smiled widely. "You can go back to your duties now Mrs Haynes." He said and shooed the woman back inside the house. "Bring some tea to the drawing room, would you!" he called after her as she scurried along the long hallway. "Do come in Michael." He gestured towards a door. Michael walked through, feeling the warmth from the roaring fire. Michael loosened his scarf. "Please take a seat." The Vicar said and gestured to a leather chair. Michael sat down opposite the Vicar. "Now, what can I do for you old friend?" He smiled. Mrs Haynes brought in a tray of tea and loudly placed it on the table, huffed and left the room.

"My very good friend, has been, well shall we say, wrongly accused of witchcraft. She is rather unwell at present and these accusations are putting even more pressure on her." Michael began. The Vicar raised his eyebrow.

"You mean Mrs Wells?" He said and frowned. Michael smiled and nodded. The Vicar sighed.

"You know Michael, I would never have got involved, it's just that one of my parishioners, and generous benefactors to the church, insisted that I paid her a visit. It was in fact his daughter that raised the alarm and accused her of witchcraft." The vicar said. Michael nodded.

"Yes, it was Jean Douglas I believe." Michael replied. The Vicar nodded.

"Yes that is correct, you know the family?" He asked. Michael shook his head.

"No, but I understand that there is love rivalry involved. Miss Douglas has made it clear that she seeks the attention of William Hubbard. Unfortunately, he is already in a friendship with young Peggy, Mrs Wells granddaughter. This made Miss Douglas, shall we say rather unhappy, and she told young Peggy that she was going to tell the village that they were witches." Michael said. The Vicar nodded.

"Ah, I see! Well you can rest assured Michael that the church will be taking no further action. In fact I could ask my congregation to say a prayer of healing for Mrs Wells in my Sunday service." He smiled.

"Wonderful! Thank you my friend!" Michael said and finished the remainder of his tea. He stood up and straightened his trousers. It was so hot in the room, he felt that he might melt if he stayed any longer. He put his hand out to the Vicar, who shook it frantically.

"Will you be in the village long?" He asked.

"For a while, yes." Michael replied.

"Well in that case maybe you could come to Sunday service?" The Vicar asked. Michael chuckled.

"Not my domain. You wouldn't want your church to be struck by lightning would you?" Michael laughed. The Vicar laughed too.

"Quite right, well if you are passing at any time, do feel free to pop in for tea." He said as Michael walked down the path.

Peggy helped Carrie up and wheeled her into the lounge. She had lit a small fire. Even though the weather was beautiful, Carrie felt the cold due to her immobility. The back door opened, and Molly called out "Yoo-hoo!"

"We are in here dear!" Carrie called out. Molly and Jo walked into the lounge.

"I thought that you would have been in the garden today, the weather is divine!" Molly said as she kissed Carrie's cheek.

"I'm still quite chilly, thought I would grab some fresh air after lunch. Give the sun time to warm my spot up!" Carrie said and laughed, which forced her into a fit of coughing. Peggy handed her a hanky and Molly looked at Peggy wide eyed. They all knew that her health was deteriorating every day.

"I think you might benefit from a little more healing." Molly said and winked. Carrie nodded, she knew her time of living was closing to an end. The back door closed, and Michael walked into the lounge. He said his hello's and then looked at Carrie.

"All sorted! I happen to know the Vicar. We go back a long way." Michael smiled. Carrie tapped his hand.

"Thank you Michael, you are a dear soul." She said and coughed.

"Nonsense, it's the least I can do, considering…." His voice trailed off as he seemed lost in his thoughts.

"Considering what?" Peggy asked, her curiosity now pricked.

"Come on Peg, we need to pop to the shops for some groceries. Molly is going to cook us one of her famous roasts!" Jo said trying to divert Peggy's attention. Peggy smiled, kissed Carrie on the cheek and left the cottage with Jo.

"So how's it going with William then?" Jo asked as they drove towards Melrose. Peggy grinned.

"He's gorgeous isn't he? I havnee seen him today though!" She said and dropped her lip, making Jo laugh.

"Molly said that we should invite the boys for dinner tonight, so on the way back we could find him. I have already told Matthew." Jo grinned.

They found William in the farmyard. He had just finished milking. Jo stopped the car and Peggy ran over to him. He held out his arms and she jumped into them.

"Would you like to come for dinner tonight. Molly is cooking a roast?" Peggy asked as she looked up at him.

"Aye, I'd love to!" he said and smiled. "Listen Peggy, I was chatting with me Ma and Da, they said that they would love to throw a garden party in Carrie's honour, to you know, show the rest of the village that they support her and everything that she has done since she has lived here." He smiled.

"Oh, that's lovely!" Peggy replied. "Better not wait too long though. Her sickness gets worse every day." Peggy said sadly. Willian kissed her on the cheek.

"I'll let me Ma know. What time tonight?" He called as she walked back to the car.

"Matthew will pick you up at seven" She called back. He blew her a kiss, she blew one back.

The afternoon was filled with Peggy and Michael beneath the tree meditating. Carrie and Jo playing cards at the garden table, and poor

Molly stuck in the kitchen preparing the roast. Michael had finished with Peggy, she wheeled Carrie back inside, she wanted a nap before dinner. Once she had made her comfortable she walked into the kitchen to where Molly and Michael were discussing Carrie's health. They stopped speaking when Peggy entered.

"You don't need to stop because of me. I am aware of how poorly she is." Peggy said as she picked up the washing basket and took it out to the garden. She was pegging out the sheets when she felt eyes on her. She looked out towards the street, there was no-one there. She looked over the wall to the field and leaning up against the west wall was a woman, and she was looking straight at Peggy. She climbed up onto the wall, to take a better look, still the woman watched her. "What are you looking at?" Peggy shouted. The woman laughed, turned, and disappeared. Peggy shook her head. Was she imagining it? She was thinking to herself as she walked through the back door.

"What's wrong?" Jo asked when she saw the look on Peggy's face.

"I don't know if I'm going mad, but there was a woman leaning up against the west wall staring at me. When I asked her what she wanted, she laughed and then disappeared before my very eyes. I mean she vanished, completely vanished!" Peggy said feeling slightly bemused. Michael looked at Molly and frowned.

"What did she look like?" He asked.

"Er, well she was wearing really scruffy clothes. She looked dirty, but her hair was really shiny!" Peggy explained. Michal looked once again at Molly and nodded.

"Surely, it can't be!" Molly said.

"What?" Peggy hadn't a clue what was going on. Again Michael nodded.

"What?" Peggy asked again, now she was becoming agitated.

"Oh sometimes, when you cross through the realms, certain spirits become curious. They tend to watch you for a while." Michael lied. Molly shook her head. Peggy shrugged her shoulders and looked at the big clock.

"I had better wake Carrie." She said and walked out of the room.

"You should have told her." Molly whispered.

"Nonsense, it could be a one off." Michael said.

"Did you want a cup of coffee?" Peggy asked Carrie as she sat up in her bed, now looking bright as a button. Carrie shook her head.

"Do you know what I would really like?" Carrie asked. Peggy shook her head. "A glass of Molly's homemade lemonade. Will you have one with me?" She added. Peggy smiled and skipped to the kitchen. She came back with two glasses filled with lemonade. Carrie took a sip and smiled, a truly contented smile.

"Now where was I?" She asked.

"You were going to Kent." Peggy replied refreshing her memory.

"Yes! That's right!"

"Well if you insist on leaving tomorrow, at least have the decency to spend the evening with me." Abe said. Carrie looked at him and smirked.

"And do what?" She laughed.

"Dinner, a nice evening stroll, that sort of thing." He grinned. Reluctantly she nodded. "Great! Be in the lounge ready to go by six thirty." He said, turned and left the room.

She went through the clothes in the closet and found the perfect dress, with a lovely matching shawl. She laid them out on her bed and sat at the dressing table. She took out her braids and brushed the long dark curls, singing to herself as she did. She placed the brush down and looked back at the mirror. It was not her reflection looking back at her, it was Katarina's.

"I'M COMING FOR YOU!" she screeched as her face changed to something Carrie had never seen before. Carrie jumped back, her heart was beating fast. She ran out of the room, straight into the path of Molly.

"Hey, what's wrong?" Molly asked, she caught Carrie as she was just about to fall. Breathlessly Carrie told Molly what had happened. "This is not good. She must be aware that you are planning to leave us, which will make you vulnerable!" Molly said. "I should tell Michael." She added and walked towards the stairway.

"Wait, I'll come with you." Carrie said as she ran to catch her up. "What I don't get, is how come she hasn't come here to get me?" Carrie said as they walked towards Michael's newly repaired door.

"She cannot physically get through the bindings. She must sense that you are leaving, which has weakened the bindings enough for her to get through telepathically." Molly replied as she tapped on Michael's door.

"Come" He called out. They both walked in.

"Sorry about the door Michael." Carrie said humbly.

"Not a problem." He replied cheerfully.

"Something has just happened to Carrie in her bedroom." Molly said.

Then they both went on to tell him what had happened. Michael sighed.

"Unfortunately, Carrie has made the decision to leave us, so in that fact there is not an awful lot that I can do." Michael sighed again. "What I will say however, is that you simply cannot take the Grimoire or anything else in the chest. We cannot take that risk. If she gets her hands on the Grimoire, we are all doomed!" he said sternly. Carrie nodded. It had now dawned on her how much the guardians had protected her, and she was in the hands of fate the moment she left.

She went to her room and changed, all the time thinking that maybe she should reconsider. Maybe she should stay in London for a while, under the protection of the guardians. She walked into the lounge. Abe was already waiting. He looked at his pocket watch.

"Fashionably late as always!" he smiled. Carrie smiled. He held his arm out to her and together they walked to the waiting carriage.

They had finished their starters, the waiter had taken their empty bowls. " I hear that you had a brush with the dreaded Katarina this afternoon?" Abe said. Carrie nodded and then laughed.

"Brush, yes funny!" She laughed. Abe chuckled.

"Carrie, I, er, I want to say something." He stammered. Carrie chuckled.

"Well go on then!" She laughed.

"Could we be serious for just a few minutes?" He huffed. Carrie tried her hardest to straighten her face, stifling the laugh that was bursting to get out. "I have watched you grow in the last six months, you have turned into the most beautiful, funniest young woman I have ever had the pleasure to know, and I for one will be truly heartbroken when you leave." He said sincerely. She was lost for words!

They finished their meal, then went for a stroll in the park opposite the restaurant. Carrie was linked onto Abe's arm. They stood beneath a huge yew tree and watched the sun disappear below the horizon. Carrie gasped at the beautiful colours that ran through the sky. Then he kissed her. He kissed her so passionately that she was dizzy and breathless when he finally released her. "You know when you first arrived at the lodge." He began, she nodded. " I told you that I belonged to a different department." He continued. Again she nodded. "I am in charge of a place called Arbatel. It is the centre of the Light Realm." He said.

"Is that what your regiment is called?" Carrie asked. Abe laughed.

"No, I am in the armed forces, but my other job is leader of Arbatel. The reason that I am in the military is so that I can gain access to privy information globally. Unfortunately, the Dark Realm are not only in this country, but they also operate everywhere." Carrie smiled and nodded, not really having a clue what he was talking about! "I would really like you to become part of my world. Carrie will you marry me?" He asked as he dropped to one knee.

"Er, er" He stood and kissed her again.

"Please?" He asked again. She grinned and then nodded. He lifted her high into the air, spinning her around and then again they kissed.

She felt as though she was walking on air when they returned to the lodge. She had never been so happy. She could not stop looking at the beautiful ring that he had slid onto her finger. He walked her to her room after they had shared the good news with Michael, Molly, and the other guardians. He kissed her. "So, you won't be leaving tomorrow then?" he asked. She smiled and shook her head.

"Great! Well tomorrow you and I have a busy day. There is lots to tell and lots to show!" he said as he walked away. "Be up bright and early!" he called out. She threw herself onto the bed, jumping up and down. She was so happy. She took out her night clothes, laying them on the bed. She undressed and slipped into them then sat at the dressing table. She washed her face, removed her jewellery, and brushed her hair. The face appeared again.

"I WILL TAKE EVERYTHING FROM YOU, UNTIL YOU ARE LEFT WITH NOTHING, THEN I WILL TAKE YOUR POWER AND YOUR LIFEFORCE!" She growled. Carrie jumped back, throwing the brush across the room. First thing tomorrow, she was going to throw that brush in the bin! She thought to herself as she climbed between the fresh crisp sheets and lay on the soft pillows, all the while thoughts of Abe danced through her mind.

Polly came into the room and pulled back the curtains waking Carrie from her slumber.

"Come on you. Abraham is waiting!" She said as she threw Carrie's robe at her. She rubbed her eyes and followed Polly down the stairs, and into the dining room. She sat down beside Abe as Polly served her breakfast. He placed his hand over hers and smiled. She smiled and then tucked into her scrambled eggs, she was starving! Michael and Molly soon joined them, and they sat chatting over breakfast.

Once ready Abe dragged her out to the waiting carriage. They did not seem to be travelling for long when the carriage stopped. Abe opened the door, climbed out and then lifted her down. They were beside a field. Carrie frowned.

"Where we need to be, is too far to travel in a carriage, so today, we travel my way!" He grinned. Carrie shook her head. Abe placed his arms around her, completely enveloping her. "Do you trust me?" He asked. She nodded. Before she knew it they were in the air! Yes in the air! Abe had shapeshifted whilst holding her which meant that she was part of the same bird as they soured through the sky. They flew over a mountain range, then descended beside a lake. Abe shifted back. Carrie jumped up and down with excitement. She was ecstatic!

Abe laughed and then calmed her. "There is someone that I would like you to meet." He said whilst he looked around the lake.

"Who?" She asked.

"Carrie, close your eyes." He said gently.

Chapter 12

There was a gentle tap on the door, then Molly popped her head around. "Just to let you both know that Michael and I are popping out for an hour. Jo is keeping an eye on the food." She said and waved.

"In that case I had better ready myself and try at least to look presentable for our guests!" Carrie said and swung her legs around, to get off of the bed.

"Wait! Who was it?" Peggy asked. Carrie laughed.

"Patience is a virtue my dear Granddaughter!" She replied.

"Argh!" Peggy growled as she helped Carrie to the closet to choose her outfit.

"Now you run along and make yourself pretty for sweet William, while I attempt to apply some make up." Carrie said and winked.

"Would you like me to do it for you?" Peggy asked.

"I'm not completely useless, well not just yet. No, all this talk about old times has made me want to do it. The times that Abe and I would attend functions and entertain at home." Carrie said lost in her thoughts as she brushed her long silver hair. Peggy kissed her on the cheek and left the room. She ran up the stairs and headed straight to the closet, looking for an outfit.

Once ready she ran down the stairs and into the kitchen. Jo wasn't there. She then heard voices coming from the lounge. She walked in to find Jo and Carrie laughing. Peggy smiled, it was so good to see Carrie happy, she thought to herself.

"About time! Come on, you can give me a hand to lay the tables." Jo chirped. Peggy smiled and nodded.

"You look beautiful." She whispered in Carrie's ear as she kissed her cheek.

"Thank you Peggy!" She said and smiled. Peggy walked over to the sideboard and began to take out the place settings for dinner. She was counting everyone in her head. She took out seven. As she began to lay the table, Jo looked over and shook her head.

"No, you need one more." She said and walked back to the kitchen. Peggy frowned, then followed her.

"There is seven." Peggy said as Jo grabbed the cutlery.

"No Peg, there's eight. Molly and Michael have gone to the station to pick him up." Jo replied and winked.

"Who?" Peggy asked.

"Well you'll find out in a few minutes won't you!" Jo laughed. Peggy growled and shook her head. They were laying the tables when William and Matthew walked in. William held a bouquet of flowers in his hand and when Peggy saw them she began to blush, well that was until he handed them to Carrie!

"Oh sweet William, they are beautiful! Thank you so very much!" Carrie exclaimed. Peggy smiled. She walked over and kissed his cheek.

"That was a beautiful gesture, thank you." She whispered. He winked at her. They all heard the back door close. Michael walked through, followed by Molly and then a man that Peggy had never seen before. Carrie gasped when she saw him. He walked past everyone, straight in the direction of Carrie. He stood in front of her.

"It's been a long time." He said quietly. Peggy watched as tears sprung into Carrie's eyes and then she knew who he was. Carrie nodded. Slowly she climbed out of the wheelchair and shakily stood in front of him. She took his cheeks in her hands and kissed his cheek.

"Hello Abe!" She said as her voice shook with emotion. Peggy was now in tears as she watched Carrie's reaction. He walked her over to the sofa and sat down beside her. He looked around the room, until his eyes fell upon Peggy. He smiled.

"And you must be the granddaughter that I have been waiting to meet." He said. Peggy blushed and walked over to him.

"Aye, I'm Peggy." She said. He stood up and enveloped her in his arms.

"Thank you, from the bottom of my heart. Thank you for taking care of your grandmother for me." He whispered. Peggy moved back and raised an eyebrow. She leant towards him.

"I'm not doing it for you, I'm doing it for Carrie." She whispered and smiled, making Abe chuckle.

They all ate dinner, Peggy was loving listening to all of the stories from days gone by that they were all telling!

"Carrie do you remember when I introduced you to Ceridwen?" Abe asked and chuckled. Carrie laughed and nodded.

"I made a complete fool of myself. I had no idea that she was a Goddess. I asked her if she was a relative of Abe's!" Carrie said, cringed and laughed. They all laughed. "Luckily for me, she saw the funny side!" Carrie added then coughed. Peggy quickly handed her a hanky. Abe looked at Molly sadly.

"So you have met a real Goddess?" Peggy asked. Carrie nodded.

"I have met one or two!" She said and winked. Peggy shook her head in disbelief and looked at William, who was totally engrossed in the conversation.

After dinner, Peggy, William, Jo, and Matthew went out for a stroll to watch the sunset. Michael and Abe washed the dishes, while Molly wheeled Carrie out to the garden to watch the sunset. Molly pulled up a seat beside Carrie's wheelchair and they both sighed.

"We are a pair, you, and I. Both fell in love with men that were beyond our reach!" Carrie sighed, Molly nodded.

"It's a cruel life, is it not!" She replied. Carrie tapped her knee.

"Don't become bitter, it just makes you unhappy. I was bitter for years, I mean if Abe had walked through that door a few years ago, I would have knocked him straight back out of it!" Carrie laughed. Molly creased with laughter. "But since young Peggy came to stay, I have realised that all those years of bitterness, were wasted. They stopped me from enjoying life. Don't let the same thing happen to you, no matter how hard it is. I know that you love Michael deeply Molly, just as I do Abe!" Carrie said. She looked at Molly who had tears running down her cheeks. "Unfortunately Molly my dearest, we are just not enough!" She finished. Molly took out her hanky and wiped her tears away.

"I feel the aging process has begun." She said quietly. Carrie frowned.

"But I thought that it didn't happen, because you are a guardian." Carrie said bemused.

"I have been this age for 150 years now, obviously my time in the guardianship is near complete." Molly sighed.

"Does that sadden you?" Carrie asked. Molly shrugged.

"No, not really, just makes me feel a little redundant." She replied. Carrie chuckled.

"I must confess, when I began to age and you didn't, I used to be so envious!" She chuckled. Molly tapped her on the hand.

"Promise me something will you?" Molly asked. "When my time in this lifeforce is over, promise that you will be there to guide me through." Molly asked.

"Of course I will!" Carrie replied.

"Why the long faces?" Abe shouted as he walked towards them.

"It's called reflection Abe, something that you have never been good at!" Carrie shouted back, making Molly howl with laughter.

"So, let me get this right. You two are guardians yes?" William asked Jo and Matthew. They both nodded. "But you're not Peggy?" He asked. Peggy shook her head. "So is Carrie a guardian?" he asked. Again Peggy shook her head. "So how did she get to meet a Goddess then?" He asked. Peggy shrugged her shoulders.

"Carrie is incredibly magically gifted. She and others are who we protect. Carrie had the option of becoming a guardian, but she chose not to. Things are written in fate from long ago. Carrie's bloodline must continue, one of her descendants will be incredibly gifted and have a significant role to play in the future" Matthew said.

"So, could that be Peggy?" William asked. Matthew and Jo shook their heads.

"No, she will be born to Peggy's younger brother." Jo replied.

"Jeez, I had no idea, I just thought that Carrie was a woman that made healing potions." He said shaking his head. Peggy chuckled.

"Well, she did that too!" She laughed.

"So will we get to meet a Goddess?" William asked. Jo laughed.

"If you try hard enough." She chuckled.

"Cool!" William said.

Back inside the cottage Carrie and the others were back in the lounge. Peggy walked through and asked them all if they would like hot drinks. Then her and William went to the kitchen to make them. Peggy put the milk on to boil, while William took out the cups and the tray. He put his arms around Peggy's waist and kissed her cheek. "I'll be back in a minute." He said and walked back to the lounge. A few minutes later he returned to the kitchen grinning. He walked over to Peggy and dropped to one knee. "Peggy, I love you with all my heart. Will you marry me?" He asked. Tears filled Peggy's eyes as she nodded her head frantically.

"Oh William, I'd love to!" She cried and jumped into William's arms.

"I just went in and asked for Carrie's blessing." He smiled. Peggy smiled. She knew that Carrie held William in high regard.

After the others had all left, Peggy wheeled Carrie to her room, and helped her to get ready for bed. She tucked her in. Carrie smiled. "It's been a wonderful evening Peggy, hasn't it?" She grinned.

"It most certainly has!" She replied. Carrie tapped the bed next to her and gestured for Peggy to sit.

"Now let me tell you about Ceridwen." She said smiling.

Carrie opened her eyes and before her was the most beautiful woman that she had ever seen. She held her hand out to Carrie, who shook it! "Are you related to Abe?" She asked. The Goddess chuckled.

"No, I am not." She replied gently.

"She is a Goddess!" Abe whispered in Carrie's ear. Carrie's face went scarlet with embarrassment. She took a low bow.

"Please forgive my ignorance my Lady!" Carrie almost whispered. Ceridwen lifted Carrie's chin and smiled.

"You were not to know child. I am here to inform you, that Katarina is seeking you now. She will stop at nothing. Under no circumstances is she to take possession of the Grimoire. You must find the crystal ball, without it she cannot trace your whereabouts." The Goddess said.

"If you need me at any time." She continued and passed Carrie a small bronze boar. "Hold this in your hand and call me." She smiled, then vanished.

Carrie dropped to her knees, still clutching the bronze boar, and put her head in her hands. "I cannot believe how stupid I am sometimes!" She shouted, now angry with herself. Abe lifted her up.

"You weren't to know. I should have told you." He said as he took her face in his hands. "Now, let's go, I'm going to take you to Arbatel." He said as he wrapped his arms around her and again they flew.

They landed beside a river. They then walked to a small market place. It was busy with traders selling their wares. They continued until they came to a small building. Inside it sold sewing equipment, needles pins and linen. They walked through the shop until they reached a door at the back. Abe opened it, there was a staircase. Carrie followed Abe and they came to another door. This one was made of metal. Abe placed something on the door, and it opened. He walked through with Carrie following closely behind. A young man walked over to them. Carrie could not believe her eyes. The place was amazing. It was all marble, with beautiful paintings covering every wall.

"Carrie this is Matthew." Abe said as he introduced them. Matthew shook Carrie's hand, she felt a strange buzzing energy coming from him. She rubbed her hands together to get rid of the sensation then followed both men as they walked up a huge staircase. They walked along a marble hallway until they reached a huge wooden door. Again Abe placed something on the door, and it opened. They walked through. "Carrie, this is my office." Abe said. She looked around in complete astonishment. It was like nothing she had ever seen before.

"I have a few things that I need to deal with, my assistant Justine will bring you some coffee. I would say to look out at the amazing view. It is most spectacular! " Abe said and pointed to a huge window. Carrie looked at him in confusion.

"But…. But we are underground?" She said quietly. Abe chuckled. The door opened and a woman slammed a tray of coffees on the table. She scowled at Carrie and left the room. Carrie helped herself to a cup and walked to the giant window. There were rolling hills, which showed to be covered in a purple hue. The view was fantastic! She watched as someone in the far distance rode a horse. The sky was blue with brilliant white clouds that looked like pillows floating in the sky.

"Ok, all done! Shall we go?" Abe said. Carrie smiled and walked back to the tray and placed her empty cup down. Abe grabbed Carrie's hand and walked her to the window. He touched it and the glass disappeared. He placed his arms around her, and they were flying. This time they landed high on a clifftop. They walked down to a tiny fishing village. It was the most beautiful place that Carrie had ever seen. "Where are we?" She asked as she watched the waves crash against the rocks.

"This is Cornwall. Isn't it beautiful?" He replied. Carrie nodded frantically.

"One day, I am going to live here!" She announced and smiled. Spray from the sea hit her face. It felt amazing! They sat on the rocks looking out to the vast ocean. The waves parted. She appeared from within the waves. She pointed at Carrie.

"I See you. I am coming for you!" She screeched. Abe jumped up and grabbed Carrie's hand. He put his arms around her and then they were back in the air. They landed at the carriage. Carrie was breathless, she blamed the flying but deep down she knew it was through fear. Fear of that red haired bitch, who would not leave her alone!

That evening at dinner Abe was telling Michael and Molly about Katarina. Michael scratched his head.

"I am not really sure what we should do?" He said. "I think I will consult with the Elders." He said and excused himself. Carrie looked at Molly. All the decisions were being made for her, and she didn't like it. Michael returned and sat down. He was about to speak when Carrie stopped him.

"Look, I know that you people are used to dealing with the dark forces or whatever the bloody hell they are called, but in my experience, you can't run away. You have to face it head on. I mean, she does scare me a little bit, but if you think about it, I have never used my power against her have I?" She said. Abe looked at Michael, then Carrie then nodded. She had such spirit. "I say draw her in, at least that way, I can get the crystal ball back. You never know, I may even finish the bitch off. " Carrie continued and smiled at Molly who chuckled.

"Oh if only you could Carrie!" Michael sighed. Carrie frowned and looked at Abe.

"Well, why can't I?" she asked.

"Because that is not what has been foreseen, or indeed written. Your role in this Carrie is to remain safe, increase your bloodline, and protect the Grimoire." Michael said.

"What? So you are telling me that I am only here to have kids and look after the book. What happened to… oh you are so magically gifted Carrie…..if I am that gifted, why can't I finish her off?" Carrie shouted angrily. Michael shook his head and looked at Abe. Abe touched Carrie's hand.

"Ok, why don't we go to London tomorrow. See if we can't draw her out." Abe said and winked at Michael.

"Don't bloody humour me Abe, I am not a child." Carrie yelled.

"I am most certainly not! I thought that was what you wanted?" He yelled back. Carrie stood up pushed her chair into the table, sending the table and everything on it flying, and stormed out of the room.

She ran to her room and slammed the door taking it clean off of its hinges.

"ARGH!" she screamed out in frustration. She walked over to the window and looked at the trees, they appeared to be the only things that could calm her down.

"Come over here" She heard. She turned. "Yes here" She heard. It was coming from the mirror. She stomped over and stood with her hands on her hips. Katarina's reflection looked at her and laughed.

"Is she feeling brave? Can she take me on? I DON'T THINK SO!" She roared.

"Do you want a fucking bet?" Carrie screamed back at her. The mirror shattered into a thousand pieces!

"What on earth is going on?" Michael shouted from the doorway.

"I declare a war! A war on the redhead, and tomorrow it begins!" Carrie shouted.

"I declare that we need to call someone to repair the door and clean up that glass!" Molly said and laughed.

Carrie picked up the hairbrush that she had thrown and began to brush her hair, as she did she laughed. Life had been far too quiet for far too long!

Chapter 13

Carrie yawned, signaling to Peggy that she needed to rest. Peggy plumped her pillows and straightened the sheets.

"I am so happy that you found a man that loves you so, my dear Peggy." Carrie said sleepily. Peggy kissed her cheek and turned off the light.

"I'm so sorry that you didn't!" Peggy whispered as she walked along the hallway and up the stairs.

The following morning when Peggy opened her eyes, she had a strange feeling. A feeling that something wasn't quite right. She stretched her arms then her legs, put on her robe and quietly walked down the stairs. She placed the kettle on the stove and warmed the teapot. She walked to Carrie's room and tapped on the door. No reply. She walked in, headed straight to the window, and drew back the curtains. The sun alone should wake her, Peggy thought to herself as she picked up a hanky that was on the floor. She dropped it in shock when she noticed it was covered in blood. She ran over to Carrie and called her, gently nudging her as she did. She was gently breathing, but Peggy could not wake her. She ran out of the cottage in a state of hysteria, screaming up the lane that she needed help.

The milkman pulled up and ran to Peggy. She explained that she needed to contact Dr Clarke. The milkman said he would fetch him. Peggy ran back into the cottage and straight to Carrie's room. She walked over to the window and looked out. That woman was there again at the wall, smirking at her. Peggy growled and walked over to Carrie. She was still. Again Peggy tried to rouse her, but still she could not wake her.

Carrie was in a meadow, it was beautiful. She walked through the lush grass and wild flowers. The sun was warm, and the breeze was gentle. She heard someone call her name. it sounded familiar. Was it Abagail? Carrie asked herself as she turned to look. It was Abagail! Slowly she walked towards her. She was now standing in front of her smiling, her face changed, it wasn't Abagail, it was her, the red-haired bitch, the same one that robbed her of the people that she loved.

"I will watch as every healthy part of your existence disappears, and you are writhing in agony. I will watch as your very life force begins to fade, then I will take it and your granddaughter's!" Katarina sneered.

"BITCH!" Carrie screamed and grabbed hold of Katarina. She threw a punch, her fist going straight through her, forcing her to vanish. "YOU CAN DO AS YOU WISH TO ME, BUT YOU WILL LEAVE HER ALONE!" Carrie roared.

"Carrie, Carrie!" Dr Clarke said as he gently shook her to wake her. Carrie jumped.

"Oh, Dr Clarke, what on earth are you doing here?" Carrie asked as she caught her breath and pulled herself up.

"Young Peggy was worried, she tried to wake you, but was unable to. She found this." The doctor said and handed the hanky to Carrie. She looked at the hanky, then at the doctor, she was completely baffled. "How long have you been coughing up blood Carrie?" the doctor asked with a look of concern on his face. Carrie shook her head.

"I haven't! That's not mine!" She said adamantly. Peggy leant over. "Look Peggy, all of my hankies are embroidered." Carrie passed one to Peggy. She nodded and passed the hanky to the doctor. The doctor sighed.

"Do you feel unwell?" He asked. Carrie shook her head.

"No I feel the same today as I did yesterday, in fact I feel better today than I did yesterday!" She exclaimed. The doctor closed his bag and looked at both the women.

"Well in that case I'll be off then." He said and smiled. Peggy walked him to the front door.

"I'm sorry for wasting your time Dr Clarke, I truly thought that something was wrong." Peggy said humbly. The doctor tapped Peggy on the shoulder.

"Better safe than sorry Peggy. If you have any concerns you know where to find me." He said as he walked up the path.

Peggy walked back to Carrie's room. She had got herself up and was sitting in the chair beside the window, her wheelchair however was still next to the bed.

"How did you get there?" Peggy asked. Carrie chuckled.

"Magic!" She replied sarcastically. "I used my legs and walked!" She added. "Now then, where is my breakfast, I'm ravenous!" She said and rubbed her tummy making Peggy laugh.

Peggy came in a few moments later with her breakfast tray. She placed it on the table in front of Carrie, who was looking out of the window intently. "There look!" Carrie said and pointed. Peggy looked.

"Aye she was there earlier and the other day" Peggy said as she handed Carrie a napkin.

"What do you mean, when the other day?" Carrie frowned.

"Not yesterday, the day before. I was hanging the sheets out to dry and saw her. When I climbed on the wall and said what are you looking at she laughed and vanished." Peggy said. "I told Molly and Michael." She added. Carrie shook her head.

"Do you have any idea who that is?" Carrie asked gravely. Peggy shook her head.

"No Michael said something about travelling through the realms and then they watch you." Peggy replied.

"Did he now!" Carrie growled.

"Who is she?" Peggy asked, still none the wiser.

"That my dear is Bloody Mary!" Carrie looked at her once again. "I see she is still doing the bidding for that bitch!" Carrie added angrily. Peggy looked at her wide eyed.

"What do you think she wants?" Peggy asked.

"I know what she wants. That hanky didn't land there by itself. It has a curse on it. Sent by the wonderful Katarina." Carrie said still looking at the woman on the wall. Peggy ran as fast as her legs could carry her. She ran to the kitchen, grabbed a box of matches and then out into the garden. She climbed on the wall, in full view of Mary.

"OI!" Peggy shouted as she struck a match. Mary looked at her. Peggy held the match to the bloodied hanky. It caught fire. "Now take a hint and piss off! Tell Katarina that her curse didnee work, in fact it had the opposite affect!" Peggy shouted. Mary stood still, glaring at Peggy. Carrie appeared beside Peggy, forcing her to look twice.

"Mary, what a lovely surprise, it's been an age darling!" Carrie shouted with just a hint of sarcasm. With that Mary vanished. Peggy looked at Carrie, her mouth gaped open. "How the…"

"What the ….?" She was lost for words.

"Close your eyes" Carrie said. Peggy did as she was asked.

"Can I open them now?" She asked a few moments later. Nothing… she opened her eyes and Carrie was nowhere to be seen!

She ran back inside the cottage to find Carrie back in her chair eating her breakfast. Peggy rubbed her eyes and shook her head. "How did you do that?" Peggy asked. Carrie chuckled.

"All in good time." She said still laughing. Peggy shook her head in disbelief. "Anyway take a seat beside me, I need to tell you about London." Carrie smiled. Peggy smiled and sat down.

She woke up, bursting with energy. There was a fight to be had and she was ready for it! She was thinking to herself as she dressed and walked down the stairs for breakfast. The dining room was empty.

Carrie sat at the table while Polly served her boiled eggs. "Where is everyone Polly?" Carrie asked. Polly shrugged.

"No idea. Abe just gave me the orders to pack yours and my belongings, that the carriage will be here in an hour." Polly replied.

"Are you coming to London too?" Carrie asked. Polly smiled and nodded. "Great!" Carrie smiled. She liked Polly, she was really down to earth, her life had been hard, they both had so much in common. Abe walked into the dining room and sat beside Carrie, Polly left the room.

"Something has come up. There is unrest in Europe, so I have been called back to base I'm afraid. You will have to go to London without me for a few days." He said as he buttered his toast. Carrie sighed. "Good news is, however, we are to be married on Saturday! "He added. Carrie nearly chocked on her tea.

"Why so soon?" She asked.

"Why not my darling?" was his reply. He winked and then drank his tea.

They were travelling to London in the carriage, with two guardians. The track was bumpy, and the journey seemed to be taking forever. It had taken Michael and Abe about 30 minutes to brief Carrie and Polly on the do's and don'ts. Carrie felt her eyelids grow heavy and soon she was asleep.

The carriage stopped, Carrie opened her eyes and looked at Polly, who smiled. "We're here." Polly said and opened the carriage door. A guardian stopped her, and they both climbed out first. When they had checked around they then allowed the girls to get out.

Carrie had put all of her clothes away when Polly knocked on her bedroom door. "The dressmaker is here." Polly said. Carrie frowned.

"He has come to measure you up for your dress." Polly added. Carrie growled and followed Polly down the stairs. The dressmaker and his assistants were in the drawing room. Carrie walked in followed by Polly.

"Come" he said in a foreign accent. Carrie walked over as he began measuring everywhere. There were a few places that Carrie was pretty sure didn't need measuring and shouted Oi at him, making Polly laugh. Carrie then spent the next hour arguing with the dressmaker over the dress's design. He wanted an elaborate dress, but Carrie preferred simple. The arguing paid off and he left with strict instructions to keep it simple.

Carrie and Polly were the only ones in for dinner. They were sat around a huge dining table in a huge room. Just the two of them. "Why don't we take our food into the drawing room, it's cosier in there, and the fire is roaring?" Polly suggested. Carrie smiled, nodded, and picked up her plate as the two of them made themselves comfortable. A maid took their plates and they both sat with their feet up sharing stories.

"Would you like a brandy?" Polly asked. Carrie screwed her face up. "Oh go on, it's decent stuff." Polly said trying to convince her.

"Go on then" She replied reluctantly. So the evening was spent, sipping brandy by the fire, sharing stories, and laughing a lot!

The following morning Carrie was a little apprehensive. She and Polly had been invited to a coffee morning and it would be the first time outside on the streets of London for a while. She dressed and met Polly in the hallway. Douglas greeted her and opened the door to the awaiting carriage. Both her and Polly climbed in. They were chatting and laughing when the carriage pulled away. After a while Polly looked out of the carriage window and frowned.

"What's wrong?" Carrie asked as she looked at Polly. Polly leant forwards.

"We are going in the wrong direction." She whispered. Carrie looked out. She was right. They were supposed to heading in the direction of Westminster, instead she could see Tower bridge in the near distance.

"SHIT!" Carrie muttered under her breath. Slowly she opened the carriage door slightly, stretching her neck to see the driver. The driver looked down at Carrie and laughed. "Jump!" Carrie shouted to Polly as she jumped from the moving carriage. As Polly went to jump, the carriage was pulled abruptly to the side sending Polly flying through the air. Another carriage was coming in the opposite direction, and when Carrie looked she realised that it was Mary driving the other carriage. Polly landed, the carriage heading straight for her. She landed face down in the dirt and the carriage ran over her.

"NO!!!!!" Carrie screamed. She ran over to Polly's flattened lifeless body, tears streaming down her face. Then she heard the thundering of horses hooves. She looked up and realised that Mary had turned the carriage around and was now driving the carriage straight at her. She quickly got up and ran, hiding behind a newspaper cart. The carriage thundered past and once it was out of sight Carrie ran back to Polly. She cried out for help and very soon two street traders came over to her. One went to get help. Two men walked towards them. One man said something to the remaining trader, and he walked away. "We are guardians, we will take care of the body." One man said to Carrie. She got up and slowly walked away in a state of shock. She walked through the streets, the same streets where she had lived and fought for most of her young life, tears streaming down her face, a few people stared, she no longer cared. "I told you, you are no match for me!" She heard. She looked all around her. She knew she was there, but she couldn't see her.

"Show yourself you coward!" Carrie screamed out, now making more people stop and stare. She heard her laughing. She took to her heels and ran looking down every side street as she did. As she approached the house at Hyde park she could feel her. She knew that she was behind her. She dared not look. She waited until she could feel her rancid breath on the back of her neck and quickly she turned. BAM! Carrie lost all control and began hammering her fists into Katarina's face, she was trying desperately to free herself, but Carrie would not relent. She could see Polly's body lying face down in the dirt. Then Katarina vanished, leaving Carrie fighting with mid-air!

Douglas ran out of the house and lifted Carrie up, she was still in such a frenzy, kicking and punching the air. He took her into the drawing room, placed her on the sofa and handed her a large glass of brandy, encouraging her to drink. She took a large gulp and finally calmed down enough to tell Douglas what had happened. She was sobbing as she explained how the carriage went over the top of poor Polly. At that moment she felt so alone again. Polly was the only person that Carrie truly connected with, in many aspects they were very similar.

The door to the drawing room opened and Michael walked in. He sat beside Carrie and shook his head. "Maybe it was a mistake allowing you to come here!" He said sorrowfully. Carrie shook her head.

"No it wasn't! I am going to find that bitch and make her pay!" Carrie shouted. She got up from the sofa and left the room.

She quietly opened the front door and sneaked out of the house. She was heading in the direction of the gypsy camp. She knew that Mary wouldn't be there, she would lie in wait! She crouched at the corner of the camp and watched for a while. A hand went over her mouth, and she was being dragged backwards. She was struggling to break free, once down a side street she was released. She was about to attack, then she saw her assailant. This tiny man could not have possibly dragged her all that way by himself. Suspiciously she looked all around her.

"My name is Hans, I am a dwarf, I am part of the guardianship. I work from Arbatel." He stated with his hands on his hips. Carrie nodded her head.

"So why did you drag me away Fingers?" Carrie asked. The dwarf frowned.

"I said Hans!" The dwarf shouted. Carrie laughed.

"I know!" She replied sarcastically.

"I need to place a binding around you. It will make it much more difficult for either of them to trace you. That way you can sit and wait. The element of surprise is a powerful one. Is it not?" Hans said. Carrie smiled, he was quite a pleasant chap, she thought to herself. She nodded. "You must follow me. I cannot do it here." He said and gestured to her. She crawled along the gutter side, until they came to a bow top caravan. Hans climbed inside gesturing to Carrie. She climbed inside and looked around, it wasn't much different to Mary's.

"Unusual transport for a dwarf." Carrie chuckled.

"Abraham's idea. This way the gypsys won't become suspicious." He smiled.

He spent the next twenty minutes or so waving his hands around Carrie chanting, then he threw dust at her, completely engulfing her and causing her to choke. He laughed.

"It will wear off soon." He chuckled. Once Carrie had recovered from the choking fit, Hans offered her a drink of apple juice, which she gulped down. "You may continue with your business. Good luck!" He said.

"Thanks Fingers, see you soon maybe!" Carrie said laughing as she climbed out of the caravan and headed in the direction of the gypsy camp. She was back where she started and watched for a few minutes. She waited for one of the family's to move on and then she quickly ran through and hid behind Mary's bow top. She seemed to be waiting for hours for Mary to return. Carrie heard her shouting at her horse and then felt the caravan move as Mary walked through it. Carrie crawled around the side and then to the front. She climbed up and walked in. Mary was busy looking for something and it took a while for her to look up and notice Carrie standing above her looking down at her.

"Get" Mary did not get to finish, BAM! Carrie hit her in the face, sending her to the back of the caravan. Carrie ran and hit her again, and repeatedly, until the most dreadful pain struck Carrie's back. She turned to be faced with Katarina. The bitch had electricity flowing from her fingers. As she pointed them in Carrie's direction, Carrie lashed out sending the electricity directly back to Katarina, who screeched and vanished. Mary was unconscious. Carrie lifted her bloodied head up by her hair. "Let this be a warning to you Mary, let the bitch do her own bidding, or you will get hurt." Carrie growled and let go, Mary's head crashing into the side of the caravan.

Chapter 14

"Wow! You certainly showed them!" Peggy said and chuckled when she realised how excited Carrie had become when she relived those moments. Carrie sighed.

"If only that were true Peggy. Never underestimate Katarina, the bitch just, will not stay down!" Carrie fumed. "Anyway, back to the wedding!" Carrie said enthusiastically. Peggy grinned, she had been waiting for this!

On the Friday morning over breakfast, Michael was not shy in voicing his anger over 'Carrie going it alone'. His words.

"Look Michael, with all due respect, I am not going to apologise. I did what had to be done." Carrie said with a mouth full of toast.

"You put yourself in an incredibly dangerous position. They could have killed you!" Michael replied, shaking his head.

"But I am not dead, I am most definitely alive and well! Now if you will excuse me I have a dress fitting to prepare for." Carrie said, gently pushing her chair under the table and leaving the room.

She looked in the full-size mirror, and she didn't look half bad, she was thinking to herself, when the door opened, and Molly walked in. She gasped when she looked at Carrie. "OH, you look gorgeous!" She exclaimed. She walked over and put her arms around Carrie. They hugged for the longest time until the dressmaker said an over-exaggerated "AHEM!." Molly quickly released Carrie and blushed.

"I'll go and fetch us some coffee!" Molly smiled and left the room. Carrie told the dressmaker that she was happy with the dress, so he left a much happier and richer man than when he arrived!

Molly and Carrie were sitting on the terrace enjoying their coffee, chatting about what had happened to Polly.

"It's just awful! Poor Polly, she was such a love!" Molly sighed. Carrie had a flashback of Polly, face down in the filth. She shuddered.

"They will pay!" Carrie fumed.

"Anyway, let's talk about something more cheerful. I take it from all of the busyness, that this is to be an outside wedding." Molly smiled.

Carrie looked around the grounds, so many people were working on the decorations.

"Hmmm. I said simple!" Carrie sighed. Molly laughed.

"I don't think that it comes into Abe's vocabulary does it!" She laughed. Carrie shook her head. "Should I get ready in your room tomorrow?" Molly asked. Carrie grinned and nodded her head, which soon turned to a frown. "What's wrong?" Molly asked when she noticed the change in Carrie's expression.

"Polly, she was going to do my hair!" Carrie sighed. Molly smiled and stood up.

"I will return shortly!" She said and walked back into the house.

Carrie decided to head straight to bed after dinner for two reasons. One, she wanted to look her best on her wedding day, and two Michael was obviously still angry with her, you could cut the atmosphere with a knife! So she left Michael and Molly to chat and climbed the stairs to bed.

She woke up to sunshine streaming through the drapes. A maid knocked and entered, she was preparing a bath for Carrie. She had also brought her breakfast up on a tray. She was under strict instructions not to wander down the stairs as Abe was there and it was bad luck! She enjoyed her soak in the bath, then wrapped in a bath sheet she sat in front of the mirror and applied her make-up. She did it just as Polly had shown her. There was a tap on the door and Molly walked through. "Let me know when you are decent. I have brought a stylist to do your hair." She called out as she closed the door.

Carrie got up and put on her robe. "I'm decent now!" She called back. Molly walked in followed by a middle-aged woman. Carrie sat on the stool, while the Polish woman worked her magic on her hair. Molly covered all of the mirrors, she insisted that Carrie wait until she was completely ready before she saw herself!

Once they were both in their dresses and the hair stylist had left, Molly uncovered the full-length mirror as they stood beside one another. Molly gasped and Carrie smiled as she looked at their reflections. "Oh Carrie!" Molly exclaimed. There was a knock on the door, Molly answered. She closed the door and nodded to Carrie. It was time!

They walked sided by side down the large staircase and outside. There was a raised area, where a man in a white robe was standing. Beside him was a man in a suit, he looked like a lawman. They walked in between the chairs that were set out and Carrie stood at the front, while Molly sat beside Michael. Abe walked to stand beside her. She turned and looked, her legs were shaking. He looked so handsome! He leant in towards her. "You look beautiful!" He whispered, she smiled the biggest smile, then the ceremony began. Firstly it was the robed man. They promised themselves to one another, having their hands fastened to one another, then jumped the besom (Broomstick!). Then the man with the suit led them to a table to complete the legal forms. He asked Carrie to read through. She looked at Abe in horror. He nodded to her that it was alright, then the man asked her to sign her name. Abe signed his first and she watched intently. Then she scribbled on the paper. The man looked at the signature then at Carrie and raised his eyebrow. Finally it was time to kiss the bride. Abe swept her up in his arms and kissed her most passionately, her entire body trembled, and her head spun as he released her. He grabbed her hand and walked her through all of the seated cheering guests.

After the formal meal, Abe introduced to Carrie to the guests. Apart from the staff, Molly, and Michael, she knew no-one. Abe approached the robed man and chatted for a while, then a man with a white beard walked over to them. "You must be Carrie." He said and smiled. Carrie smiled, she could feel a surge of energy emanating from him. She nodded.

"I am Abe's oldest friend, I'm not sure if he has ever mentioned me." He grinned. Carrie shook her head. He took her hand and kissed it. "I am Merlin!" He said. Carrie smiled.

"Pleased to meet you Merlin." She said smiling. Merlin was taken aback. This had to be the first time when he introduced himself that he wasn't asked. 'What? The Merlin!'. Abe turned and smiled when he saw him. He put his arms around him.

"It is so good to see you my friend!" Abe said as they hugged. Carrie smiled.

"I wouldn't have missed this day for the world!" He replied. Abe nodded.

"Are the pigs with you?" Abe asked. Merlin chuckled.

"Of course my friend!" He grinned. Carrie did not have a clue what was going on. Why would someone take pigs to a wedding she was thinking to herself when Molly walked over.

"Abe, could I borrow Carrie for a while, there is someone that would like to meet her?" She asked. Abe nodded and smiled. "Oh hello Merlin, I thought that I saw the pigs earlier!" Molly said and smiled.

"Molly, looking stunning as always!" Merlin said and kissed her hand.

"Charmer!" She shouted back as she led Carrie by the hand. They walked across the garden until they came to a small group of people. A small group of small people! They all moved out of the way to reveal an incredibly beautiful, stunningly dressed small woman. Molly beamed,

"Carrie, this is Esmelda, Queen of the Fae!" She announced excitedly. Carrie looked at Molly then Esmelda, she hadn't a clue what Molly was talking about. She held out her hand. Esmelda wore a puzzled expression and took it. Carrie shook her hand, (rather aggressively the Queen thought!).

"Pleased to meet you Es, er…"

"Esmelda, Queen Esmelda!" Molly whispered.

"Pleased to meet you Queen Esmelda!" Carrie said eventually and shook the Queen's hand again!

"Yes quite!" The Queen said and nursed her hand once Carrie had released her grip.

"You are supposed to bow and kiss her hand." Molly whispered. Carrie turned scarlet with embarrassment then turned back to the Queen.

"Apologies Queen Esmelda!" Carrie said reached for the Queen's hand, kissed it gently and then bowed. The Queen smiled.

"It's lovely to meet you Carrie. Anyone who is a friend to Abraham is a friend to the Fae!" She said and smiled. Carrie bowed again. Molly took her hand and led her back in the direction of Abe and Michael. "Let's hope her granddaughter has a bit more about her!" Esmelda said loud enough for Carrie to hear. She scowled at Molly and was about to turn around and go back. Molly stopped her and shook her head.

"She doesn't mean it. That's just the way the Fae are." Molly said. Carrie frowned.

"What even are they?" She asked ignorantly, making Molly chuckle. "And why does that Merlin bloke have pigs with him?" Carrie continued. Molly was now howling with laughter.

"Oh my dear Carrie, there is still so much you have to learn!" She said as tears of laughter ran down her cheeks.

The sun began to set, and Abe grabbed Carrie by the hand. "Come on wife, we have a honeymoon to go to!" he said as the crowd cheered. He led Carrie out of the door onto the deserted street. She looked around for a carriage, then looked at Abe. He outstretched his arms and wrapped them around her, then they flew…..

They landed on what appeared to be a massive hill. Carrie looked all around her, then at Abe. "Where are we?" She whispered. Abe grinned.

"We are in bonny Scotland!" He announced. Carrie frowned.

"Never heard of it!" She sighed. "It's got giant hills hasn't it?" She said as she looked up. Abe roared with laughter.

"They are called mountains my love!" he said through the laughter. He took her by the hand as they walked to a building made out of wood. He opened the door and Carrie gasped. It was gorgeous. There was a roaring fire, a kitchen area. Comfy sofa's and a huge bed. She looked at Abe wide eyed.

"Is this yours?" Carrie asked. Abe smiled.

"It's ours my darling! I had it built as somewhere to disappear to if necessary. Hans and his team built it for me." He smiled. Carrie grinned when she thought about the dwarf.

"I like Fingers!" She exclaimed and chuckled.

"Huh?" Abe was confused. Carrie laughed.

Two glorious weeks they spent at the secret lodge, Carrie was ecstatically happy! They were the best two weeks she had ever had! The night before they were due to leave, Abe appeared to have something on his mind. He was sitting on the rug in front of the fire, Carrie was running her fingers through his beautiful dark hair. "A penny for 'em?" Carrie said, breaking his chain of thought. He let out a long loud sigh and held her hand.

"I wish, we could stay here like this forever Carrie. I have had the best time!" he sighed. She nodded in agreement. "However, that is not to be. Where do you think you would be the happiest? We have to settle, and I will probably be away a lot of the time, but I don't want you to be alone, and I want you to be happy." He said as he gazed into her big brown eyes.

"Somewhere near the sea. I will be happy there." She grinned when she thought about it. Abe sat in deep thought for a moment.

"Didn't you plan to run away to Kent?" He asked. Carrie chuckled and nodded. "I have the perfect place then! There is a safe house in a lovely town on the east coast. It's called Whitstable. Have you ever been there?" he asked. Carrie shook her head. "I think that you will love it there!" he grinned. "So tomorrow, we should go back to Salisbury. Then I can make the arrangements for the move to Kent. How does that sound?" He asked. Carrie frantically nodded and then kissed him!

They arrived back in Salisbury the following day and were greeted at the door by a very excited Molly. She grabbed Carrie's hand, dragging her into the lodge. "Come! You must tell me everything!" She squealed excitedly.

"Not everything Carrie!" Abe shouted. Carrie laughed.

"It makes me feel a little sad that you are leaving. What ever will you do with yourself all day?" Molly asked, after Carrie had told her of their plans.

"Well, I was wondering if you would come to the coast and help me to learn to read and write. I can't be the wife of the leader of the light realm and not be able to even sign my name!" Carrie sighed.

"I would love to!" Molly grinned.

"Abe will only be at the house for a week, then he has to go to Europe again. Would you be able to come then?" Carrie asked. Molly nodded frantically. She took out her diary and jotted it down. She smiled.

"A brand-new adventure! " Molly sighed.

They arrived at the house and Carrie grinned. It was a fisherman's cottage, which overlooked the harbour. Carrie inhaled deeply, thoroughly enjoying the salty sting of the sea air. Abe unlocked the door, Carrie wasn't disappointed. The inside was equally as beautiful. The small lounge with an open fire and pretty floral sofas. The kitchen was small but quaint and practical. Abe led her up the small staircase to the bedrooms. There were three. The main bedroom was just big enough for the large bed, dressing table and built-in closets for their clothes. Abe sat on the bed and smiled as Carrie looked out of the window, watching the fishing trawlers coming and going out of the harbour.

"What do you think?" He asked. Carrie turned, grinned, and ran over to him pouncing on top of him. She kissed him all over his face.

"Oh Abe! I absolutely love it!" She exclaimed!

There was a knock on the front door. Carrie looked at Abe who smiled and walked down the stairs. Carrie followed. Abe carried a large box into the kitchen. Carrie looked at him with a raised eyebrow.

"Groceries! We have to eat!" He said and chuckled. Then it dawned on her. She had never cooked anything in her life!

"I don't know how to cook!" She said quietly. Abe laughed.

"It's a good job that I am here for a week then, should give me enough time to teach you a thing or two!" He said and tickled her. She creased with laughter.

They put the groceries away and then Abe took Carrie around the small town. It was so beautiful! Then they walked down to the beach. Carrie walked to the sea and dipped her hand in. the water was cold, but it felt so good! She loved the feeling of the wind blowing the sea spray into her face.

So for the rest of the week, Abe taught Carrie the basics of cooking. On his last evening Carrie cooked chops, mashed potatoes, cabbage, and swede, all by herself. She placed the dinners on the table and waited for his reaction. He placed a forkful into his mouth, Carrie waited anxiously, then he choked. Carrie watched in horror, jumped up then beat his back, sending his face into his food!

"I was pretending!" He said as he wiped the food from his face.

"I'm so sorry Abe! I actually thought that you were choking!" Carrie said trying her hardest not to laugh. Abe scowled at her. "Anyway, how is it?" She asked, still stifling a laugh.

"I was going to say that it was delicious. Well that is until you forced my face into it!" Carrie could hold the laugh no longer. She burst out laughing, covering her mouth, trying her hardest to stop herself. Abe began to laugh, and within seconds both of them were howling with laughter!

The following morning she crept down the stairs and prepared Abe's breakfast. She boiled him two eggs, with toast and placed a pot of tea on the table. He came down, kissed her on the cheek and sat at the table.

"Are you sure that you will be alright? I don't like the idea of you being all alone." He said as he ate his breakfast. Carrie nodded.

"Molly is coming this afternoon. She is going to stay for a few days to teach me how to read and write." Carrie said with a mouth full of toast. Abe chuckled. He reached into his pocket and pulled out a necklace with a locket. He passed it to Carrie. She opened the locket, there was a photograph of each of them inside.

"Aww! Sweet!" She grinned as she fastened it around her neck. "Thank you, it's beautiful!" She added as she held the locket in her hand.

"A very gifted man I know called Cedric, crafted that for me. It is magical. If at any point you feel threatened, rub the locket and I will know." Abe said and smiled. Carrie leant over the table and kissed him.

"I am going to miss you so much!" She said and smiled sadly.

Chapter 15

"Do you still have the locket?" Peggy asked. Carrie frowned and shook her head.

"No, It was taken from me." She said sadly. Peggy frowned.

"By whom?" She asked. Carrie shook her head.

"I'll get to that later in the story." Carrie replied.

"Right! I have chores to be getting on with. Where would you like to sit this morning?" Peggy asked.

"I shall take myself to the lounge in a short while. You carry on Peggy." Carrie said and waved her hand to shoo Peggy off. Peggy saluted and walked to the kitchen.

She was preparing the stew, when the back door opened, and Molly walked in. "Hello Peggy. How's things?" She chirped. Peggy smiled.

"Not bad, all things considered!" Peggy replied. She then went on to tell Molly about what had happened early that morning. Molly frowned and shook her head.

"They are relentless! When will they ever give that poor woman peace!" She scorned. Peggy sighed.

"I know. It's so frustrating, especially when you have no magical powers. If I did have, I would sort the lot of them!" Peggy fumed and raised her fists in the air. Laughter came from the doorway, they both turned to see Carrie in her wheelchair laughing at Peggy.

"Oh my Peggy, such spirit you have!" Carrie sighed. Molly nodded in agreement.

"Abe and Michael will be here shortly. We were wondering if you felt up to a short drive to the coast?" Molly asked. Peggy smiled as Carrie's eyes lit up.

"I haven't been to the sea for around 15 years!" She sighed. "I would love to!" She added.

So with the afternoon of an empty house, Peggy had the chance to catch up on all the chores that were difficult to do when the cottage was full of visitors.

She hung the rugs on the line outside and began beating the dust from them fiercely.

"All alone are ya?" She heard a woman shout. She looked around but could see no-one. She continued to beat the rugs. "Oi, over here." She looked quickly. Bloody Mary was now leaning over the garden wall.

"Go away! You have no business here!" Peggy said in her sternest voice.

"Aye but I do." Mary said in her thick Irish accent. "I tell you what! I'll make life easier for you all, after all she is gonna be dead soon." She said and laughed. Peggy shot her a look, "You give me the book and I'll leave you all to it." She added. Peggy walked over to the wall. Her legs were trembling, but she didn't care. She was face to face with Mary.

"OVER MY DEAD BODY!" Peggy roared. Mary laughed.

"As you wish!" She chuckled and then leapt at Peggy. She jumped on top of Peggy, pinning her arms down with her legs. She took a knife from her trouser leg and looked at Peggy. "You see this?" She lifted the blade into the sunlight. "I'm gonna cut you, drink your blood and then run this sharp blade through your heart." Mary said, her eyes red. Peggy was struggling, trying so hard to free herself. "Well that is unless you change your mind and give me the book." She added.

"You're bluffing!" Peggy shouted.

"Now, why would you think that?" Mary asked.

"You are not a revenant. That's why you do Katarina's bidding for her." Peggy struggled to say. Mary laughed.

"That was before I got too old. One day Kat said to me, I can stop that. All that has to happen is, I drink your blood, you drink mine, and that's what happened, and that's why I am not a frail old *has been* like Carrie!" Mary said, her eyes becoming redder by the second. Peggy flipped! She summoned all her strength and tried her hardest to throw Mary from her. She was so strong. She could not shift her! Peggy cried out in frustration.

"Hey, HEY, GET OFF OF HER NOW! "She heard William shout. Within seconds Mary flew off of Peggy, landing in a heap on the floor. Peggy jumped up. It was as though an invisible force was beating Mary. William ran to Peggy and threw his arms around her. When they both looked Mary had vanished. "What the bloody hell was that all about?" William asked. Peggy shook her head. William grabbed Peggy's hand and walked her to the kitchen door. They both jumped when they saw her. An incredibly beautiful, alas very angry looking woman was leant up against the wall beside the door. They both stood with their mouths gaped open. The woman chuckled.

"Please stop doing that." She said sternly. Together they both closed their mouths. "Better" She said. "I am here to tell you a little secret." She added. They both nodded, both of them still speechless. "I will not allow that woman to harm your grandmother, is that clear?" They both nodded. "That woman is in debt to me. I gave her an incredibly small task, all that she had to do was keep the crystal ball safe, but she failed. As a result, whenever she means to threaten or hurt either of you, I will stop her. My name is Arianrhod. Please relay this message back to Carrie." She said and nodded at Peggy. Peggy nodded, the woman vanished.

William looked at Peggy who appeared to be dazed. "Who was that?" He asked. Peggy shook her head in bewilderment. He helped Peggy into the kitchen and put the kettle on the stove. "Sweet tea, that's what you need, it's good for shock, well that's what me Ma says." William said as he warmed the pot.

Carrie and Molly were sitting on the promenade, while Abe and Michael went to buy them all an ice cream. Carrie smiled as she watched the waves crash onto the shore, it took her back to Whitstable. A time in her life when she thought that she could finally be happy!

"It is good of Abe, you know to visit. I'm sure he probably has more important things to be getting on with." Carrie sighed. Molly frowned.

"I think that it is the least he can do Carrie. One day, you will open your eyes and see him for who he truly is!" Molly said and shook her head.

"And is that the same for you and Michael?" Carrie sneered.

"Michael is nothing like Abe, nothing like him!" Molly said defensively. Carrie chuckled.

"He is more like Abe than you care to admit Molly. Let's not forget, they were in this together. The end goal is equally important to both of them." Carrie snapped.

"Yes but Michael is sorry Carrie, surely you must see that!" Molly replied.

"And so is Abe, he wouldn't be here now if he wasn't would he!" Carrie began to cough. Molly reached her a hanky.

"Yes you're right, I know you are. Sorry." She said remorsefully. Carrie tapped her hand.

"Come on, men are not worth falling out over are they?" She said and smiled. Molly nodded in agreement.

They both walked along the promenade, smiling away, none the wiser of the conversation that was just held about them. Michael passed Molly her ice cream and smiled.

"Thank you!" She said abruptly and snatched the ice cream from him. He frowned and looked at Abe, who shrugged. Abe passed Carrie hers. She smiled, a genuinely happy smile. Abe touched her shoulder.

After a while Carrie began to shiver. "Should we head back to the car?" He asked. Carrie smiled and nodded.

Peggy had cooked a large pot of stew, and the smell was most welcoming, when the four of them went inside. Carrie yawned and wheeled herself to the bedroom, she was exhausted. Abe walked out to the kitchen to find Peggy sitting at the table trembling.

"Peggy what's wrong?" Abe asked when he saw her. She burst into tears. She went on to tell Abe what had happened in their absence. He put his arms around her as she sobbed.

After an hour of Peggy chatting to Abe, she began to calm down and feel better. "Is young William coming for dinner this evening?" He asked.

"No, well I haven't asked him." Peggy replied. Abe got up and walked into the lounge where Molly and Michael were. He took the car keys and left the cottage.

About twenty minutes later Abe walked through the back door, followed by William, Peggy threw her arms around him as soon as she laid eyes on him. They all sat around the table chatting about what had happened that day.

"Oh Peggy, do you realise that you have had your first audience with a Goddess!" Carrie said. Peggy looked at her grandmother. She appeared to be stronger, younger, happier since Abe's arrival.

"Really?" William said wide eyed. Carrie smiled.

"Really sweet William!" She replied. William looked at Peggy.

"Ha!" He said and laughed!

Molly and Michael cleared the dishes. Carrie yawned, the sea air has exhausted her! "Would you like me to help you into bed?" Peggy asked and smiled. Abe leant across the table.

"Why don't you and William go for a nice stroll, I can help Carrie into bed." He smiled.

"Er, I don't think so! You are a man, and she is a respectable lady!"

Peggy frowned. Abe and Carrie both laughed.

"I am well aware of that, we are married and have had three children together!" Abe replied as he laughed. Peggy continued to frown.

"Aye but…"

"But nothing Peggy, Abe's right. He is more than capable of helping me. You and sweet William should go and enjoy each other's company." Carrie smiled and nodded. William nudged Peggy and reluctantly she got up and left the room with him.

Abe wheeled Carrie into her room and helped her into her nightdress. Carrie tried her hardest to retain her dignity, making Abe chuckle.

"Carrie it's not like I haven't seen it before!" he grinned. Carrie blushed.

"I am aware of that Abe, but unlike you, I have not retained my youthful figure, and unfortunately everything has gone south on me!" She said and laughed as he tucked her into bed. Abe sat on the chair beside Carrie's bed and held her hand. He looked deep into her still big brown eyes. "People must think that you are wheeling your mother around, not your estranged wife!" Carrie continued. Abe sighed, a loud sigh.

"Oh Carrie, what a tangled life we have lived!" He said. She nodded. "I want you to know something." He added. Carrie raised her eyebrow in curiosity. "The last night of our honeymoon." He began. Carrie nodded. She remembered it so clearly. "I said that I wished we could stay like that forever. Do you remember?" He asked. Carrie nodded.

"Like it were yesterday" She sighed. Abe's grip tightened on her frail skeletal hand.

"I meant every word of it! I believe that had we stayed there, we would still be sitting there to this day, just as happy. Life has a way of putting a spanner in the works." He continued. Carrie frowned.

"No Abe, not life. What you should have said is *women* have a way of putting a spanner in the works! Or even, your roving eye has a way of doing so!" Carrie said. She looked at Abe, tears filled his eyes.

"I am so sorry. Sincerely. Believe me, I punish myself every day for the wrong doing, for the betrayal, for the suffering that I have caused you!" He said his voice quivering as he fought the compulsion to sob. Carrie could feel the sting of tears in her eyes. She tapped his hand.

"If I ask you something, do you promise to give me an honest answer, not what you think I want to hear?" Carrie asked. Abe wiped his tears and nodded.

"Did you ever truly love me?" She asked, secretly dreading the answer, she knew that if she asked him to be honest, he would! He sighed, then buried his face in his hands. Carrie became nervous. "Actually, don't answer that. I don't think that I could cope with the truth. Now I really need to sleep." Carrie said. Abe stood, bent over kissed her on the cheek, turned out the light and left the room. Carrie turned her head, buried it in her pillow and sobbed!

Molly and Michael were sitting in the lounge. Molly was silent, which worried Michael somewhat.

"Molly, is everything alright?" Michael asked nervously. She scowled at him.

"No Michael, it isn't!" She fumed. Michael frowned. "For over 100 years I have loved you. For that time I have waited patiently for you to take the hint. Even when Abe proposed to Carrie, still you never took the hint. Am I that hideous?" Molly asked. Michael sighed. He took Molly's hand in his.

"Molly my dear, there has been far too much deceit. I would never want to mislead you in any way. I have always been aware of your feelings, I just never wanted to fill you with false hope. I do love you Molly, you are my best friend, but friendship is all I have to offer." He said remorsefully. Molly broke down in tears. She had dreaded having this conversation for an entire century and now finally it was out there, and her heart was breaking!

"Ahem!" Abe said and awkwardly walked into the room. Molly continued to sob. Abe looked at Michael and frowned. Michael shook his head. Abe sat down beside Molly and put his arm around her shoulder. She buried her face into his shoulder and wept. Michael left the room. Abe passed Molly a hanky.

"Do you want to talk about it?" he asked as she lifted her head and wiped the tears away.

"It's done, it's out there. He loves me as a friend and that is that!" She sniffed. Abe shook his head.

"Molly, I just don't know what to say." He sighed.

"You could say, there are plenty more fish in the sea, or it's time to move on Molly, find your true love!" She sniffed again then chuckled.

"Well, I could say that if you like, I don't think that it will help though!" Abe chuckled. Molly laughed and nudged into Abe.

"What a mess we have all made of things! It could have been so different, you know if we hadn't pledged our lives to the guardians." She said.

"Yes, we would be dead! Well you, Michael, and myself!" Abe replied.

"Are you afraid of death Abe, is that why you continue to serve?" Molly asked. Abe sighed.

"Surely everyone is afraid to leave this realm. No Molly that is not what drives me. There are certain things that must happen, and I made a promise to see it through to that point. To be honest, I cannot wait to meet my great granddaughter, when it all begins. The beginning of the end eh!" Abe said solemnly.

"So you sacrificed everything for that?" Molly asked. Abe shook his head.

"No Molly, I am not that heroic. Many of the things that I have done, were done for purely selfish reasons." He replied. Michael walked back in.

"I think that we should maybe make a move." He said quietly. Abe looked at his watch and yawned.

"Peggy hasn't returned yet. I will stay here tonight, make sure she gets home safely." Abe said.

"Are you sure Abe, I don't mind doing it." Molly smiled. Abe smiled.

"No Molly, I am sure that you and Michael have things to discuss and anyway, I have to return to Arbatel for a few days, so I would like to spend as much time as possible with them both." He continued. Molly nodded then her and Michael left the cottage.

Abe walked into the kitchen and put the kettle on the stove. He opened the kitchen door, looking out for Peggy to return while he waited for it to boil. After a few minutes he heard Peggy and William's voices and he sighed with relief. They came through the back door laughing.

"You still here?" Peggy asked as she took off her coat. Abe looked at himself and then around the room.

"It appears so." He said and smiled.

"Cheeky so and so!" Peggy said as she walked through to the hallway and hung up her coat.

"I had better head off now Peggy, before the rain gets any worse." William called out. She walked back through.

"Oh, Ok, will I see you tomorrow?" She asked.

"Just try and stop me!" he replied as she walked him out of the door.

Abe poured the boiling water into the teapot. "Tea?" He asked Peggy when she walked back in and shook the rain water from her hair.

"Aye please." She replied. Abe handed her a steaming cup of tea. "Thanks."

"I told Molly that I would be staying here for a few days, is that ok with you?" Abe asked. Peggy frowned.

"Why?" Peggy asked as she blew on her tea.

"I have to return to Arbatel for a few days, so I wanted to spend as much time as possible with you both." He replied. Peggy forced a smile. She would pretend to be happy for Carrie's sake. She had noticed such a difference in her since Abe's arrival.

"Look Peggy, I am not asking for you to like me. I want to be here for Carrie, it's the least I can do, given the circumstances." He said

"It's a shame you couldn't be there for her when she was well!" Peggy muttered under her breath.

Chapter 16

Peggy took Carrie's breakfast tray into her. She placed it onto the table and drew back the curtains. Carrie sat herself up. Peggy put the tray on her lap.

"Abe is staying for a few days before he has to return to Arbatel." Peggy said so matter of factly. Carrie smiled.

"Stay while I eat my breakfast." Carrie asked and grabbed Peggy's hand.

"Of course." Peggy replied and sat down on the chair. "So how long were you in Whitstable?" She asked.

"Well….."

So now that Carrie could read and write she decided that she should volunteer at the local hospital. She desperately needed to fill her time, she was becoming so bored and lonely. She applied to the local hospital and was thrilled when she got the job, and it was paid!

She got up one morning early, to get ready for her shift, when her head spun, and she felt the need to vomit!. She spent the next thirty minutes vomiting in the toilet. She thought that she must have picked something up from work. Once she had drank a glass of water she began to feel better, so she headed for the hospital.

After an incredibly busy shift, she walked out of the hospital exhausted. She walked along the road and noticed a familiar face walking towards her.

"Molly!" She shouted and waved. Molly ran and threw her arms around her. It had been two months since they had seen one another.

"What I want to know is… why haven't you told me in your letters?" Molly asked once she had released Carrie from the bear hug! Carrie frowned.

"Told you what?" Carrie asked.

"The baby!"

"What baby?"

"The one in there!" Molly replied and touched Carrie's tummy.

"What? You mean I'm…"

"Yes! Didn't you know?" Molly asked excitedly. Carrie shook her head.

They got back to the cottage and Carrie put the kettle on the stove. "I had better write to Abe and tell him." Carrie sighed as she placed her hand on her tummy.

"Wait, I have a better idea!" Molly said and closed her eyes. She kept them closed for a few seconds. "I bet he is here before dinner!" Molly proclaimed.

"Eh?" Carrie was confused. Molly laughed.

"The power of telepathy!" Molly said and poured the hot water into the teapot.

And as Molly suspected the door opened an hour later. Abe ran through the kitchen and swept Carrie up in his arms.

They sat around the table eating dinner. Well Abe and Molly were eating, Carrie was picking, every time that she ate, she felt sick!

"I think that we should go back to Salisbury, to the lodge. I don't want you here all alone." Abe said as he placed his knife and fork on his empty plate. Carrie frowned.

"But I love it here. Please Abe can't I stay for just a little longer?" She pleaded.

"I could stay with her." Molly said and smiled. Abe looked at Molly then at Carrie.

"Please!" Carrie said. Abe shook his head.

"Alright, just for a while longer. When you reach six months Carrie I must insist that we go back." Abe said. Carrie jumped up and threw her arms around him.

"Thank you!" She whispered in his ear.

The following day, Molly travelled back to the lodge to get more things. Abe walked Carrie to the hospital to tell them that she could no longer work there, then they went for a stroll on the beach. Carrie was sad the following morning when Abe had to return to Arbatel.

So for a few months life went by quietly. Carrie was happy when the sickness stopped (thanks to Molly's potion of willow bark!) and every day she became increasingly proud and protective of her growing tummy. Every night before she went to sleep, she would tell her tummy, that she would protect the tiny life that was growing inside of her and vowed to be a better parent than hers were.

Carrie and Molly were walking down the high street, popping in and out of the shops. The weather was beautiful. The sun was shining, there was not a cloud in the sky. Carrie was so hot, she desperately wanted to go to the sea, but the beach was crowded with day trippers. Molly popped into the butchers shop, to buy some sausages for dinner, Carrie waited outside, the smell made her feel sick. Someone tapped her on the shoulder. She turned, thinking that it was Molly. She was wrong.

"What is this, I see before me?" Katarina sneered and poked Carrie hard in the tummy. Carrie bent over double. Molly came running out of the shop.

"LEAVE HER!!!!" Molly roared. Katarina bent down beside Carrie's ear.

"I will take it. That thing that lives inside you. I will take it! She whispered. Carrie let out a roar and hit out with all her strength, sending Katarina flying into the air. Then she vanished. Carrie was in so much pain, it was hard for her to stand straight. Molly helped her back to the cottage. She laid Carrie on the sofa and laid her hands over her tummy, trying to heal Carrie and save the baby. Eventually Carrie smiled.

"The pain has subsided now." She said with a sigh of relief. "Thank you Molly, from the bottom of my heart, thank you!" Carrie said. Molly smiled.

"I'll go and make us a cup of tea." She said before she disappeared into the kitchen. Carrie got herself up and walked outside to the toilet. She came back through to the kitchen in floods of tears. Molly looked at her.

"I am bleeding" She sobbed. Molly closed her eyes and called out to Abraham. Within half an hour he ran in through the door.

"She needs to be at the lodge. We need a doctor to examine her!" Abe said as he began to panic.

"The journey is too long, she needs a doctor now Abe!" Molly insisted.

"Carrie can you stand?" He asked her. She nodded. He helped her up and walked her out to the back garden. He closed his arms around her, and they were flying. Molly locked up the cottage and did the same. They were back at the lodge. Abe carried her up to the bedroom, washed her and put her in her nightdress as they waited for the doctor to arrive.

The doctor was examining her as Abe, Michael and Molly waited outside the room. Abe was pacing back and forth, insisting that Molly told him exactly what had happened for the fourth time! The doctor came out of the room and walked with Abe down the hallway.

"The child lives, the next twenty-four hours are crucial. She must have total bed rest and plenty of fluids." The Doctor said as he made his way down the large staircase.

For the next three months Carrie was confined to bed rest until the day finally came. Up to that day Abe was a nervous wreck, Carrie dare not tell him about the awful visions of Katarina she was having every night. Even though she was petrified at the thought of childbirth, she was so excited to meet her baby! After a long grueling eleven-hour labour, he finally made an appearance! The midwife came out of the room and smiled at Abe, who ran into the room. Carrie handed him their new son. He took the baby in his arms and kissed Carrie. "What should we call him?" Abe asked.

"George!" Carrie announced proudly. Abe smiled and nodded.

Carrie and George had to remain at the lodge. Britain had declared War on Germany and Abe was in Europe most of the time. Within two years Carrie became pregnant again. World War I was raging, and she must have fell pregnant on Abe's last visit home.

George was a troublesome child. He was stubborn, always getting into mischief and had a terrible temper. His behaviour seemed to deteriorate. The larger that Carrie's bump became, the more he began to misbehave. Carrie was worried. With Abe away at war all of the time, she knew that he was the only person that George would listen to.

One evening, the day before Carrie gave birth, she walked passed the nursery. She could hear George talking. She placed her ear to the door and listened. Slowly and quietly she opened the door and peeked in. To her complete horror Katarina was sitting on the floor with George. She held a dolly in her hand. "Baby" She said and pointed to the dolly. George nodded. She took out a knife and stabbed the dolly. "George hurt the baby." Katarina said. George let out a giggle. She handed him the dolly and the knife and laughed as the child repeatedly stabbed the dolly. Carrie threw the door open and screamed out. Katarina disappeared. She ran over to George and snatched the dolly and knife from him.

"That lady is bad George, bad do you hear me!" She shouted, just as her waters broke.

Everyone was attending Carrie, Molly had contacted Abe, but it was impossible for him to leave. After another eleven-hour labour Carrie gave birth to her second son. Both were well. The following morning after Carrie had rested a while Molly tapped on the door and walked into the room, hand in hand with George. "I have come to introduce George to his new brother." Molly beamed. Carrie smiled at the sweet looking boy. He looked so grown up! She held the baby out to him. He looked at the baby.

"George hurt baby." He said as he hit the baby in the tummy.

"NO!" Carrie and Molly both shouted in unison, as Molly pulled the boy away. The baby was screaming. Michael ran into the room as Molly quickly told him what had happened. Michael took George by the hand and led him down the stairs, while Molly healed the baby and Carrie told her what had happened the evening before.

For months they all had to keep a close eye on George. His aggression towards his younger brother was slowly getting worse by the day. War was still raging in Europe and Britain was being bombed daily, Abe had only seen baby Albert once since his arrival, and now this baby boy was a happy giggly little chap, the complete opposite to George.

One evening after the children had been settled into bed, Carrie and Molly were sitting in the lounge chatting.

"Maybe you should recruit a nanny." Molly said thinking. She had to go away on Guardian business for a while and would be away for a substantial amount of time. Carrie sighed.

"I suppose I could do with an extra pair of hands." Carrie said once she had thought about it. "Before you go, will you teach me how to do that telepathy thing?" She continued. Molly smiled and nodded.

"I'll teach you now." She replied. So for the next hour Molly talked Carrie through it and she gave it a go. She had managed to get through to Molly, and Michael, she was thrilled.

Breaking glass. Shards flew past the large windows. Carrie ran as fast as she could up the stairs, with Molly following. She ran into the nursery. George was hitting the windows with a wooden hammer, smashing them with brute force.

"GEORGE!" Carrie shouted in her sternest voice. The child looked at her and laughed. He then looked at Albert's cot. Carrie looked at Molly who ran towards the cot, as too did George. Molly reached out and grabbed George, just as he was about to attack a now crying Albert. George turned and pushed Molly. He pushed her with such force, she went flying through the air, slamming against the door as she landed. Carrie didn't know what to do first. Molly was unconscious, Albert was screaming, and George was heading back towards the cot.

Carrie ran at him. Without her realising it, he grabbed the locket that was around her neck and ripped it from her. He pushed Carrie, she did not move. She grabbed him and walked him out of the room, as she shouted for help. No-one came. She struggled to hold George, he was unnaturally strong. She kicked Michael's door open. It was empty. She placed George on the chair and locked the door behind her. She ran up the stairs. Albert was still screaming, but thankfully, Molly had regained consciousness. Carrie grabbed hold of Albert and crouched down beside Molly.

"Are you alright? Do I need to call the doctor?" Carrie asked. Albert had now calmed and was quiet. Molly shook her head.

"No I'm fine." She looked around the room. "Where is he?" She asked.

"I have locked him in Michael's office." Carrie replied anxiously.

"CARRIE!" They both heard Michael shout from down the stairs. They both ran, Carrie still holding onto Albert. Molly overtook her and reached Michael first. He was pointing to the window in his office. Molly looked in horror. Carrie looked. The window was broken, George was walking hand in hand with Katarina, across the lawn. Carrie handed Albert to Molly and ran as fast as her legs would carry her. Katarina watched as Carrie ran towards them both and shot lightning from her fingers towards Carrie. She dare not retaliate. If she sent it back it would hit George. She took a shot of electricity, sending her to the ground. She was so infuriated, she ignored the pain, got up and continued to run. She only had one option. She looked at George. "I am so sorry son" She mumbled under her breath as she lunged to hit him. The force was so great, George flew through the air. Katarina sent another bolt from her fingers, this time Carrie rebound it, sending it back. She quickly looked, George was lying on the ground. There was no movement.

Ceridwen, please help me Carrie thought to herself as she ran in George's direction. Now something was behind her, her arms were pulled back, and she was held in a lock. Katarina again sent a bolt towards her. The pain was excruciating, forcing her to yelp. It was at that moment she realised who was holding her. Mary let out a laugh. Carrie summoned all of her energy, her anger, her complete and utter rage. She let out a roar, then threw Mary away from her as she ran in the direction of Katarina who was now standing over George. She almost flew through the air as she landed on Katarina and began to hit her with all her might.

As always Katarina vanished into a cloud of dust. Carrie walked over to her son's lifeless body. A shadow passed behind her, she thought it was Mary, so she turned to attack. It wasn't Mary it was Ceridwen.

The Goddess leant over George's body and gently laid her hands over him. He began to cough, Carrie choked back the tears. Ceridwen turned to Carrie who took a low bow. "Thank you sincerely. I owe you so much!" Carrie sobbed. The Goddess smiled, then vanished. Carrie walked over to George and picked him up.

"I am so sorry my love." She sobbed as she held him tightly. As she walked back towards the lodge Carrie sighed with relief when she saw Abe running towards her. He took George from her, and they walked into the lodge. Michael, Molly, Albert, and a young woman were in the lounge. Carrie collapsed in a heap on the floor, weeping. She was inconsolable.

The young woman was Molly's niece Joanna. She was a guardian with a special gift. She had a natural ability to calm. She usually worked in the magical prisons, calming violent prisoners. Once Carrie had calmed, with the help of brandy Molly sat in front of her.

"Carrie this is Joanna, she is going to help you with the children." Molly said and smiled. Carrie wiped her tear-stained eyes and looked at the young woman. She smiled.

"Do you have any idea what you are letting yourself in for?" Carrie sniffed.

"It's ok. I have an ability to calm violence." Joanna said as she shook Carrie's hand. Carrie looked up and smiled. "I'll take the boys up to the nursery, if that's ok?" She continued. Carrie nodded. Joanna took George by the hand and carried Albert in the other arm.

A few minutes later Molly walked back in with a tray of tea, which she placed on the table and then handed out the cups. Carrie cradled the warm cup in her cold hands. She turned to look at Michael. "Why didn't you help me?" She asked quietly. Michael sighed.

"She placed a holding spell on me, that's why I didn't go after them myself. The only thing that I was able to do was shout." He said sadly. "I am sorry Carrie." He added. Carrie smiled.

Carrie and Abe had checked in on the children, Joanna was sleeping in the nursery. The boys were both sound asleep. They were sitting in bed. Carrie was exhausted, but she was so happy to see Abe, she didn't want to waste a single second.

"I think that you and the boys should stay in the house in London. Molly is staying there, and to be honest, it would make it easier for me to see you all more." He suggested. Carrie smiled.

"If it means that I get to spend more time with you, I will move anywhere." She said and kissed him.

"So, is it the Joanna, Jo, Joanna?" Peggy asked. Carrie nodded and smiled.

"Wow!" Peggy said. "I hate Katarina!" She scorned. Carrie frowned.

"There is not a lot to like I'm afraid." Carrie replied. There was a knock on the door and Abe poked his head around.

"I have made us all some lunch. It's a beautiful day, shall we dine alfresco?" He asked. Carrie smiled and nodded. Peggy frowned. Once he had gone Peggy looked at Carrie.

"What was he going on about? What on earth is alfresco?" She asked. Carrie let out a chuckle.

"It's outside dining!" She replied. Peggy shook her head and tutted.

"Why didn't he say that!" She said.

Chapter 17

They sat in the garden and ate the lovely lunch that Abe had prepared. Carrie put down her knife and fork after finishing the last mouthful of quiche. She smiled at Abe. "That was delicious. I had forgotten what a good cook you were!" She chuckled and winked.

"I try." He sighed.

"Aye, my patience" Peggy mumbled under breath. Carrie heard it and frowned if she heard it then so must Abe. He touched Carrie's hand and smiled, she had also forgotten that he could read her thoughts! Peggy cleared the plates as Carrie and Abe enjoyed the warm rays of the sun.

"Cooey!" They both heard Molly call out, then she appeared coming through the back gate, followed by Michael and Jo. Michael and Molly sat down with Carrie and Abe, Jo walked inside to find Peggy.

"I have been hearing stories about you." Peggy said and winked.

"All bad I hope!" Jo said and laughed. "What are you wearing tonight?" Jo continued. Peggy looked confused.

"To the dance!" Jo clarified.

"Crikey, I had forgotten about that! I wonder if William has remembered?" Peggy said as she dried the last plate. Jo laughed.

"Well he knows that Matt and I are picking him up at half six." Jo replied.

"Oh Matt now is it!" Peggy said and laughed. "I think I'll wear the baby blue two piece." Peggy added.

"Ooh yes. I really like that outfit." Jo said.

"What about you?"

"Ooh, I'm going to throw caution to the wind and wear a low-cut red dress!"

" You are too daring!" Peggy laughed as she picked up the tray of teas and carried them out to the garden.

Peggy handed out the cups. "Thank you" Molly said and smiled as Peggy passed her a cup of tea.

"Right, I had better go and prepare the dinner." Peggy said and turned back towards the cottage.

"No need Peggy, I will grab us all a fish and chip supper." Abe called out. "Come back and enjoy the sunshine!" He added. Peggy looked at Jo and rolled her eyes. She had no idea why he irritated her so much, but he did!

Peggy heard whistling and knew that William was close by. He jumped over the wall from the field. Everyone greeted him. "William, just in time for some lemonade!" Molly said as she walked past him into the cottage.

"Lovely!" He said, grinned and wiped the beads of sweat from his brow.

Matthew's car pulled up outside the cottage. Peggy looked out of her bedroom window and waved. She walked down the stairs and into the lounge where Carrie, Abe, Molly, and Michael were playing cards.

"I'm off now." She said as she kissed Carrie's cheek.

"Have lots of fun, and don't take any crap from the locals!" Carrie said, making Molly burst out laughing. Michael tutted and looked at Abe.

"Stay safe." Abe said as Peggy headed towards the door. "Oh, Peggy." He added.

"What?" She replied abruptly.

"You look beautiful!" He said and smiled. Peggy grinned.

"Thanks Granddad!" She laughed and closed the door. Abe looked at Carrie and grinned, he felt an overwhelming sense of pride, even if she was trying to wind him up!

Peggy huffed when Matthew parked the car, she noticed Jean's brothers car parked up. Jo smiled and tapped her on the shoulder. William planted a kiss on Peggy's cheek and gave her a look of reassurance. They all climbed out of the car and headed towards the village hall. The same man as before was taking tickets at the door. He looked at Peggy and screwed his eyes up. "There is to be no trouble from you this week!" He scowled at Peggy. She opened her mouth to retaliate when Jo jumped in front of her smiling at the man.

"You won't even know that we are here" Jo said, took Peggy's hand and led her inside to find a table. Peggy sat down. She frowned at Jo.

"Why didnee you let me say my piece?" Peggy fumed.

"Because Peg, tonight we are going to show them all who the real troublemakers are!" Jo grinned.

William and Matthew put the drinks on the table. William sat beside Peggy, Matthew was just about to take a seat when Jo jumped up, grabbed him by the hand and led him onto the dance floor. Peggy chuckled as Matthew frowned.

"She's a brave Lassie, I'll say that for her!" William said before he took a long gulp from his beer.

"What do you mean?" Peggy asked and looked at Jo showing off. The local girls were all scowling at her.

"Wearing a dress like that! I mean it's a wee bit revealing isn't it!" William replied.

"I think that she looks gorgeous!" Peggy said defensively.

"I think that she looks like a tart!" Peggy heard from behind. She turned and was faced with Jean, perched on the table behind them.

"Well, no-one asked for your opinion did they!" Peggy fumed. Jean leant over, looking directly at Peggy.

"Have you met my knew friend?" She sneered and moved to the side to reveal Mary.

"Aye, I have. Hello Mary, how are you?" Peggy asked and chuckled when she saw the look of disappointment on Jean's face. Mary let out a low growl, which turned Peggy's chuckle into a loud laugh. "Now if you will excuse me, I need to powder my nose." Peggy said as she stood up.

"This could take a while, have you seen the size of it!" Jean shouted, Mary cackled.

"Shut up!" William snapped at Jean, who turned scarlet, threw William a look and then walked in the direction of the ladies toilet.

There were two cubicles in the ladies, and one was in use, Peggy went into the other. She heard the main door open, and she instinctively knew it would be Jean and Mary. Peggy flushed and opened the door. They were both standing with their backs against the hand basins. Peggy walked over to them.

"Excuse me!" She said confidently. They both laughed. Peggy went to push past Jean. Mary grabbed her around the throat.

"How dare you!" She growled. The other cubicle door opened and much to Peggy's relief, out stepped Arianrhod the Goddess. She grabbed Mary's hair, forcing her head back.

"Now let go." She said calmly to Mary. She released Peggy and Arianrhod spun her around. Mary looked horrified. Jean ran out of the ladies making Peggy chuckle. "Now I must insist that you apologise to this young lady and then go as far away from this place, as far away as possible." The Goddess said. Mary put her head down and looked at the floor. "NOW!" The Goddess roared.

"Sorry" Mary mumbled, not even looking in Peggy's direction.

"GO!" Arianrhod shouted. Mary took to her heels and ran. Arianrhod chuckled. Peggy bowed.

"Thank you my lady" Peggy said nervously.

"No need to thank me, as I have already said, I will not allow her to hurt neither you nor your grandmother. I shall hang around for a while." She said as she walked out of the door.

As Peggy walked back into the hall, all of the locals were staring and pointing. It took all of her strength not to say anything to any of them, instead she walked with her head held high and smiled at William when he turned to look at her.

Back at the cottage Molly yawned. Michael smiled at her. "Come on, you look exhausted, shall we drive back?" He asked. Molly smiled.

Once they had said their goodbyes it just left Carrie and Abe in the lounge. "Would you like me to help you into bed?" he asked. Carrie frowned.

"No, I am not tired and besides, I am waiting up for Peggy!" She said and looked at the clock. It was only 9.30.

"Ok, how about a glass of wine?" Abe asked and winked a cheeky wink at her. She thought about it. What did she have to lose, she knew that she was dying anyway.

"Just a small one Abe." She smiled and winked back. He laughed as he walked out into the kitchen.

They were sitting beside one another on the sofa, in front of a crackling fire sipping wine. "Mmm!" Carrie said as she took her first sip. She had not had a drink since she and Abe parted company. She had forgotten how light red wine made her feel. She smiled at Abe. He looked at her with such a sad expression.

"What's wrong?" She asked.

"I look at you Carrie, and every time that I do, I despise myself a little more." He sighed. She tapped his knee.

"Oh Abe, you cannot continue to punish yourself, what is done is done, we cannot change it, no matter how hard we try." She said and took another sip of wine.

"I know, I just wish that I had been a better husband, a man that you truly deserved." He sighed again.

"Right! I shan't drink another drop if you are going to be all melancholy and miserable!" Carrie said sternly. Abe chuckled.

"Sorry." "Do you remember when I told you about the ball in London?" He asked and chuckled. Carrie chuckled.

"Are you talking about the Molly and Merlin thing?" Carrie asked as she roared with laughter. Abe too was now laughing, he nodded his head. "Wasn't it Esmelda that caught them?" Carrie asked. Abe howled with laughter, nodding frantically.

"Do you know, still to this day, I am not allowed to mention it!" Abe said as he wiped tears away from his eyes.

"How is the old meddler? Have you seen him recently?" Carrie asked. Abe nodded.

"Yes I had to go and see him a few weeks ago, still the same as ever." He said and smiled.

"Give him my regards when you see him next will you." Carrie said and smiled as she thought about him.

"Well I was going to suggest…." Abe began. Carrie raised her eyebrow in anticipation of what was coming next. She gestured for Abe to continue. "He really would love to come and see you." He continued. Carrie smiled.

"Well I suppose it might be nice to see him again, it's been a long time!" she sighed.

"Wonderful! I'll let him know" Abe grinned.

The back door opened and within seconds Peggy and William walked through. Carrie sighed with relief when she saw how happy Peggy looked.

"Did you have a good time?" Abe asked. They both nodded eagerly.

"Would anyone like a cocoa?" Peggy asked. Both Abe and Carrie nodded.

So over cocoa Peggy and William told them all about their evening. Carrie smiled.

"Well let's hope that sees an end to it all!" She said and yawned.

"I'd better head home Peg." William said as he too yawned. He said goodnight then Peggy walked him to the door.

"Come on you. Let's get you into bed!" Abe said as he helped Carrie out of her seat. She chuckled when he said it.

"Oh Abe, if only I were younger!" She said and laughed.

He tucked her into bed and looked at her. "You know, even now when I look at you, I see the Carrie that I married. I would say sweet and innocent, but that would be a lie!" He said and laughed.

"Bloody cheek!" Carrie said as she snuggled down beneath the blankets.

Abe walked back into the lounge, where Peggy was sitting warming her hands in front of the fire.

"Peggy, I just want you to know, that I am genuinely sorry for the way that Carrie has been treated, especially by me." Abe said quietly. Peggy looked at him and sighed.

"You know, you make it very hard for me to dislike you." Peggy replied. Abe smiled. "It still doesn't excuse you though. I mean I only know a wee bit, Carrie hasn't told me the entire story." She continued.

"I know, and I expect a massive telling off when she does." He said as he cringed. Peggy raised her eyebrows.

"Well, I'm off to bed now. Oh, would it be ok, if I went to the beach with Jo tomorrow?" She asked as she walked towards the door.

"Of course. There is someone coming to see Carrie tomorrow, so she will be busy entertaining." Abe replied.

The following morning Peggy took Carrie's breakfast into her. She placed it on her lap, grabbed her own breakfast and sat on the chair beside Carrie, it seemed to be the only time that they had a chance to chat!

"So London?" Peggy asked as she tucked into her boiled eggs. Carrie smiled, a sad smile.

The move to London was stressful. George misbehaved for the entire journey, even Jo's magic did not work. Abe was meeting them there and Carrie sighed with relief when the carriage pulled up and Abe was standing at the door waiting.

After a few months Carrie was beginning to get restless. She hated doing nothing but amuse the children all day, most of the time Jo did it. She and Molly were talking over dinner one evening.

"You seem really fed up. What's wrong Carrie?" Molly asked. Carrie sighed.

"I love the boys I really do, I just wish that I could do my bit for the war. I hear you, Abe and Michael talking about it, and it makes me feel useless." She huffed.

"So why don't you volunteer at the hospital. They are crying out for volunteers at the Fulham military hospital, wounded soldiers arrive by the boat load every day!" Molly said and smiled.

"Do you think that Jo would mind?" Carrie asked.

"Mind what?" Jo asked as she walked into the room. Molly went on to tell Jo of her suggestion. "I don't mind, but I will say that we should maybe contact an agency and look for a backup, we never know when I'm going to be called away." She said and smiled. Molly looked at Carrie, all three of them smiled in agreement.

So that's what she did. They found a reputable Nanny agency and began the interviews. There were two that both Carrie and Jo had shortlisted. The first and favourite was an older woman called Mrs Kennett. She had lots of experience, but Carrie worried that George would be too much for her, considering her age. The second was a younger woman called Clara. She had experience and had worked abroad.

After hours of deliberating they came to a decision and Carrie contacted the agency. She walked into the nursery. "How did you get on?" Jo asked as she peeled George's mouth from her leg.

"George!" Carrie shouted and frowned.

"I HATE YOU!" The child roared into Carrie's face. She moved him out of the way so that she could speak to Jo.

"Mrs Kennett is a no! she has taken another job, but Clara is available. She starts tomorrow." Carrie said and smiled. "Will you be ok to show her the ropes?" Carrie asked. Jo nodded.

"Sure." She said cheerfully

Carrie didn't have the chance to meet the new nanny, she had to be at the hospital for seven, there were more wounded arriving. After a grueling ten-hour shift, Carrie wearily made her way home. Douglas opened the door, Carrie gave him a smile and headed straight to the nursery.

Jo was seeing to Albert, while Clara was playing with George. Jo looked at Carrie and smiled.

"I won't be a second Clara." Jo said as she handed Albert to her, who immediately started to cry the minute she took him. Carrie frowned as she and Jo walked to her bedroom.

"Well?" Carrie asked as she changed behind the screen.

"George loves her! Albert doesn't." Jo said abruptly. Carrie tutted.

"Honestly, it always one or the other!" She sighed. "And you?" Carrie asked. Jo raised her eyebrows.

"I'll let you know in a day or two!" She said. "I had better go and rescue poor Albert." She added and walked out of the door. Carrie was in such a good mood, Abe had telepathically told her that he would be home for a few days, and she couldn't wait to see him!

That night, sitting in bed, they finally had a chance to catch up. Abe told her about all the atrocities he had been witnessing and then she told him about the horrific wounds inflicted on the soldiers she was caring for. They both agreed that they would be happy when this horrible war was over, Abe told Carrie that he believed it wouldn't be too much longer. They chatted about the new Nanny and the boys, Carrie told Abe how George's behaviour seemed to be getting worse. There was a tap on the bedroom door and Jo poked her head around.

"I am popping out. I must attend a meeting with the Elders. I shouldn't be too long." She smiled and closed the door.

"So, how is Albert's behaviour?" Abe asked as he scratched his chin. Carrie smiled.

"Oh Abe, he is a beautiful boy, he is walking now!" She beamed. Again Abe scratched his chin, in deep thought.

"I just do not understand why George behaves the way he does. It is a complete mystery!" he said. Then at that moment, in Carrie's mind it all began to make sense.

"Wait! Now I may sound as though I am an utter lunatic but think about this. When I was pregnant with George, who poked me in the tummy and nearly caused me to lose the baby?" Carrie said wide eyed. Abe looked at her in complete horror!

"Yes! Katarina! Carrie I think that you may be on to something. I will contact Merlin now, see if he can't do a reversal or something." He said as he jumped out of bed and pulled his trousers on. Abe left the room to contact Merlin, so Carrie thought that she would quickly check on the boys. As she got to the nursery door, she could hear Albert crying, not a wingy cry, but a truly harrowing cry. She opened the door.

George, Albert, and Clara were sitting on the rug. George smacked Albert in the face, sending him flying across the rug, while George laughed.

"GEORGE!" Carrie screamed as she ran into the room and picked a now screaming Albert up from the floor. She shot a look at the new nanny.

"What on earth is going on!" Carrie shouted at the nanny.

"We were playing a game, then he just launched an attack on poor Albert just as you came in." Clara said.

"Why was he crying before that, I heard him as I walked along the landing?" Carrie asked, she was furious!

"George wouldn't let him play with the spinning top, so I thought that we could all sit on the rug and play a game together." Clara replied anxiously. Carrie frowned. Abe walked in, Carrie handed Albert to him.

"Albert can stay with us tonight." Carrie turned to the nanny and said.

Chapter 18

They were up early the following morning. Merlin was coming to observe George. Albert was happily playing on the lounge floor with a wooden toy, Carrie and Abe watched him. He was so good natured, such a sweet little boy. George, who had been looking out of the window, walked over to Albert, and hit him around the head. Not a tap, he sent the poor mite flying.

Carrie ran to Albert, while Abe picked George up and marched him out of the room. Poor Albert was black and blue. Carrie held him tight in her arms and sang to him to calm him down.

A few minutes later Abe came in followed by Merlin, Carrie was relieved.

"Carrie if you take Albert and give him to Jo, we can bring George through, so that Merlin can begin." Abe said. She smiled and did as he asked.

They were in the lounge, Merlin sat on the floor with George. He whispered things to him. George chuckled every time that he did.

Merlin looked over at an incredibly anxious Abe and Carrie and frowned. Carrie took George by the hand and led him to the nursery. When she returned Merlin joined them both in the study, they had more privacy in there. Abe sat behind the desk, Carrie on the windowsill. Merlin perched himself on the edge of the desk.

"It is as you suspected. The child has been cursed." Merlin said.

"And can you reverse it?" Abe asked. Merlin frowned and shook his head.

"I tried my friend, unfortunately the curse is too strong." Merlin replied.

"There must be some way of reversing it!" Carrie fumed and walked towards the two men. Merlin sighed and shook his head.

"My dear, if what I did failed, I fear that nothing will work." Merlin said sadly.

"No! There is a way, and I will find it. I will not let that bitch ruin my son!" Carrie screamed and stormed out of the room!

As she stormed along the hallway she walked straight into the path of Michael, knocking him sideways. Michael hit the wall knocking his glasses off and breaking them.

"MY GOODNESS!" Michael shouted as he picked up the broken glasses. Carrie stopped in her tracks. She bent down and picked up the broken glass.

"I'm so sorry Michael. I didn't mean to bang into you!" Carrie said as she passed him the shards.

"What on earth has happened?" He asked, he could clearly see how anxious Carrie was. She looked around to see if anyone was about.

The coast was clear.

"It appears that Katarina cursed George when I was pregnant. Merlin has tried to reverse the spell, but it is too strong!" Carrie said frustratedly. Michael shook his head.

"There must be a way." He muttered whilst deep in thought. "Ah, you remember how to meditate?" He asked. Carrie frowned and nodded. "Good. Sit beneath the tree, try to make contact with one of the Goddesses, maybe they will have the answer." Michael said and smiled, feeling pleased with himself. Carrie frowned.

"I thought that with your experience Michael, you would maybe have an answer!" She fumed.

"Forgive me, I could have sworn that I have just advised you!" Michael said agitatedly. Carrie shook her head and stomped off towards the staircase. She walked into her bedroom, reminding herself not to slam the door, she had taken so many off of their hinges!

She was stood looking out of her bedroom window, watching as Abe and Merlin played ball with her two boys. For once they were both squealing with delight! The door knocked, and Carrie grinned when Molly poked her head around the door.

"Come in" Carrie said gesturing her to the window. Molly joined her and watched. She looked at Carrie and smiled.

"Well that's a first!" She said. "Carrie I want you to come somewhere with me, if you can spare a few minutes." Molly added. Carrie nodded.

"Where?" She asked.

"You'll see." Molly said as she took her hand and led her down the stairs, out of the kitchen door and into the garden. They walked passed Abe, Merlin, and the boys. Carrie waved at them all.

"Molly why all the mystery?" Carrie asked, as she wondered where the hell they were going. Molly laughed and continued to lead. They stopped when they came to a group of outbuildings. Molly unlocked one of the doors and gestured for Carrie to go in. It was like a giant greenhouse inside. There were plants growing everywhere!.

"Welcome to my workshop!" Molly grinned. Carrie looked around in fascination. Molly walked over to a work surface and pulled something from beneath. It was a wooden chest. "Give us a hand will you?" She asked Carrie as she struggled to lift it. Carrie took the other end and they lifted it onto the work top. Molly grinned. "This belongs to you." She said.

"How? How does it belong to me?" Carrie asked.

"Do you remember when Michael showed you the book?" Molly asked. Carrie thought for a moment and then nodded. "This is it. This grimoire and this chest belongs to you. It was given to the Elders by Abagail, to be given to you when the time was right. That time is now!" Molly added. Carrie was bewildered. Molly placed the grimoire on the worktop, then looked at Carrie. "Ask it to show you the answer to your problem." Molly smiled. Carrie raised her eyebrow, not knowing what Molly was getting at. "George Carrie!" Molly said. The penny dropped and Carrie nodded her head.

"Please show me how to undo the spell put on my son George." Carrie asked. The pages of the book began to flick back and forth , then stopped. Both Carrie and Molly looked. It was a reversal spell. Molly read down the page, writing things on a piece of paper. She walked over to the many shelves and began to take things out of baskets. She soon returned to Carrie and the Grimoire.

"Right, we have all the necessary ingredients here. Now all we have to do is crush them!" She said as she took down a mortar and pestle and began grinding. She passed it to Carrie. "Put all of your hopes into it as you crush!" Molly advised. Carrie did just that. Molly placed it into a paper bag and handed it to Carrie. Carrie looked at the window, she watched a shadow pass across. She walked over and looked out.

"Molly look at this!" Carrie said. Molly walked over and looked out. She looked at Carrie and frowned.

"What on earth is she doing?" Molly asked.

"I don't know, but I'm about to find out!" Carrie said as she rushed to the door, Molly grabbed the spell and followed. They both looked on as Clara was tiptoeing, trying to look through the windows. Carrie looked at Molly, then at Clara.

"What are you doing?" Carrie called out, making Clara jump.

"I er…. I was looking for you." Clara said awkwardly.

"Well you have found me, what can I do for you?" Carrie said sternly.

"I was wondering if I could have this afternoon off. My sister is unwell, and I said that I would go and look after her." She replied.

"Yes, when will you return? Carrie asked.

"Tomorrow, first thing" Clara replied. Carrie nodded, Clara paused for her moment, then turned and walked back towards the house. Molly and Carrie walked over to Abe and Merlin. Albert ran to Carrie and held his arms up to her. She scooped him up and kissed him on the cheek. She could feel eyes on her, she turned and watched as George scowled at her. She handed Albert to Molly and walked over to the disgruntled little boy. She knelt down in front of him.

"Would you like a hug George?" Carrie asked, smiled, and held her arms open. He pulled his arms back and hit her as hard as he could on the nose, blood spurting out as he laughed with delight. Abe ran to Carrie as Merlin took George by the hand and led him to the house. Molly handed Albert to Abe and placed her hand over Carrie's bleeding nose. The bleeding stopped. Abe looked at Carrie.

"Please tell me that you have an answer to this. I cannot leave you here with him behaving like that!" Abe said. Molly nodded.

"Carrie was just about to perform it, when he hit her." Molly said anxiously

"Do you think that he knew?" Abe asked. Carrie shook her head.

"No Abe, he just hates me!" Carrie mumbled sadly. Abe put his arm around Carrie.

"Nonsense! He loves you, he is just under that awful woman's spell!" He said and smiled. Carrie smiled, an unconvincing smile, as they walked back to the house.

Merlin met them in the hallway. "I will place a holding spell on him, so that you can carry out the reversal". Carrie smiled and nodded, she wasn't sure if it would work, this was making her nervous! They were in the nursery, Molly had taken Albert for a walk around the park. George was sitting on the rug, Merlin placed the holding spell on him. He was still and expressionless. Carrie knelt down to face him. She placed her hand inside the bag and took a handful of the dust. She had memorised the chant as she ground the preparation earlier. She was about to blow the preparation at George, when the nursery window made an almighty cracking sound and the glass from the window shattered all over the room, hitting both Carrie and Abe!

Carrie removed the glass from Abe's neck and face, then he did the same to her. Merlin removed the holding spell from George and Jo took him into the lounge. Housekeepers then entered the nursery and began to clean up the glass, as Abe waited for the glaziers to come and repair the window.

Carrie stood at the lounge door watching George. Jo sat on the rug opposite him. "How did the window break George?" Jo asked sweetly. He giggled.

"The lady did it!" He said as his giggle turned into a laugh.

"This lady?" Jo asked as she showed him a photograph of Katarina.

"Yes!" He replied. Jo nodded and then looked over at Carrie, who shook her head in complete despair.

Later that afternoon, once the window had been repaired, Jo took both the children to the nursery. Carrie, Abe, Merlin, Molly, and Michael were in the lounge discussing what they should do.

"Why don't we try again now!" Merlin suggested. Screaming, loud screaming and harrowing cries came from up the stairs as they all ran as fast as their legs would carry them. Carrie was first in the nursery, she was taken aback when she stepped inside. There was blood everywhere. Jo was bleeding, so too was little Albert. Molly ran to Jo as Carrie picked Albert up to see where he was bleeding. As she examined him, she saw that there was a deep gash in his arm. Once Molly had healed Jo she joined Carrie. She placed her hands over the deep gash on Albert's arm and it closed. Carrie exhaled deeply.

"Where is George?" Abe asked. Jo shook her head and burst into tears. She pointed to the window. Abe and Merlin ran over and looked out. Katarina was walking across the garden , holding George's hand. Abe and Michael both ran.

"Would you like me to take Albert?" Molly asked Carrie. She sighed and reluctantly passed her the little boy. She slowly got up and walked out of the room.

Do not let her take him! She heard. She ran as fast as was physically possible and caught up with Abe and Merlin.

"Let him go NOW!" Abe roared. She threw her head back and laughed. Carrie lost all control. She ran at the red-haired bitch and hit her with all her might. Katarina flew through the air and landed against a tree. Abe grabbed George. Katarina sent electricity towards Carrie, she sent it back. She walked through the next wave that she sent and punched her, again, and again until she eventually vanished.

Carrie marched across the lawn, fuelled by rage. She grabbed George's hand and sat him on the grass, as he struggled. She began to chant as she took a handful of the spell and blew it into the child's face. He screamed and held his eyes as Carrie continued to chant.

Once she stopped she burst into tears, she wept like never before. She scooped the traumatised boy up into her arms and held him tightly as they both sobbed.

"How will we know if it was successful?" Abe asked.

"Only time will tell." Michael replied.

After dinner they were sitting in the lounge with their coffees. Jo put her head around the door and gestured to Carrie. Carrie left the room and walked with Jo up the hallway. "Clara is back." Jo whispered. Carrie frowned.

"I thought that she said she would be back tomorrow." Carrie replied. Jo nodded.

"There's something else" Jo whispered again. Carrie nodded. "I found this in her case." She added as she passed a photograph to Carrie. Carrie looked at the photograph, it was the photo that she had shown George earlier that day after the window had smashed. Carrie was about to storm up the stairs when Jo stopped her. "She is her sister. She told her that you were going to reverse the spell. That's why the window smashed and then she appeared here." Jo whispered. Carrie nodded impatiently.

"I know that!" That's why I am going up there now to throw her out!" Carrie fumed.

"Wait Carrie!" Jo said as she grabbed her arm. Carrie scowled at Jo. "It may be in our best interest to keep her close." Jo said. Carrie shook her head. "Go and ask Abe and the others what they think." Jo continued. Carrie marched back to the lounge and told them what Jo had said.

"Maybe she has a point." Michael said. Carrie scowled and looked at Abe, she was going to lose it if he agreed. Abe shook his head.

"No, she has to go. I do not want her anywhere near Carrie or my children." Abe said quietly.

"Besides Michael, I thought that you would be having kittens. She could easily take the Grimoire!" Molly said. Michael's smile turned to a frown.

"Yes you are right Molly, well thought!" He said.

"So, can I go and throw her out now?" Carrie asked. Abe chuckled.

"Do as you wish!" He replied. Carrie ran up to the nursery. She opened the door. George and Albert were playing with their toys happily. Carrie bent down and kissed them both. Then she looked around for Clara. "George, where is Jo?" Carrie whispered.

"She is getting our milk" He replied and smiled. Carrie smiled.

"And where is Clara?" She whispered. George shrugged his shoulders.

"Don't know Mummy!" He replied sweetly. Again Carrie smiled as her heart melt. It was the first time he had ever called her that!

"Shall we go and find Jo and your milk?" She asked both the boys, they both nodded. She picked Albert up and held George's hand as she walked back down the stairs. They walked into the kitchen, it was empty. She went into the lounge and told the others that she couldn't find either of them. Molly looked at Carrie horrified.

"You don't think that she has taken Jo do you?" She asked anxiously. They all looked at one another.

"Michael and I will search the house and the grounds." Abe said and gestured to Michael to get up. Just as they walked out of the door.... The Grimoire! Carrie heard. She ran after them both, screaming the word that she had just heard, then ran out of the house towards the workshop.

There was a knock on the door, Abe popped his head around the door. "Peggy, Jo is here." He said and smiled. Peggy looked at the clock.

"Crikey, is that the time!" She said as she grabbed hers and Carrie's tray and headed towards the kitchen. Abe followed her.

"I'll clear the dishes, if you go and help Carrie to get dressed." He said smiling as he took the trays from Peggy. She smiled and nodded as she walked back towards Carrie's room.

She ran down the stairs ten minutes later, ready for the beach. She walked into the garden where Carrie was sitting in the sun and kissed her on the cheek.

"Are you sure that you'll be alright?" Peggy asked. Carrie chuckled and nodded.

"I am in safe hands Peggy, now stop worrying and go and enjoy yourself!" Carrie replied.

Chapter 19

She could feel his presence before she saw him. She smiled widely when she saw him walk up the garden path, sporting farming attire, the flat cap was a particular winner! He walked over to her with open arms. "Carrie, I am so happy that you agreed to see me! It has been an age hasn't it?" Merlin said, grinned and kissed Carrie on the cheek.

"Merlin, I love your outfit, really suits you!" Carrie said and burst out laughing. Merlin looked down at what he was wearing.

"I thought that I looked rather dashing!" he said chuckling. He sat opposite Carrie and looked at her intensely. "You look radiant!" He added. Carrie frowned.

"Now we both know that is a lie! I am very close to not wearing this skin any longer, it's getting a bit too big!" Carrie said and pulled her loose skin down. Merlin howled with laughter.

"Oh Carrie, how I have missed your wit!" he laughed. Abe walked out to join them with a tray of drinks. He looked at Merlin and winked. Abe handed out the drinks and sat beside Carrie. She looked at them both and smiled.

"Just like old times isn't it?" She sighed as she thought back.

"Indeed! And once again, I have things to say that need to be said!" Merlin said as the smile left his face. Carrie tutted.

"Do you know, for a fleeting moment, I actually thought that you were just coming to see me, no ulterior motive, just to see me!" She huffed.

"I have! But I also have things that must be disclosed to you that can then be passed onto young Peggy." Merlin replied.

"So why don't you tell Peggy yourself!" Carrie sighed.

"You know why! She must find young Robert." Merlin said. Carrie frowned.

"I have already told her." Carrie replied. Merlin smiled.

"The child will need guidance Carrie. Her connection to the realm will be so great, that she will not have a moments peace!" He added.

"Of that I am well aware Merlin, I just don't understand why I wasn't allowed to take the Dark realm on, so that she wouldn't have to!" Carrie frowned.

"As great as your power is Carrie, it is not your fight to be had, I understand that you wished to save your great granddaughter from the pain and suffering, but that is not what is weaved within the threads of fate!" Merlin exclaimed.

Carrie nodded, there were forces at work, that she simply could not fight, nor could she voice an opinion. Carrie smiled to herself when she thought back to the story that Abe had told her about Molly and Merlin.

"Would you grant a dying woman one final request?" Carrie asked.

Merlin looked at her suspiciously, then reluctantly nodded.

"If it is within my power, then yes." He replied quietly.

" I wish to discuss the ball, you know when you and Molly were caught red-handed." Carrie said, grinned and looked at Abe. Merlin shook his head.

"No! No! Absolutely not!" Merlin snorted.

"Ah, but Merlin, that is within your power!" Abe said and winked at Carrie. Merlin scowled at Abe then tutted and shook his head.

"Very well! What would you like to know?" He sulked. Carrie grinned a wide grin.

"So come on, what exactly were you and Molly doing when Esmelda caught you?" Carrie asked.

He paused for a moment. "And no lies, Abe will know" Carrie added.

"We were creating a temporary love spell, something like that!" He mumbled. Carrie burst out laughing.

"Who for?" She asked through the laughter.

"Michael of course, Molly was so sad, I suggested that I could make a potion, where for one night, Michael would find her simply irresistible. Only for one night though!" Merlin said with a look of shame on his face.

"Did you do it?" Carrie asked. Merlin hung his head in shame and nodded.

"No way! So Molly and Michael have…"

"Yes, yes, but it had repercussions." Merlin replied angrily. Carrie frowned.

"What do you mean?" Carrie asked. Merlin buried his face in his hands and shook his head.

"I promised that I would breathe a word to no-one." He mumbled. Carrie raised her eyebrows. "Joanna!" Merlin added.

"Eh! Oh you mean that she is Molly and Michaels daughter!" Carrie said and placed her hand over her mouth in complete shock. Merlin nodded.

"Please, please not a word to anyone, Michael does not know. His memory does not recognise the night in question." Merlin sighed. Carrie looked at Abe and shook her head.

"Does Jo know?" She asked. Merlin shook his head.

"No and never will she." He said and raised his eyebrows at Carrie.

Jo and Peggy had found the perfect spot on the beach, they had laid down the blanket and were both basking in the warm sunshine. After about an hour Jo was becoming restless. She sat up and nudged Peggy.

"Do you fancy a dip?" She asked. Peggy looked at the waves, then at Jo and shook her head.

"No, the water is cold and besides I canee swim!" She said as she held her hand over her eyes to shield them from the sun. Jo grabbed Peggy's arm and began to pull her.

"Come on Peg, I'll teach you." She wined as she pulled harder.

"Five minutes and no longer !" Peggy fumed as Jo dragged her into the freezing cold sea. Jo went straight under, Peggy stood in the water shivering. Jo grabbed her again pulling her down, Peggy screamed and then they splashed one another. Peggy began to realise that it really was fun and the longer that she was in the water, the less cold she was.

After frolicking for twenty minutes or so, Peggy had enough and walked back to the blanket, Jo stayed in the sea for a swim. Peggy dried herself off and relished the warm rays of the sun as she lay back on the blanket.

Sand was kicked into her face. She sat up, wiped the gritty sand from her eyes and looked. Jean was stood over her. She knelt down and looked at Peggy.

"I believe that your tarty friend might need some assistance." She said, laughed and walked away. Quickly Peggy looked in the direction of Jo. She saw Mary swimming towards her.

"JO!" Peggy screamed out as she jumped up and ran towards the ebbing tide. Mary had now grabbed Jo from behind and was pulling her beneath the water. Peggy reached the sea and wadded in, but Mary had dragged Jo further out, out of Peggy's depth. She screamed as loud as she could, trying her hardest to get the attention of the other bathers, no-one appeared to hear her. Peggy became hysterical when Mary vanished, and Jo went below the waves. Then she was grabbed from behind and was too being dragged under. She was gargling, choking, and fighting for breath when something pulled her out and dragged her to the shore. She was lying on the sand choking, catching her breath, when she saw her rescuer. A beautiful woman placed her finger on her lips.

"My name is Nimue, I am sorry that I couldn't save your friend, I was called too late." She whispered and then vanished into the sea. Peggy dragged herself up, sobbing as she walked to the blanket. She looked around, the beach was deserted, she sat down and sobbed her heart out.

Two men approached her, one tapped her on the shoulder. She

wiped the tears from her eyes and looked up. One the men knelt, making Peggy edge away.

"We are Guardians, we will not hurt you, we have come to take you home." The man said and smiled a kind smile. Peggy looked at them both in bewilderment.

"How did you know where to find me?" Peggy asked through the sobs.

"You rubbed the necklace. We will send people out to retrieve Joanna's body, now come with us." He replied as he helped Peggy to her feet.

Carrie was still shell shocked over Merlin's revelations, when Molly and Michael walked through the back gate. Carrie was surprised how well Molly hid things and was so natural around Merlin, even though they both harboured such a guilty secret. Abe went to the kitchen to prepare lunch, Merlin followed him.

"And I thought that he was coming to see you?" Molly huffed, Carrie chuckled and shook her head.

"You know Merlin, there's always an ulterior motive!" Carrie said and smiled at Molly. Molly nodded in agreement. They heard a car pull up and Molly peered over the wall. She ran as soon as she saw the guardians with Peggy. "What's wrong Molly?" Carrie called out as Molly ran towards them. They walked Peggy out to Carrie, then went back inside to break the news to Molly. Peggy sat beside Carrie and wept. Carrie held her and waited patiently until she had enough composure to tell her what had happened.

They sat in the garden, Carrie was lost for words. Abe brought both her and Peggy a cup of sweet tea each and placed it on the table.

Carrie smiled a small smile as Abe placed his hand on Peggy's shoulder.

"I am so sorry that you have had to go through this Peggy, and I am sorry about Jo, she was a wonderful person, she played a huge part in our lives didn't she Carrie." Abe said as he wiped the tears that were forming in his eyes.

"I couldnee save her. I tried I really did!" Peggy sobbed. Molly walked out to them. Carrie was now sobbing. Molly knelt before Peggy and took her hands in her own.

"Now you listen to me, none of this is your fault, and I will not have you blaming yourself, Jo knew the risks Peggy." Molly said and smiled a small smile, she looked at Carrie who was wiping her tears away. "Now, go and freshen yourself up. William will be here soon, Matthew has just gone to collect him." She added. Peggy walked with her head hung low, into the cottage.

Molly sat beside Carrie, Carrie grabbed her hand, from one mother to another, she felt her pain, so too did Abe. "I am so sorry Molly!" Carrie said as she could not stop herself from crying again.

"One day I will be with her again, and at least now I am safe in the knowledge that she will be safe until that point." Molly said as tears rolled down her cheeks. "She joined the Guardianship against my wishes. I told her that it was perilous, but she was headstrong." She added. Carrie smiled. Just like her mother! Carrie thought quietly to herself.

A little later Carrie was exhausted from all the emotion and desperately needed to lie down. Abe looked at her and could see that she was struggling. "Would you like me to take you to your room for a lie down?" He whispered. Carrie nodded gratefully. He wheeled her back into the cottage and straight into the path of Peggy.

"Can I take her, please?" Peggy asked. Abe nodded and left her with Carrie. Peggy helped her onto the bed and smiled. "When you have rested, will you tell me what happened to Jo when she went missing?" Peggy asked. Carrie smiled

"I'll tell you now, I just wanted to be a little more comfortable that's all." She smiled.

Carrie ran as fast as she could down to the workshop. She was relieved to find the lock still intact. This however was a problem as she didn't have a key, Molly had it and she was watching the children. Carrie grabbed the lock and pulled as hard as she could. It wouldn't shift. In a fit of frustration she thumped the glass door. It shattered, giving Carrie the access she needed. She ran over to where the chest was, pulled it out and opened it. She was overjoyed when she saw the Grimoire in its rightful place. She pushed it inside her jumper., The chest, take the chest! She heard. She placed the Grimoire in the chest and began to drag it out of the workshop. She was pulling it across the grass, struggling, it was so heavy. She felt a sharp pain in her back and slowly turned. Katarina was standing behind her, electricity flowing from her fingers. "Give it to me NOW!" She roared. Carrie laughed, as she secretly felt for her locket. It wasn't there.

"Never in a million years!" She shouted. She held the handles either side and picked the heavy chest up, then continued to walk away from Katarina. Sharp pain again, it took Carrie all of her strength not to drop the chest, yet she still continued. She anticipated the next shot and turned quickly to face the red-haired bitch. Katarina shot the electricity, hitting the chest, then rebounding and exploding as it reached her. She screeched and vanished. Quickly Carrie carried the chest back to the house. She dragged it through the hallway and put her head around the lounge door to check on Molly and the boys. They were all fine. She picked it up once again and carried it to her bedroom. She hid it under her bed and then walked back down the hallway towards the staircase. As she passed one of the guest rooms she heard voices. The man's voice was definitely Abe's. She opened the door and nearly fell backwards in shock when she saw them. Clara had Abe pinned up against the wall, she was kissing around his neck, he was smiling then they kissed. Carrie lost all control she ran over, grabbing Clara by the scruff of the neck and threw her across the room. Then she was faced with Abe. She pulled her fist back and lunged to hit him, but he repelled it with his own magic. She screamed, an unearthly scream and ran down the stairs to Molly and the boys. After telling Molly what had happened, Molly went to find Michael.

She walked to his office and strolled in, it was empty. She ran all through the downstairs, the place was deserted. She ran up the stairs, running into every room. She ran into the room where Carrie had caught Abe and Clara. She was sitting on the bed chanting. He was in the corner of the room with his hands over his ears. Molly ran to Carrie and asked her to give her the remainder of the reversal spell, which Carrie did.

Molly went back to the room and walked over to Abe as Clara was still chanting. Molly blew the spell into his face, chanting her own chant louder. He cried out and looked at Molly as he wiped his stinging eyes. Molly turned and walked to Clara. She began to sing a chant, getting louder and louder, until Clara was holding her ears and screaming. Molly let out a piercing scream and Clara disappeared. She then turned to Abe. She looked at him in disgust and shook her head.

"Molly, she enchanted me!" He said. Again Molly shook her head.

"I am not a fool Abraham. I know that when Carrie walked into this room, you were most certainly not enchanted. The reason that vile bitch attempted to enchant you was because you would not leave with her. You disgust me! Now where is MICHAEL?" Molly shouted

"Molly please, you won't tell Carrie will you?" He pleaded.

"Where is Michael?" She asked again.

"He's in the cellar. They locked Jo in there." He said. Molly walked to the door. "Molly please?" He called out. She slammed the door as she walked out!

Molly ran down to the cellar and eventually found Michael, who was untying Jo's hands. She sighed with relief when she saw them both.

"Are you hurt?" She asked as she took Jo's face in her hands. Jo shook her head.

"Clara was about to attack me after she had tied me up, so I began to chant, and she buggered off!" Jo replied. Molly smiled, as the three of them headed in the direction of Carrie. She wasn't in the lounge when they got there. Jo headed up to the nursery, while Molly told Michael what had happened.

Michael sat behind his desk and shook his head. "I knew that it would happen, given Abe's shady past. I just knew that he would hurt her. I blame myself entirely." Michael said sadly.

"For what?" Carrie asked as she stood in the doorway.

"Oh er… Carrie, I hadn't noticed you there!" He said and chuckled as he went the brightest shade of red.

"Well?" She asked again. Michael buried his head in his hands.

"For what Abraham did. He blames himself, Michael should have stayed with him, instead of separating from him." Molly replied for him. Carrie shook her head.

"You can't blame yourself for the fact that he is a cheating bastard!" Carrie said as she slumped into the chair beside Molly. Again Michael shook his head.

Later that evening there was a knock on the bedroom door. Carrie climbed out of bed and walked to answer it. As she suspected Abe was standing with a huge bunch of flowers.

"Please, can we make up. She enchanted me Carrie, you know that because Molly used the reversal!" Abe said all puppy eyed. Deep down she knew that he was lying, but there was something about him that she couldn't stay angry with. She opened the door wide and walked back inside the room. He handed her the flowers. "I promise that I will never allow myself to become enchanted again! " He said and kissed her.

Chapter 20

Carrie woke the following morning, she turned to find the bed empty. She climbed out of bed and found a note on her dressing table. *Been called back to the base. Sorry about yesterday, see you soon, Abe xxx* . She placed the note back on the table, shook her head in disbelief and then walked towards the nursery. Both boys were still fast asleep. She closed the door and crept down the stairs and into the kitchen. The housekeeper Janet was preparing the breakfast, Carrie smiled at her. "Will the children be taking breakfast in the nursery?" She asked. Carrie shook her head.

"No they can eat with me in the dining room." Carrie replied. She then walked back up to the nursery to wake them.

Carrie, George, and Albert were eating breakfast in the dining room, when Michael and Molly walked in, they sat at the table after serving themselves some food.

"Good morning! Where is Abe?" Michael chirped. Carrie frowned.

"Where do you think?" She scowled. Michael tutted.

"Carrie you were aware that he was the leader of Arbatel, when you first got together, he made it clear that, he would have to share his time between you and the Realm, did he not?" Michael said. Carrie shook her head.

"I didn't say that he had gone to Arbatel Michael." Carrie said and looked at Molly. Michael frowned. "He has been called back to base." Carrie continued. Michael had a look of surprise on his face.

"No you must be mistaken, his entire battalion are in France." Michael replied as Molly nudged him with her elbow. He yelped and frowned at Molly.

"Well he must have gone to France then." Carrie said as she wiped the egg from Albert's mouth.

"No, I hardly think so, from what he said to me yesterday, the battalion were just winding things up. The war is more or less over now." Michael smiled. Carrie's mind went into overload. If he wasn't at the base, where the hell was he? She was thinking to herself. "He could be at Arbatel." Michael said, as he thought out loud.

"No Michael, he wrote a note that said that he had been called back to base." Carrie replied adamantly. Michael shook his head in bewilderment and looked at Molly, who was scowling at him.

"He's definitely not at Arbatel, I have just come from there." Jo said as she pulled a chair out and sat down with her breakfast.

"Are you ok to watch the children?" Carrie asked as she got up from her chair. Jo nodded.

"I'll give her a hand, I have nothing planned for today." Molly said. Carrie smiled, tapped Molly on the shoulder and ran up the stairs.

Once she was dressed she walked out of the house and into the gardens. She found a quiet spot and ground herself. She needed to shape shift, but she had no idea how to. She took the small bronze boar that Ceridwen had given her and rubbed it, thinking about the Goddess as she did. She felt the ground grumble beneath her, as a mist appeared, and the Goddess stepped out from the mist.

"How can I be of assistance?" She asked. Carrie bowed.

"I am so sorry to call upon you, but I need to shape shift, but I have no idea how to." Carrie said humbly. Ceridwen smiled and nodded. She went on to explain to Carrie what she must do.

"Do I have the power to do it?" Carrie asked doubting her own ability. The Goddess smiled.

"You underestimate yourself. You power is incredibly strong, listen to yourself, believe in yourself and the power of the elements, do not allow words to impress upon what is not true." Ceridwen said and touched Carrie's face. Her energy was so warm, so comforting. "If you follow my instructions and truly believe in yourself you cannot fail." The Goddess added as she vanished back into the mist.

Carrie took a deep breath and closed her eyes. She could feel her body changing and very soon she had taken flight. She knew that she had to fly west, she looked at the sun for guidance. She flew over Stonehenge, and soon landed just outside of the base. She shifted back to herself and ran across the field. There were guards on the gate, and she instinctively knew that they would not grant her access. Again she shifted and flew into the base. She hopped around a corner and around the side of the hanger. The place was deserted. She shifted back and walked to where the officers mess was.

She peered into windows as she crouched past the buildings. Then she heard him. A door opened and Abe walked out arm in arm with a woman in uniform. They were laughing, then he picked her up, spun her around and kissed her.

She tried so hard not to lose control, but her love for him was so great, that she couldn't. She ran towards them, roaring as she did.

They both looked at her completely horrified. Abe was shouting at her, but she heard nothing. She ran at the woman, who was now screaming, before she reached her she quickly turned and punched Abe as hard as she could, sending him flying through the air, landing in a heap beside the hanger. The woman began to run, Carrie caught her up and jumped onto her back, wrestling her to the ground. She turned her over to face her.

"How long?" Carrie roared. The woman was sobbing, pleading Carrie not to hurt her. "I SAID HOW LONG?" Carrie roared again.

"A… A Few months." The woman replied her voice quivering with fear.

"Were you aware that he was married with children?" Carrie asked. The woman frantically shook her head. "Well he is, and I am the poor suffering wife that he cheats on. You are fucking welcome to him!" Carrie said as she climbed off of the woman. She leant to the side and vomited. Once composed she walked over to the heap that was Abe. The desire to kick him was so great, but this time, she took control. She bent down and looked at him.

"You bastard! I am fucking done with you, and your fucking lifestyle. I am going to take my boys as far away from you as possible. I never want to lay eyes on you again. DO YOU FUCKING HEAR ME!" She bellowed. Then she ran, as she ran she wept, her heart was breaking and the faster she ran, the more broken it became. She fell into a ditch, rolled into a ball, and sobbed and sobbed, until there were no tears left.

Once she had composed herself, with her swollen eyes and aching heart she shifted and flew back to London. She walked into the house, straight past Michael, up the stairs to the nursery. Both boys were sitting playing with toys. She found a sack and began to put as many of their clothes in as possible. Jo walked in.

"Carrie what are you doing?" Jo asked.

"I'm taking my boys and getting as far away from here as possible." Carrie said angrily as the vision of Abe and that woman ran through her thoughts.

"What? Why?" Jo asked.

"Because Jo, my so-called husband is a lying, cheating bastard and I never want to lay eyes on him again!" Carrie said as she fought back tears.

"You can't run away Carrie." Molly said from the doorway.

"Give me one good reason why I should stay Molly." Carrie struggled to say. Molly walked over to her and pulled her in close for a hug.

"Because my dear, you are pregnant, with a baby girl." Molly replied. Carrie pulled away.

"I know that, but I am still going. I cannot be anywhere near him!" Carrie said.

"I have a friend in Yorkshire. She is a widow, her house is huge, and she is incredibly lonely. I am sure she would love for you and the boys to go and stay with her for a while." Jo said.

"Is she a guardian?" Carrie asked suspiciously. Jo chuckled.

"No, when my mother died, Molly was busy in Arbatel I was sent to her and her husband. I stayed with them for four years, until Auntie Molly was able to have me full time." Jo replied. Carrie smiled and nodded.

Later that day a carriage pulled up outside the house, and with the help of Molly and Jo, Carrie and the boys climbed in with all their things and rode away.

It was dark when they finally arrived, Carrie couldn't see anything, both the boys had fallen asleep. She climbed out of the carriage, and the driver handed her an oil lamp. She found the path that led to the large front door. She pulled on the bell. A few minutes later an elderly woman opened the door. "You must be Carrie!" She said happily. Carrie smiled and nodded. "Well let's get your youngsters into the house and get you all comfortable." She added. The driver unloaded the luggage and placed it all in the huge hallway. Carrie woke the boys. She helped George climb down and grabbed Albert, together they walked into their new home.

"My name is Doris." The elderly lady said to the boys. George smiled, Albert hid his shy face in Carrie's shoulder.

"This is George, and this is Albert." Carrie said as she pointed at them.

"Welcome to your new home George and Albert!" Doris said and grinned.

Peggy looked at Carrie with such compassion as she tapped her hand. "I'm sorry." She whispered.

"For?" Carrie asked.

"All the awful things that have happened to you." Peggy replied.

"Peggy, Robert will have a daughter, her gift will be so much greater than mine, but with that comes hardship. She will need you to guide her and comfort her." Carrie said. Peggy nodded.

"Aye, I promise I will. Now I had better go and prepare the dinner!" Peggy said, kissed Carrie on the head and left the room.

She walked out to the kitchen and into the pantry, grabbing all the things she needed to make the pies. William walked through and grabbed her, wrapping his arms around her.

"How long have you been here?" Peggy asked.

"About an hour, I was talking to Molly and that man with the beard." He replied. Peggy smiled and nodded.

"Oh, you mean Merlin." Peggy said with a chuckle, waiting for his reaction.

"Are you joking, not the …. Not the wizard?" William said.

"I prefer wise man, sage, or Druid maybe. Have never understood the term wizard!" Merlin said as he mysteriously appeared from nowhere. Peggy laughed as William stood with his mouth gaped open, his eyes wide.

"Young Peggy, I have not yet had the chance to speak with you my dear, may I say how very honoured I am to meet you!" Merlin said in an over charming manner.

"And I you" Peggy replied. Merlin nodded.

"Yes I understand that you are now aware of the incredibly important role which you will play in this, what shall we call it, er day of reckoning!" he said and smiled. Peggy nodded, she didn't really have a clue about what he was saying!

"Wonderful! One more thing… it's rather delicate." He added. Peggy raised her eyebrows, she had been warned by Carrie about Merlin. "Well, I understand that Carrie is educating you on her life as such." Merlin said apprehensively. Peggy nodded. "It's about Abraham." Merlin said and squirmed as Peggy scowled. "Try not to be too hard on him, he is only human after all!" Merlin said and chuckled.

"Really, I would say more PIG than human!" Peggy sneered.

"Ah, let us not be mean to pigs. Extraordinary creatures that they are!" Merlin said and the three of them burst out laughing. Merlin left the kitchen which then left Peggy and William.

"I am so sorry about Jo, Peg, I know how much you liked her." William said sincerely. Peggy nodded. She didn't want to start crying again, so she smiled and continued making the pastry.

Later that evening, after the dinner dishes were done and put away, Peggy helped Carrie back to her room. She looked so frail and tired. Peggy tucked the sheets in and kissed Carrie on the head.

"You're not going are you?" Carrie asked anxiously.

"You look exhausted, I thought that now Abe has gone to Arbatel, you would want to catch up on some sleep." Peggy replied. Carrie chuckled.

"Oh my Peggy, I shall soon sleep for a long time, I need to make the most of every second that I have left!" She said and winked at Peggy. "Now come, there is still so much I must tell you." She said and patted the chair beside the bed. Peggy sighed, nodded, and sat listening intently.

So, the months disappeared quickly for Carrie and her two sons, in their new surroundings. The house was huge, old, and tired but comfortable none the less and both the young boys seemed to thrive in their new life. Carrie helped with some of the repairs that desperately needed doing and she and Doris cooked together, played with the boys, went for long walks on the Dales, well until Carrie's bump was so huge that she physically could no longer do it!

Carrie woke in the night to the familiar sensation of early labour pains. For a few hours, she walked around, dealing with the pain, until the pains were closer together, and becoming unbearable. She called Doris, who called the local Doctor. By the time the Doctor and midwife arrived, Carrie had given birth, with the help of Doris, luckily both the boys had slept through it! Carrie was sat in bed with a beautiful baby girl. She looked just like Abe, Carrie hadn't seen him for six months. She had secretly hoped that he would come looking for them, but he never did, which made Carrie believe that he never truly cared for any of them.

Doris told Carrie to sleep, which she did, until Doris woke her. "You have visitors my dear, are you up to seeing them." She whispered so as not to wake the baby. Carrie looked at Doris, hoping that Abe was there.

"Who?" Carrie asked as she pulled herself up in the bed.

"Molly and Jo." Doris replied. Carrie smiled.

"Yes Doris, show them up please." Carrie replied. Doris left the room, and the baby started to cry. Carrie lifted her from her crib and carried her over to the bed. Molly and Jo walked in, Molly looked so happy to see her. Molly kissed Carrie and then looked at the tiny bundle wrapped up in Carrie's arms.

"Oh my, she is beautiful!" Molly exclaimed as tears formed in her eyes. "What have you called her?" She asked. Carrie smiled.

"Polly, she is my tiny Polly!" Carrie replied.

Molly was staying for a while, Jo was heading back to Arbatel on business. After a few days Carrie was back on her feet, she, Molly, and Doris had such wonderful times with the children, the incredibly beautiful landscape, and each other.

After a week since Molly's arrival, one evening after the children were settled, Molly and Carrie were sitting in the lounge, looking out onto the garden. "Carrie there is something I have to ask you." Molly said nervously. Carrie raised her eyebrows. "It's Abe, he asked me to ask you, if he could come and see you all?" Molly squirmed. Carrie stared out to the garden, saying nothing, after a few minutes she sighed.

"Well, I can't really stop him can I? They are his children after all." Carrie mumbled. Molly smiled.

"I'll let him know." Molly replied.

Carrie got out of bed the following morning, fed Polly, and then took her down the stairs. She walked out to the kitchen and placed the heavy cast iron kettle on the stove. She laid the breakfast table and then went up the stairs to wake the boys. She held their hands and led them down the stairs. She had told them that Daddy was coming to visit, which pleased George very much, he missed Abe badly, Albert on the other hand, didn't really remember Abe. She sat them at the table and served them their breakfast. Molly came into the large kitchen and poured herself some tea from the pot, then sat staring into the crib at the sleeping baby.

"Where's Doris?" Molly asked as she broke from her daze. Carrie frowned and looked at the clock. It was 7.30, and every day Doris had always been the first up, to light the fires and put the kettle on the stove. Carrie looked at Molly.

"I had better go and check." She said as she wiped her hands on her pinny and walked towards the stairs.

Doris's body was grey and lifeless but looked incredibly peaceful. Carrie felt for a pulse when she realised that Doris wasn't breathing. There was nothing. She ran down the stairs and told Molly. Carrie ran to the village to call on the doctor.

He walked out of Doris's room and smiled a sad smile. He handed Carrie a piece of paper. "Local undertaker." He said in a thick Yorkshire accent. Carrie nodded. As she was showing the Doctor out, a familiar face walked up the path towards her. Her stomach flipped and she felt sick!

"Carrie, you look beautiful." Abe said and handed her a huge bunch of flowers. She huffed, handed the flowers back to him and walked back into the house, leaving the door open so as he could follow her. She handed the Undertakers details to Molly, who nodded and walked up the stairs to get ready, then walked into the kitchen where the children were.

The minute George laid eyes on Abe he ran to him, throwing his arms around him, Carrie felt tears prick her eyes. Albert hid behind Carrie. After ten minutes of Abe playing peek-a-boo with him, he warmed to Abe and was playing with him, just as George was.

"Do you want tea?" Carrie asked abruptly.

"Please" He replied from the floor. Polly began to cry. Carrie looked at the clock and realised that she needed to feed.

"You'll have to make it yourself and watch the boys while I feed the baby." Carrie said as she picked up the tiny baby and walked out of the room.

Chapter 21

Later that day, after the undertakers had taken Doris, Carrie, Molly, and Abe were in the lounge. The boys were playing in the garden.

"Where are you going to go now?" Molly asked Carrie.

"To be completely honest, I hadn't even thought about it." Carrie replied.

"Does she have any family?" Abe asked. Molly shook her head.

"Not that I am aware of." Molly sighed. Then there was a knock on the door. Carrie walked to the door and opened it. There was a stern looking man, dressed in a suit, holding a case.

"Mrs Wells I presume." He bellowed. Carrie nodded.

"I am Mr Dean, Mrs Page's Solicitor." He continued. Carrie frowned.

"Mrs Page?" Carrie asked. He huffed.

"Mrs Doris Page!" He replied.

"Oh, sorry, do come in." Carrie said and led him to the lounge. He sat on a chair and crossed his legs. Carrie sat beside Abe on the sofa. "This is my husband Mr Wells, and this is my friend, Miss May." Carrie introduced them both. He raised his eyebrow.

"Yes, quite, well to the matter in hand. My business here concerns Mrs Page's property and belongings." He retorted.

"Oh, when do we have to leave?" Carrie asked anxiously. She had no idea where she was going to go. The Solicitor frowned.

"Mrs Wells, you are not required to leave. Shortly after your arrival, Mrs Page came to my office to change her will. She named you as her sole beneficiary. She also requested that the undertakers were to contact myself when the eventuality happened. The house, all of her belongings, and the significant amount of savings she had are now yours. I just need your signature on the paperwork." He said and smiled. Carrie was gob smacked!

"What a wonderful gesture, you must have made quite an impact!" Molly said after the solicitor had gone.

"I know! I can't believe that she left it all to me!" Carrie said sadly.

Abe had been at the house for over a week and as much as Carrie hated to admit it, he was wonderful with the children. Molly had taken the three of them for a walk, which left Carrie and Abe alone in the house. Carrie was in the kitchen preparing the dinner. Abe was watching her as she placed the diced beef into the big pot and placed it on the stove.

"I must say Carrie, your cooking has come a long way since we first met!" He said and laughed. Carrie threw a cloth at him and laughed. "The children are wonderful, such a credit to you. I absolutely adore them!" He continued. Carrie smiled and nodded.

"Me too!" She replied as she chopped the onions, making her eyes water.

"Carrie I am so sorry for the way that I behaved in the past, I just want you to know that. You have not left my thoughts for a single day since you left. There is a huge gaping hole, and I know that it is my fault." He said. Carrie nodded.

"Could I stay for a while, spend some time with our beautiful children? Please?" He asked. Carrie put the knife down and looked at him.

"You can stay in the spare room." She replied. He grinned.

"Don't get any funny ideas Abe. I haven't forgiven you." She said and handed him a basket of potatoes. "Here you can start earning your keep and peel them!" She said and laughed.

A month had past, Molly had returned to London, Abe had called in a few favours, so between him, Carrie, and Hans team of incredibly skilled dwarfs they had started renovations on Carrie's house. It took six long months in total, and when it was finally finished, Carrie threw a party for all of those who had helped, the locals and of course Molly, Michael, and Jo.

The party was in full swing, the children were tired, so Carrie took them up the stairs to settle them. She tucked the boys into bed and kissed them both.

"Mummy" George said sleepily.

"Yes my love" Carrie replied.

"Thank you"

"For what?" Carrie chuckled.

"For bringing Daddy back" He replied as his eyes closed. She smiled and quietly closed the door.

Once everyone had left, all the mess had been cleared, Carrie threw herself on the sofa and sighed. Abe handed her a glass of brandy. She took it from him, smiled and thanked him. He sat down bedside her, and they both slowly sipped their drinks, Carrie was exhausted.

"You know that I love you, don't you?" Abe said and stared at her intently. Carrie sighed.

"You know Abe, when we first met, I actually believed that you did love me. Just goes to show how wrong someone can be." She sighed and looked at him.

"What I did was wrong, so very wrong and it took, six long months of separation from you to realise how wrong I was and how much you mean to me." Abe said sadly. "Please Carrie give me another chance to prove it to you. Please?" He pleaded.

Every part of her very being, wanted to scream YES, YES, except for her mind. That was screaming NO, NO DO NOT TRUST HIM! She looked deep into his eyes, she realised how much she missed him, all those long lonely nights wondering where he was, what he was doing, and why he wasn't there with her. She drank her brandy, he quickly refilled it. He leant in and kissed her!

"Mummy, mummy, why is Daddy in your bed?" George shouted and jumped on them both. Carrie lifted her head from the pillow and quickly put it back down. Her head was pounding!

Molly was sitting grinning at her across the kitchen table, Carrie caught her glance and chuckled.

"What?" Carrie asked as she sipped her tea.

"So, was it too much brandy, or just pure unbridled passion that forced you to give in?" Molly smiled.

"Both!" She replied.

So, over the next few years, life ticked away nicely. Abe did actually prove himself, he was a great father and a loving, faithful husband. However, Carrie always felt anxious. Life was not like this, and she was constantly waiting for something to go wrong.

One morning, she was walking through the village with young Polly, she need to go to the grocery shop, for a few bits. She had her basket in one hand and Polly's hand in the other. She was a beautiful little girl, always cheerful, and so loving, Carrie adored her. They began the long walk back to the house. The sun was shining and there was not a cloud in the sky. As they walked, Carrie picked wild flowers. Polly watched and did the same, they both had a large handful. There was a gust a wind, which blew Polly's flowers. She ran to collect them, when out of nowhere a horse and cart appeared and ran straight over the top of the little girl.

Carrie let out the most harrowing scream as she ran to her little girl, face down in the dirt. She heard laughter, before she even looked at the cart she knew who it was as she watched Mary charge away. Slowly Carrie turned the small child over. She was breathing. Carrie dropped everything , swept her up in her arms and ran as fast as she possibly could. When she reached the house she collapsed on the step, she was breathless and exhausted. Abe opened the door.. he bent to help her up. Carrie shook her head. "No help Polly, please Abe, she's been run down!" Carrie sobbed. Abe took Polly from her and ran inside the house, telepathically calling out to Merlin. He placed her on the sofa. She began to choke. He tried to sit her up, but she screamed out in pain, all the while Abe was praying for Merlin to get there. Carrie caught her breath and slowly climbed the steps, petrified of what might be happening inside of the house. She felt a strong wind as Merlin appeared and rushed past her. She began to weep. If Abe had called on Merlin, she must be bad, Carrie was thinking as she began to become hysterical. Darkness.....

She woke up and through the daze she recognised Molly standing over her. Molly smiled.

"Has she died?" Carrie asked anxiously. Molly smiled and shook her head.

"Merlin and I healed her. Her injuries were bad, but hopefully she will make a complete recovery." Molly replied and passed Carrie a glass of water. She drank it all down.

"Where is she?" Carrie asked.

"She is downstairs. Do you want me to fetch her?" Molly asked. Carrie shook her head and climbed off of the bed and walked quickly towards the stairs. She was so relieved when she walked into the lounge and saw Albert and Polly chasing one another around the room. Carrie looked at Merlin, she walked over to him. "I Owe you so much!" She said and kissed his hand. Merlin smiled and shook his head.

"Nonsense!" He chuckled. Carrie walked over to Abe who had his arms open. She fell into them and sobbed.

Although Polly seemed to make an almost complete recovery, since the accident, she had developed a nasty cough, it was worrying Carrie, so much so that she opened the chest and took out the Grimoire, for the first time in years. She placed the book on the floor. "Show me how to heal my little girl." She asked. The pages flicked back and forth then stopped. She read through. She wrote down all the things that she needed to make the elixir, then replaced the Grimoire and the chest in their hiding place and walked down to the kitchen.

The one thing that she needed but didn't have was rowan berries, which luckily were in abundance on the moors. She looked out of the window, to gauge the weather, grabbed her basket and headed off in the direction of the moors. As she walked higher up onto the crags, the wind began to howl. She collected some berries and began the descent. A mist appeared in front of her, it was dark, she knew that this was not good, so she stopped in her tracks. Katarina walked out from the dark mist.

"You see, as soon as you use your magic, I can track you down, and finish what Mary failed to accomplish." She said sneering.

"You will leave my children alone. Do whatever you want to me but leave my children. I will not allow you to harm them. DO YOU UNDERSTAND!" Carrie screamed. Katarina laughed.

"I fear that cannot happen. One of your offspring will have a child. That child will then have a child, who will attempt to destroy the Dark realm and I WILL NOT ALLOW THAT TO HAPPEN! I will take from you, your children, your husband, and that damned book!" She bellowed. Carrie lost control. She lunged at Katarina, who sent lightning to her fingers and sent it towards Carrie, sending her hurtling backwards and landing against a rock.

It took the very breath from her, she panicked as she saw Katarina walking towards her, her hands ready to send the lightning again. Carrie screamed out in frustration. Much to her own amazement she rose up in the air and lunged at Katarina. She threw a punch sending her through the air, landing in a heap. She appeared to be unconscious. Slowly Carrie approached her still, motionless body. She leant over. Katarina's hand came up and grabbed her throat. Carrie was choking, fighting for breath. Everything began to spin. She was swirling, then BAM she managed to free herself and hit Katarina in the face. The red-haired bitch let out a piercing shrill then vanished into a cloud of dark mist. Carrie sat on the heathland, still coughing, trying to come to terms with what has just happened.

The elixir appeared to be working and for the entire week, Carrie rarely heard Polly coughing, for which she was thankful. Abe had arrived back from an important meeting in Arbatel, it seemed that although the war was over, the Dark Realm were spreading poisonous thoughts amongst the people, attempting to cause an uprising in Germany. This was worrying Abe greatly and Carrie could tell, his usual cheery demeanour had disappeared, and he seemed constantly anxious.

He was sitting in the lounge after dinner, Carrie had settled the children into bed, poured them both a brandy and sat down beside him on the sofa. "Why don't we take the children for a day out at the seaside tomorrow, it will do them good, and may even ease your troubled mind a little?" Carrie suggested. Abe stared into his brandy glass, sighed, took a sip, then looked at Carrie. A smile crept across his face, then he nodded.

"Yes I think that's a wonderful idea, we could take a picnic!" He said as he placed his glass on the table and got up. "I'll go and arrange the transport now." He smiled. Carrie smiled and put her head back against the sofa, a took a large gulp of brandy. Abe returned smiling.

"The carriage will be here at 9 tomorrow morning." He said as he sat down beside her, chinked his glass against hers and leant in for a kiss.

They loaded the extremely excited children, the picnic basket, and themselves into the carriage and were on their way to the sea by 9.20. The boys were so excited, constantly nagging Abe, asking if he would teach them to swim. He laughed and nodded. The arrived at the beach around midday and the weather was beautiful. Carrie laid out a huge blanket, with the help of Polly, while Abe introduced the boys to the ocean. He was teaching Albert to swim, when George threw something into the water, forcing the water to swell and engulf albert, who then began to choke on the salty water. "George! What did you just throw into the water?" Abe fumed as she helped Albert. George laughed as Abe watched helplessly as Carrie's locket floated past him, then disappeared into the ocean. "Why did you do that?" Abe bellowed. Again George laughed.

There was a gentle breeze blowing through Carrie's hair, which felt wonderful. Polly was happily playing in the sand, until George ran up to her and kicked sand into her face, she began to choke. Carrie was furious. She shot George a look, then looked at Abe, who took the young lad by the arm and walked off, telling him off. Polly was crying, the sand was scratching her eyes. Carrie took her hand and walked her down to the sea. Gently she scooped some water into her hand and splashed it into Polly's eyes. It seemed to help and eventually she stopped crying.

Throughout the picnic, Carrie watched Polly continuously, and every time the little girl coughed, Carrie scowled at George. Abe could sense that the atmosphere was tense, so he asked the two boys if they wanted to go for a walk, which they both did.

They had been gone at least an hour, Polly was becoming tired, and the sun was beginning to burn her tender skin. Carrie looked at her watch. They only had twenty minutes before the carriage was returning to take them home. She began to pack everything away with the help of Polly. She grabbed the basket and told Polly to hold onto her skirt as they walked across the sand towards the pick-up point, all the time, searching for Abe and the boys. She placed the basket down, wiped the sweat from her brow and sighed.

"Look Mummy! There's Albert!" Polly called out and pointed. Carrie looked and saw Albert sitting on a wall alone. She left the basket, grabbed Polly's hand and they walked towards him.

"Albert, what are you doing here on your own?" Carrie asked anxiously. He looked up, his face was tear stained and he sniffed.

"Daddy was talking to a lady, he told me and George to go and play. George ran away and left me. I was worried that you would go home without me!" He sobbed. Carrie wrapped her arms around, holding him tight. She wiped the tears away from his face.

"Albert, I would never leave you. What on earth is wrong with George today? And where the bloody hell is your father?" Carrie said, as her heart raced with anxious flutters. She walked Albert and Polly to the pick-up point and sat them both on the basket. She took Molly's necklace from around her neck and handed it to Albert. He was only seven, but he was very grown up for his age.

"I need to find George and Daddy. I need you to look after Polly for me. I promise that I won't be long. If you feel in danger at any point, rub this stone, and I'll come straight back. Ok?" Carrie said quietly. Albert nodded wide eyed, Polly did too. Carrie kissed them both and ran in the direction that Albert had said they had gone. She began to run looking all around her. She stopped for a moment, to catch her breath and take a look around her, when someone grabbed her from behind. She quickly turned, ready to attack to be faced with George laughing hysterically.

"What do you think you are doing George, I could have really hurt you? " Carrie fumed, holding her chest to still her thumping heart. "Where is Dad?" Carrie asked. Again George laughed and pointed to an old derelict building. Carrie frowned. "He's in there? George is this another prank?" Carrie asked suspiciously.

"No! He's in there with a woman." He said and pointed again. Carrie took flight, running at full speed. There was a window with no glass, and she could clearly hear Abe's voice. The woman's voice was familiar. She reluctantly peered through and instantly wished that she hadn't. Abe was in an embrace with her. THAT woman. Carrie lost control and charged inside like a raging bull. She flew at Abe, throwing a punch sending him hurtling into the wall, all the time SHE was laughing. "BASTARD!" Carrie screamed and then turned. She walked calmy towards her, and as she stood in front of her she smirked. Carrie pulled her fist back about to punch, when she felt the pain of electricity run through her body, then she heard her familiar laugh.

"I really wouldn't do that Carrie. Shouldn't you be taking care of your children, not snooping on your cheating husband!" She said and laughed. "Now, be a good girl and put my sister down." She sneered. Carrie let go and turned to face Katarina. "Very good! Now, Mary is watching over your children for me, and so long as you do as I ask, no harm will come to them. Is that understood?" Katarina asked, her eyes the brightest green. Carrie stared at Katarina. "WELL?" She roared. Carrie reluctantly nodded.

"You and I will travel together to collect the Grimoire, once it is in my possession, I will instruct Mary to release the brats." Katarina continued. Carrie scowled.

"No Way! They travel with me." She roared.

"Very well, Mary kill all three of them!" She shouted.

.

Chapter 22

Carrie closed her eyes and called out to the earth. *Please, please don't let her hurt my children.* She thought. Carrie lifted her hand up and grabbed Katarina by the throat, tightening her grip, she was lost in rage. Clara jumped on Carrie's back, but she threw her off effortlessly, all the time choking Katarina. She looked and noticed that her hair was changing, each time Carrie applied more pressure, her hair became greyer. Again Clara jumped on Carrie's back, this time gauging at Carrie's eyes with her long fingernails. "Hmm, your husband's lips taste so good!" She whispered in Carrie's ear. Carrie instantly let go of Katarina and threw a punch at Clara after she had thrown her off. Clara went flying through the air, landing on top of a dazed Abe.

Carrie looked at Katarina, waiting for the lightning to appear, none did. She now had the appearance of a frail old woman.

"Carrie you have drained her energy, run!" Abe shouted as he threw Clara off of him. Carrie thought about the children and ran, as she ran she sobbed, she was so afraid. She looked in the direction of the carriage pick-up point. The three of them were sitting on the basket.

Carrie stopped in her tracks, caught her breath, and shouted thank you to the sky.

"What happened?" She asked breathlessly as she approached them.

"A pretty lady helped us. She sent the nasty lady away." Polly said. Carrie smiled then looked at Albert.

"A horrible dirty woman pulled up in a carriage, she grabbed Polly and threw her inside. I hit her and she hit me back, then a lady walked out of the sea. She grabbed the dirty woman and held her up against the carriage. She helped Polly get out. She whispered something to the dirty woman who then climbed on her carriage and rode way." Albert said. Carrie touched his red swollen cheek.

"Then the pretty lady said that you were coming to get us, and she vanished!" Polly said wide eyed. Carrie chuckled, looking at the beautiful little girl who was sat with the widest eyes.

"She said her name was Nimue, and that she was your friend." George said quietly. Carrie smiled and nodded.

"Look! There's Daddy!" Polly shouted and ran towards a limping, disheveled Abe. A carriage appeared from nowhere, charging horses running over Polly as too did the carriage. As the dust settled and Carrie had realised what had happened she screamed. Darkness……..

She opened her eyes, her head was pounding, but she was relieved to be home. She lifted her head from her pillow, the room was in darkness. She climbed out of her bed and lit the gaslight. She looked at her watch. It was 11pm. Then she remembered! She remembered those moments before she passed out. She ran to the door, weeping.

It was jammed. She began to hammer on it and took it off of its hinges, throwing it across the hallway. She ran to the stairs and then down them. The entire house was in darkness. She ran through every room, the house was empty. She called out "Albert, George, Abe, Polly." Nothing. She ran to the front door but the moment that she touched it, a charge of electricity threw her backwards. She ran to the back door. The same thing happened. Carrie screamed out in frustration. She collapsed in a heap on the floor sobbing. Then she heard footsteps coming towards her. She looked up. Katarina's piercing eyes were boring a hole through her.

"WHERE IS IT?" She bellowed. Carrie screwed her eyes up.

"WHERE ARE MY FAMILY?" she replied. Katarina laughed.

"You really don't remember do you?" She said through the laughter. Carrie shook her head, she was fuelled with rage, quickly she jumped up and grabbed Katarina.

"If you wish to see your family again, I advise you to let go." She choked. Carrie dropped her.

Katarina rang a bell and within seconds two half dead looking men arrived. "Take her back to her room. I will follow and place the bindings around the door and windows." She ordered. They both nodded grabbing Carrie roughly, dragging her up the stairs. Once in the room they threw her across the floor, her head crashing into the bedpost. Katarina followed in after them chanting at the window, then sending electricity at it. The two men left. Katarina walked to the doorway and again chanted using electricity to seal the entrance. "Sleep on it. I'll be back in the morning, I'm sure that gives you enough time to remember." She laughed and left.

Again Carrie screamed out in frustration, the room began to spin, and she passed out.

"Mummy, Mummy" She woke up to hear. It was Polly. Carrie looked around the room.

"Polly, Polly sweetheart I'm here." Carrie shouted.

"Mummy, I can't find you." She heard.

"Polly, Mummy is in her room sweetheart." Carrie called out again.

"Mummy, it's so dark and I'm scared" Polly's voice faded away.

Carrie wiped the tears away from her eyes, Peggy could clearly see how distressing it was for her to speak about it. Peggy passed her a hanky, then wiped her own eyes on another one.

"Is there anything I can get you before I go to bed?" Peggy asked. Carrie sniffed, then smiled.

"No thank you Peggy, all this emotion has completely drained me. I just need to sleep." She said as she yawned. Peggy kissed her on the cheek, turned out the light and made her way up to her room. She changed into her nightdress, climbed into bed, and sobbed. How Carrie appeared so strong and resilient was beyond her. Peggy thought that her life was bad being separated from Robert, but poor Carrie had suffered so much more pain and misery.

Peggy woke up and rubbed her eyes. She looked at her watch it was 5.30. She had tossed and turned all night, visions of Carrie suffering at the hands of Katarina and her awful sister had constantly run through her head. She climbed out of bed and headed towards the kitchen, as she walked past the lounge, she could hear voices. She stopped and listened.

"How much longer do you think she has?"

"I have no idea."

"Well, do you think that she has enough time to tell Peggy everything she needs to know?"

"I DON'T KNOW Michael. You can be so callous sometimes!" Peggy heard Molly say. She opened the door and stood in the doorway with her hands on her hips.

"Well, don't mind me, you two continue discussing my grandmother's final days, I'll tell you what, why don't we plan her funeral too while we are at it! "Peggy shouted furiously.

"That won't be necessary Peggy, I already have." Carrie said from behind her. Peggy turned and squirmed when she saw Carrie in her wheelchair.

"And for your information Michael, I think I have ample enough time to tell Peggy what she needs to know. To be honest with you all, I am done with all this shit. My entire life has been filled with it. What has to be done, what has to be said. My daughter died at the hands of those bastards, they have made my life a living hell. The sooner I get to the other side the better!" Carrie roared, wheeling herself back to her room. Peggy looked at both Molly and Michael.

"I hope you are both proud of yourselves! This is bloody farcical!" Peggy huffed and quickly shuffled to Carrie's room. She could hear her sobs before she even opened the door. Tears began to sting Peggy's eyes, the sound of the heartbreak was too much! Peggy gently tapped on the door and walked in. Carrie was sitting in her wheelchair looking out of the window. She slowly walked over to her and placed her hand gently on her shoulder.

"I'm so sorry that you had to hear that." Peggy said as tears ran down her cheeks. Carrie tapped her hand.

"It was nothing you said, so there is no need for you to apologise." Carrie said and attempted to smile.

"Aye I know, but…."

"Peggy could I speak with Carrie alone please?" Molly interrupted. Peggy scowled at Molly then looked at Carrie for guidance. Carrie smiled and nodded.

"It's ok Peggy, you go and prepare the breakfast, I'm starving." Carrie said. Peggy turned and huffed as she stormed past Molly.

"I am so sorry!" Molly said meekly, she couldn't look Carrie in the eye. Carrie chuckled.

"You know, if I were twenty years younger, this situation would have been completely different. I have spent years fighting, and I am not about to spend my final days doing the same!" Carrie said.

"I feel so ashamed. I should have just told him to shut up!" Molly replied. Carrie smiled.

"Michael is Michael, you love him warts and all! He has an end goal, which he is determined to see through to the end, I understand that Molly, I lived with Abe for long enough!" Carrie said. Molly smiled and nodded.

"Now go and lay the table for breakfast will you." Carrie said and shooed her out of the room. Molly smiled, nodded, and did as she asked. Carrie wheeled herself over to the chest and opened it. She found the photo of the three children, and she looked at it, then held it close to her heart. She placed it into her pocket, wiped her face and headed towards the kitchen. She could smell bacon and grinned as she entered and watched Peggy making bacon sandwiches for them all.

"I do believe that you have the power of telepathy Peggy!" Carrie said and Molly laughed. The back door opened, and William walked in, wearing his usual happy smiling face. He kissed Peggy on the cheek, then handed Carrie a small posy of flowers.

"Nothing fancy today I'm afraid." He said. Carrie smiled.

"Beautiful, none the less." She replied as she put them to her nose and smelt the wonderful aroma.

"William, are you free today?" Peggy asked. He smiled and nodded.

"Aye, why do you ask?" He replied as he chewed on his bacon sandwich.

"I thought that you and I could take Carrie out for a walk, and maybe a picnic?" Peggy suggested. William smiled.

"Aye sure" He replied. Carrie smiled. At that moment she could think of nothing better than to spend the day with the two of them. "I'll go home and fetch my fishing rod. You never know I might be able to catch us all something for our tea!" He grinned, kissed Peggy, and left.

They found a lovely spot beside the river, not too far from the cottage. William had set up his rod and seemed to be in his element, sitting watching the water. Peggy was looking at Carrie, a sad expression shot across her face. Carrie frowned.

"What's wrong?" She asked. Peggy sighed.

"I know that you probably don't want to talk about it, but I kind of need to know what happened to Polly, I didn't sleep a wink last night." Peggy said. Carrie smiled.

She woke up, it was daylight. She needed to find a way of getting out of the room. She paced back and forth, racking her brains, when she heard footsteps walking towards her room. Katarina stood in the doorway.

"Have you had enough time to think about things?" She asked. Carrie raised her eyebrows. "WELL??" She roared. Carrie laughed.

"I will not give you the book, so I suggest that you turn around and fuck off back to wherever you came from!" Carrie chuckled.

"Are you deranged?" Katarina asked. Again Carrie laughed. "I will kill your entire family if you do not give me that book. Carrie shrugged her shoulders.

"Do you think that I am bluffing?" Katarina asked. Again Carrie laughed. Katarina let out a piercing shrill then stormed off towards the stairs. Carrie knew that she was playing a dangerous game, but at that moment in time she had no other choice.

Still Carrie paced back and forth, a little while later she heard footsteps again. This time there was more than one person. Katarina appeared at the door.

"I will ask you once again. Where is the book?" She asked calmly. Carrie threw her head back, mimicking Katarina, and laughed.

"Very well!" Katarina sighed and beckoned to someone that Carrie couldn't see. Abe stood in the doorway, closely followed by Clara. "Now show her how much you desire my sister. Show her that she means nothing to you." Katarina sneered. Abe and Clara began to kiss. Carrie looked the other way. She slid down the wall buried her head in her knees and held her hands over her ears.

When she heard the familiar shriek of frustration from Katarina she knew that it was safe to look. Carrie sighed, they had gone.

"Mummy, where are you?" She heard Polly's voice. Carrie closed her eyes, sending herself into deep meditation, just as Michael had taught her, all those years before.

She was in the meadow. The air was filled with the scent of wild flowers. She looked into the distance and smiled when she saw Abagail. She walked towards her. As she approached, Abagail stepped to the side to reveal Polly standing beside her. Tears streamed down Carrie's face as she looked at her little girl. "Mummy! There you are!" Polly shouted excitedly. Carrie bent down and scooped the little girl into her arms, sobbing as she did. Abagail touched Carrie's shoulder.

"She does not understand that she is no longer of your realm, which is why she keeps calling out for you." Abagail said gently. Polly was holding onto Carrie so tightly. Carrie moved the child's hands from around her neck and looked at her.

"Sweetheart, do you remember when the horse ran over you?" Carrie sobbed. Polly nodded. "Well, you became so poorly that Abagail had to bring you here to stay with her and wait for Mummy. Do you understand?" Carrie asked. Polly nodded sadly. "Mummy won't be long. You be a good girl for Abagail won't you." Carrie wept.

"I love you Mummy." Polly cried.

"I love you too sweetheart so much!" Carrie wept, forcing herself out of meditation.

Now she knew that Polly had in fact died, but the boys were thankfully still alive, she had to fight. She sat in wait, until finally the footsteps were back. She could feel the anger building inside of her as thoughts of Polly ran through her head. Katarina appeared at the door.

"I have a slight inconvenience, I wonder if you could help me?" She sneered. Carrie shot her a look. "Which one of your boys should I devour first? The elder or the younger? Which one do you think would taste better?" Katarina sneered. Carrie lost all control, she no longer cared about the electrical bindings, and she bounded straight through them grabbing Katarina by the throat.

"Isn't one enough? Can't you just leave it at that!" Carrie roared. Katarina was struggling, trying her hardest to break free and call out. Carrie pulled her fist back and hit Katarina with all her force. She flew through the air and landed in a heap on the floor at the end of the hallway. Carrie's arms were pulled tight behind her, she could smell Mary's stench before she could see her, then Clara appeared in front of her.

"You know, I pity Abe, I mean being forced to sleep with you just to create children. He deserves so much better than YOU, a dirty nobody from the gutter!" Clara sneered. Carrie roared an unearthly roar and as she did her body began to rise, forcing Mary to release her. She floated above both women who were standing gawping at her in disbelief. First she kicked Mary, sending her flying down the stairs, then Clara, who landed on top of her sister. Her feet touched the floor, and she ran as fast as she possibly could. She reached the front door. The two men that dragged her back to her room were standing guard. One took a run at Carrie, she punched him sending him through the door, electrocuting him. The other then tried to grab her, she hit him and then ran through the electricity, not feeling a thing. She continued to run, until she had no energy left. She was out on the moors, the clouds were building, looking increasingly menacing. The wind began to gather momentum, she knew that she needed to move, but where would she go?

Chapter 23

She was leaning against a large boulder, sheltering from the biting wind, when a hand grabbed hold of her. She inhaled deeply, ready to fight, when she recognised the voice. She quickly turned and sighed with relief when she saw him. "Fingers!" She sighed.

"Carrie you must come with me." Hans whispered, all the time looking all around him.

"Hans I need to find the boys." Carrie replied. Hans nodded.

"Yes, come!" He said impatiently. "Keep low, we mustn't be seen." He added. Carrie followed keeping as low as she possibly could, until she realised that they were heading back towards the house.

"Hans!" Carrie whispered. He continued, not paying her any attention. "HANS!" She shouted. He turned and scowled. He placed his finger over his lip and shushed her. "Why are we going back to the house. I have only just managed to get out. They are not there." Carrie whispered. Hans continued to walk, nodding his head, yet still walking in the direction of the house. Carrie ran to catch him up and grabbed his arm. He turned and frowned.

"I heard what you said, but you are wrong. The boys are tied up in the attic. We must go to the house. I know that Katarina and her sister have left the house. We must get in, remove the bindings, and replace them with my bindings." Hans whispered. Carrie nodded.

"Wait, if Katarina is not there, who is guarding the house?" She asked.

"There are two men, I believe that they were guarding you." He replied. Carrie nodded, then smiled when she thought about how easy they both were to overcome. "If you cause a distraction outside the house, it will give me passage to get in and remove the bindings." Hans whispered. Carrie nodded. Once at the garden wall Hans crept around the back of the house. Carrie walked up the path and began shouting as loud as she possibly could.

"I am coming in there for my children!" She bellowed, then grinned when she watched as both men walked out of the front door towards her. She could feel the fury building inside of her as they looked at one another, ready to attack. She lunged at the biggest man, sending him to the ground instantly. She threw a punch, knocking him out, as the other man grabbed her by the hair and pulled her across the lawn. She grabbed his fingers and crushed them, making him scream out in pain, forcing him to release her. He looked at her, his eyes red with anger. She threw a punch, sending him flying into the garden wall and collapsing in a heap. She quickly ran around the back of the house. She opened the back door and threw a stick inside to see if the electricity was still live, to her relief, it wasn't, and she walked through the kitchen. The house was quiet. She walked through the rooms looking for Hans. There was no sign of him downstairs. She quietly walked up the stairs and found Hans, at the bottom of the second flight of stairs that led to the attic. Once she had reached him, he opened the door and both of them walked up the narrow staircase. Hans tried the door at the top, it was locked. He took out a tool and began trying to open the lock, nothing was working. Carrie could hear Albert crying, she was becoming so frustrated.

"Boys, stay away from the door!" She shouted, as she threw a punch at the door. The door flew from its hinges and just missed Albert as it flew into the room. Albert was in the corner, his hands and feet were tied, there was no sign of George. Carrie ran to Albert quickly untying the ropes that were cutting into his skin. "Where is George?" She whispered.

"Carrie look out!" Hans shouted. She turned and was faced with George yielding a hammer, holding it over Carrie's head. She quickly moved as he brought the hammer down with such force that the claw stuck into the floorboard.

"GEORGE!" Carrie roared as she walked over to grab him. He snarled at Carrie, his eyes almost black with anger. She had seen this George before, visions of the same eyes appeared in her head from when he was cursed as a small child. Hans walked towards him, he threw a punch sending the poor dwarf flying, landing beside Albert.

"Get Out!" George roared as Carrie approached him. She took a step backwards, bent down grabbing Albert's hand as she did and walked towards the door. George grabbed hold of Albert, pulling him away from Carrie. "He stays with me" George growled. Carrie laughed.

"I don't think so sweetheart." She said and picked Albert up. She walked towards the door as George jumped onto her back, sinking his teeth into her as he did. She managed to throw him off and when he landed and didn't get up she realised that he must be unconscious. She ran down to her room with Albert. She opened the door to the secret passage where she kept the chest. She opened the chest and took out the reversal spell.

"Albert, I need you to be a brave boy and stay here. I need you to guard the chest." Carrie whispered. Albert was frantically shaking his head.

"No, no please don't leave me Mummy, I'm so scared." He said, his voice quivering with fear.
"Sweetheart, I must go back and help Fingers. I will be as quick as I can." She said, kissed him on the cheek, closed the door and locked it. She ran back to attic as fast as she could. Her heart sank. Hans was still out cold, George had gone. She looked everywhere. She eventually woke Hans and after a quick recovery they both ran down to Carrie's bedroom. Her heart was beating so fast as she silently prayed that George had not found Albert. She let out a huge sigh, when she unlocked the door and saw Albert sitting on the chest, there was no sign of George anywhere.

She locked everything back up, then her, Hans, and Albert went down the stairs. The house had been completely trashed. Carrie stood with her hands on her hips assessing the damage, shaking her head as she did.

"Carrie, we need to find the boy. He could be hiding anywhere in here and I believe that he could pose a great danger to both Albert and yourself." Hans said as he nervously looked around.

"I'm sure he will come out when he is hungry." Carrie said loudly and winked at Hans. Hans scowled and shook his head.

"No you must leave here, just for a while, until we have located the child." Hans said anxiously. Carrie shook her head.

"This is my home, he is my son. I will not allow them to drive us out Fingers. You are free to leave any time you like, but me and Albert are staying put!" Carrie said adamantly, this was her first true home, and she wasn't going to just up and leave it! Hans shook his head.

"I shall place the bindings, then I must seek out Abraham." He said and tutted. Just hearing his name sent Carrie into a fit of rage.

"Do not bring that bastard anywhere near me or my children. Do you understand?" Carrie sneered. Hans frowned.

"I don't understand Carrie. It was Abraham that sent me to help you. Whatever has happened?" Hans said with a look of confusion about him.

"Well Fingers, it's one of two things. One, he's been enchanted, and this is a trap, or two, he's not enchanted and is a genuine bastard!" Carrie fumed. Hans shook his head.

"No, he contacted me and asked me to assist you, he said that you were in grave danger and that he was unable to help you as he was involved with a secret mission." Hans replied still none the wiser. Carrie laughed.

"Why does everyone believe his lies? Surely there must be one of you lot that can see straight through him!" Carrie fumed. "Well I for one am not that gullible. If you wish to believe him, then that's your look out, just do not bring him anywhere near me." Carrie said as she began clearing the mess in the hallway. Hans walked off shaking his head in bewilderment. He placed the bindings and then left.

Carrie and Albert spent the remainder of the day clearing the mess, then Albert helped Carrie to prepare the evening meal. They sat at the table eating, well Albert was pushing his food around his plate. Carrie smiled at him.

"What's wrong? Don't you like it?" She asked.

"I'm scared. What if George is hiding somewhere in here and kills us when we are asleep?" He sighed, his eyes wide with fear.

"Sweetheart, I have no idea where he is, but I'm pretty sure that between us we can stop him. I have the reversal spell, so if he does come back I can stop all of this." Carrie smiled. Albert shook his head.

"No, I don't think that we can. He is evil, he beat me when I was tied up. He said that he hated me and you. He said that he was glad that Polly was dead, that we were all weak and that he was going to stay with Dad and that nasty lady." Albert said as his eyes filled with tears. Carrie's did too. Carrie wiped his tears away and then her own.

"I Promise you that I will not let him hurt you ever again! Until we find him, you can stay in my room with me. Is that a deal?" Carrie asked. Albert smiled and began to eat his food. They were both exhausted and decided to take a cup of cocoa to bed. Albert didn't drink his, he fell asleep before it had chance to cool. Carrie sat and stroked his hair as the tears fell, tears for her beautiful daughter that they cruelly took from her, she eventually sobbed herself to sleep.

She woke up when she felt the bed move. She quickly lit the candle on her bedside table. Albert was not there. She climbed out of bed, quietly calling his name. she looked all around the bedroom, she checked the door to the secret passage, it was still locked, then she walked to the bedroom doorway, the door was stood up against the wall. She could hear his sobs and followed the sound. He was in Polly's room. She quickly opened the door and was relieved when she saw him sat on the rug. She ran over to him.

"What are you doing sweetheart?" She asked gently. He appeared to be in a sleep state, Carrie gently shook him to wake him. He jumped and then grabbed hold of Carrie, wrapping his arms around her tightly.

"He said that Polly wasn't dead, that it was just a trick and that she was in here." Albert said wide eyed.

"SHIT!" Carrie shouted as she grabbed hold of his hand and ran back to the room. She looked around and checked the door again. It was still locked, but something was telling her to open the door and check. Her heart was beating out of her chest as she turned the key. She pushed the door open and sighed with relief when she saw the chest.

"*Open the chest*" She heard. As she walked towards it, she felt a gust of wind hurling past her. Abagail appeared. She stood and shook her head. "It is a trap. Do not open it." Abagail said before she vanished. Then Carrie heard Albert scream. She ran back into the room to see George dragging him towards the door.

"LET HIM GO NOW!" Carrie roared as she ran towards them. George laughed. She grabbed hold of Albert's legs and pulled him, sending George flying into the wall. She stood Albert behind her and placed her hand in her pocket, grabbing the reversal spell. As she approached George he looked at her and she blew the spell into his face. She was not expecting his reaction. He blew it straight back to her, got up and ran.

She grabbed hold of Albert's hand and took chase. She heard the front door slam, she knew he had fled. She sat on the bottom stair, Albert sat beside her. She put her hands in her face and wept. In the space of a few hours she had lost two of her children and her husband, she felt so shattered. Albert put his arms around her and held her tight.

"It's ok Mummy, I'll look after you, don't cry." He said gently. Carrie held him so tightly, she then wiped her eyes and smiled at her beautiful boy.

"I know you will sweetheart. Let's make a pact to always take care of one another." She sniffed. They linked little fingers and the pact was sealed.

The months passed and the season was beginning to change, signs of Autumn were appearing daily. Albert had finished school and walked home by himself, he seemed happy as he hopped up the garden path. Carrie was pruning the roses in the garden, she looked up and smiled at him.

"Did you have a good day?" She asked as she stood up and stretched her back. Albert grinned and nodded.

"I have baked a cake, go and cut yourself a slice while I tidy these tools away." Carrie said as she collected all the gardening tools. She closed the shed door and heard the front gate close. She looked around the side of the shed to see a woman a little older than herself walking up towards the front door. She knocked. Carrie wiped her dirty hands on her skirt and hurried through the back of the house to the front door.

"Can I help you?" She asked sternly as she opened the door.

"Are you Carrie?" The woman asked in an Irish accent. This made Carrie suspicious.

"Who wants to know?" Carrie growled. The woman blushed and looked around. Then she cleared her throat.

"My name is Florence, I am not sure if Ma told you about me." She replied awkwardly. Carrie frowned.

"I'm sorry, but I haven't got a clue what you are talking about. I have never heard of a Florence." Carrie said.

"Carrie I am your sister." She replied. Carrie let out an over-exaggerated laugh.

"My sister died many years ago." She scoffed. Florence nodded her head.

"Aye Hester, I know." She replied. Carrie stood back when she heard her say Hester. "Please if you let me in I'll explain." She added. Carrie shook her head.

"No way, everyone must think that I am thick! Now go back to the red-haired bitch and tell her to do her own bidding will you!" Carrie said, she was trying to close the door, but Florence stopped her.

"I know who you speak of, but I can promise you, I am not here to do her bidding, I am here to help you and Albert." Florence replied and smiled. "Please Carrie, give me a chance to explain, then if you still don't believe me, I'll leave. I promise." She pleaded. Carrie pulled the door wide open and gestured for her to come in. Carrie walked to the kitchen, Florence followed her. Albert looked up, his mouth full of cake and smiled.

"You must be Albert, sure you're a handsome fella aren't ya." Florence said and smiled at him. He nodded frantically.

"Albert, run upstairs and get changed, I need you to run to the shop for me." Carrie said as she took his empty plate. He climbed off of the chair and did as Carrie asked.

"Would you like a cup of tea?" Carrie asked as she filled the kettle and placed it on the stove.

"That would be lovely, thank you." She smiled.

They both sat at the table, Carrie poured the tea. "Well, explain!" Carrie said as she looked over the steaming teapot. Florence cleared her throat.

"Our mother fell with me when she was thirteen years old. Her parents were very religious, and when they found out they went mad. They sent Ma to a convent to have me, then put me up for adoption, Ma went back home. I was adopted by the local Doctor and his wife. They were always good to me and took good care of me, but when I was about five I began to have visions. They were always of Ma, you, and Hester. I told the Doctor, so he and Rose, his wife, sat me down and told me that they weren't my real parents, then they told me that Ma had moved to London and had a family there.

I used to think about you all the time. The visions came back, the first one was when Hester was killed, then I began to see all the awful things that were happening to you. In the village where I grew up, there was a wise old lady, and one day I went to see her. She told me all about you, and that my visions were true.

After a while the visions stopped, I fell in love, got married and had a baby girl. Life ticked away nicely, but I was always thinking about you. My husband died and his rich family sent my daughter away to boarding school, I was all alone so I thought it was about time that I came to find you." She sighed.

Chapter 24

Carrie instinctively knew that Florence was speaking the truth and when she looked at her she could see a strong resemblance to her mother.

"So you had two sisters, I wonder why your mother never told you about her?" Peggy asked. Carrie chuckled.

"Because Peggy, she always too drunk!" Carrie said laughed, then coughed. The sun was getting low in the sky and the air was becoming chilly, Peggy could see that Carrie was cold and tired.

"We had better get you back home. William are you ready?" Peggy shouted. William nodded and began to pack his fishing things away. He walked over to Peggy and Carrie.

"What delights are we having for tea then sweet William?" Carrie smiled. William frowned.

"I'm really sorry, but I didn't catch a single thing." He replied disappointedly.

"I think that we should all have a fish and chip supper tonight. Would you be a dear and fetch it for us William?" Carrie asked.

"Aye, it's the least I can do." He sighed and began to push the wheelchair back towards the cottage.

Carrie went to her bedroom for a lie down, Peggy caught up with the washing. William took his fishing gear home. Peggy was hanging some sheets on the washing line when Molly walked through the back gate.

"Peggy, I really am truly sorry about this morning. I should have told Michael to shut up." Molly said. Peggy smiled and nodded.

"Why were you both here so early?" Peggy asked. Molly frowned.

"The Elders, Michael's grandfather is an Elder, he told Michael yesterday that Carrie was going to die in her sleep today. Michael panicked and of course dragged me here at dawn, just to make sure she was ok." Molly whispered. Peggy's eyes widened.

"Shit!" She shouted as she dropped the sheet and ran towards the cottage. She ran to Carrie's room and opened the door. Carrie was lying on her bed, completely still. Peggy stopped in her tracks and watched to see if Carrie was breathing.

To her huge relief Carrie's chest rose as she took in a deep breath. Peggy sighed as she looked at Molly, who walked over to Carrie and held her wrist. She checked her watch. Carrie was still sound asleep. Molly ushered Peggy out of the room. "Her pulse is rather faint, we should keep an eye on her." Molly whispered. Peggy frowned.

ABRAHAM

He was walking along with his two sons when he recognised the woman walking towards them. He was dreading this moment. The moment that it had been decided in his last meeting, the day before at Arbatel, he felt sick to his stomach. How he had argued with the Elders, particularly Henry, Michael's father, he was adamant that he was not going to do it, when Henry cleverly pricked his conscience. Guardians who were working covertly in Germany had sent word back that Katarina was having a relationship with a top German general, in an army that should not even exist. She had inside information, that the light realm desperately needed to know, and the Elders believed that Abraham was the only person who could gain her trust.

"Abraham, we must stop meeting like this." Clara sneered and winked at him. He attempted a convincing smile as his stomach tied itself in knots.

"Clara, what a coincidence!" He replied. She walked over and held her body tight against his.

"We need to talk. Children, I am just going to steal your gorgeous father away for a while, why don't you hop along and amuse yourselves." She said as she looked at the young boys. Albert shook his head as George began pulling him towards the sea. Abe smiled at Albert and nodded, gesturing for him to go. Reluctantly the boy did as his father wished.

Clara led Abe into a disused building and leant against the wall. She stroked his face. "Now that I have you all to myself I am going to make the most of it. My sister wants you, and fortunately for me she engages in other matters at present, so I thought that I would take this opportunity to steal you for myself, until she summons you." Clara said as she then leant in and pushed her lips hard against his. The compulsion to vomit was so strong, he pushed her back and sighed, it was the only option that he had.

"Hmm, but surely if your sister finds out about us she will punish you?" Abe said trying his hardest to sway her attention away from him. Clara laughed.

"Who do you think sent me here? She wants you and I to break Carrie, then she will do whatever she wishes with you." She said, and again kissed him. Then he saw Carrie as he pushed Clara away from him. Carrie rushed towards him and hit him. He landed in a heap, dazed from hitting his head.

After the battle, Abe left the building and hobbled back to the carriage pick up point. He could see Carrie and the children in the distance. Polly ran towards him, just as Mary came thundering along and rode the horses straight over the top of his little girl. His heart stopped, he watched as Carrie screamed out the most harrowing scream that he had ever heard, then she collapsed. Mary climbed down from the carriage, grabbed the two boys, and threw them into the carriage, then she dragged Carrie and threw her inside. She rode away. Abe dropped to his knees when he saw the lifeless body of his beautiful little girl, face down in the dirt. A gust of wind blew around him, then Merlin put his hand on his shoulder.

"I will take her my friend." He said gently, picked up Polly's body and vanished into the wind. Abe put his head to the ground and sobbed.

"Get up now!" He heard. He looked up to see Katarina and Clara standing over him. He sighed into himself, wiped the tears from his face and got to his feet.

"Where is the child?" Katarina boomed. Abe just shook his head.

"Maybe Mary took the body to dispose of it." Clara said. Katarina nodded.

"Now then, we need to break your wife. I must have the Grimoire. You and Clara will put on a little performance of lust for her. Is that understood?" Katarina shouted. Abe nodded. He had to play along even though he desperately wanted to grab her by the throat and choke the breath from her.

After Abe and Clara had done their performance, all three of them went to a house nearby that Katarina owned. Apparently she had inherited it from one of her former husbands! Then Katarina and Clara went back to Carrie's house, which gave Abe the chance to gather and then send information telepathically to the Elders.

Later that evening there was a loud knock on the door. Katarina sent Clara to answer the door, and Abe nearly jumped off of his seat, when she walked back into the lounge, followed by George. Abe looked at Katarina in bewilderment.

"Ah young George. What have you got to tell us?" Katarina asked. George looked at Abe, then at Katarina.

"She and that dwarf have put bindings up. The dwarf has left, so it's just her and Albert in there." He said and smiled a sickly smile at the red-haired bitch. Abe wanted to jump up and shake some sense into the boy!

"Good. After dark, I want you to go back to the house. Try to get the Grimoire, if you cannot, at the very least bring the other boy here." Katarina said and smiled. George smiled, then turned and scowled at Abe. She then sent him off to find food in the kitchen. Abe made an excuse that he needed the toilet, then went on the hunt for George. He found him sitting at the kitchen table. Abe sat down opposite him.

"What are you doing?" he whispered sternly at his son, his son that was barely recognisable. George sneered.

"None of your business." He mumbled with a mouthful of food. Abe leant over and grabbed his arm.

"George, you need to stop this now! These are very bad people, you have no idea what you are getting yourself into!" Abe whispered. George pulled his arm away and laughed. He leant forward.

"Why are you here then?" He asked. Abe shook his head. He had no reply. He got up and walked back to the lounge. After a while Abe yawned and stretched.

"Yes it is getting rather late." Katarina sighed. "George you should be going now, should you not?" She said to the boy, who nodded, stood up and left the room. "Good! Abraham, if you follow me, I will show you to your room." She said and gestured for him to follow.

They went up the stairs, Katarina opened a door and beckoned him to go in. As he did, she followed. "This is our room." She sneered as she began to undress. Abe gulped, again he wanted to vomit. Thoughts of Carrie, Polly and Albert were running through his head and now the Elders expected him to climb into bed beside her. Katarina climbed into the huge bed, Abe walked to the window and looked out. "I am sending something to dull the pain and the memory." He heard Merlin say in his head.

Luckily for him, Merlin had sent a spell that, whenever Abe was expected to have a physical relationship with Katarina, his memory blacked out and he had no recollection of it. The following morning he discovered that George had failed on both endeavours, sending Katarina into a huge fit of rage. She sent one of the guards out to find her something to feed on, as she had exhausted her energy. Abe was watching from the window as the guard was dragging some poor beggar up the path. He knew the fate that beheld that poor soul and could not sit by and witness it. He turned and looked at Katarina.

"I need some air." He said and walked towards the door.

"WAIT!" Katarina roared. "You can go back to the house and get that book!" She ordered. Abe nodded, he was happy to get away for a while and hopefully be able to talk to Carrie.

He inhaled deeply as he reached the path towards Carrie's house. He slowly and apprehensively walked up to the front door and knocked. The door opened and Molly was stood in front of him. He was silently happy that it was Molly and not Carrie.

"You are not welcome here Abraham. If she lays eyes on you, goodness only knows what she will do. You must leave now!" Molly whispered for fear of Carrie overhearing. Abe smiled a small smile, turned, and left. He shapeshifted and flew to Arbatel. He desperately needed to speak to the Elders. He knew that it was risky, but he was unsure how much more he could take.

"You simply cannot expect me to stay with that awful wretch for six months! My wife and son live nearby, they will not see me. Do you have any idea how it feels to be so close to the people you love and not be able to make contact?" Abe shouted at Henry and Edward, the youngest of the Elders.

"This is what you signed yourself up for Abe, you were advised not to become emotionally attached. You were aware that it was written in fate and couldn't be altered. I am sorry that it grieves you, but you must go back!" Henry said as he stood. "You are head of the light realm, so I suggest that you start behaving in the manner that is expected of you!" Henry sneered and walked out of the room, swiftly followed by Edward.

He returned to Katarina, who was thankfully in a better mood. "Did you get it?" She asked. Abe shook his head.

"Unfortunately, I couldn't get anywhere near the place. Bindings have been put in place." He sighed. Katarina shook her head.

"Useless!" She muttered and then called for George. The lounge door opened, and Mary walked in. Abe wanted to lunge at her and choke the very life out of her, instead he summoned all of the self-control, that he possibly could, and tried his best to ignore the fact that she was even there.

"Ah Mary!" Katarina said and looked at Abe. "Sit down and watch" She ordered him. He did as he was told. Katarina walked over to Mary and with her hands created a mist, which completely engulfed the filthy woman. The mist cleared and a woman stepped out. She was in her sixties, well rounded, wearing unusual clothes.

"This is Mary in the future." Katarina sneered. Abe looked on in astonishment. "What is your name dear?" Katarina asked.

"Sandra dear." Mary replied in a thick West Country accent.

"And who are you?" Katarina asked.

"Why I'm your auntie." She replied. Katarina looked at Abe.

"Ha!" She shouted. Abe frowned, he had no idea where this was leading. Katarina summoned the mist, engulfed her inside and the usual dirty Mary stepped out. "You can go now." Katarina said and shooed her out of the room.

"I am covering for all eventualities. If by chance, I cannot stop one of your brats from pro creating in the future, I have created Auntie Sandra, who will befriend and then betray, telling all sorts of untruths and leading whomever to me!" Katarina sneered.

Six long months turned into two long years of Abe having to be at Katarina's side. It was one of the worst experiences he had ever had to suffer. Apart from losing his family, he had never experienced anything like it. The woman was pure evil, only interested in herself and what she could gain. Abe was relieved when he had to go to Germany on orders from the Elders. He no longer had to sit by and watch as Katarina, Clara and George constantly plagued Carrie and Albert.

It had been six years since he had been in England. He wanted to visit Carrie and Albert. He asked Michael if he would ask her. Michael looked at him with a solemn look on his face.

"Oh dear. I am afraid my friend that we have not been able to trace Carrie's whereabouts for the last five years. Her sister arrived from Ireland, and shortly after that the house was sold and they had gone. Not even Molly can find them." Michael sighed. Abe slumped in his chair.

"I just want to explain." He sighed. Michael nodded.

"I understand that, but if we do not know of her whereabouts then I cannot help you. Er, there is something that I need to tell you however." Michael said anxiously. Abe nodded gesturing for him to continue. "It's George, he has married and has a child." Michael said. Abe nodded.

"Who?" Abe asked.

"A local girl, but he is rotten to both her and the child. I believe them both to be in great danger. Katarina wants them both dead." Michael continued. "Katarina disappeared for a while and that's when he met the young lass. He seemed content, up until the point that Katarina re-appeared and now he is at her disposal again" Michael sighed. Abe scratched his chin and shook his head.

"So Carrie has disappeared off of the face of the earth, George is about to kill his family! Any other great news that I might need to hear?" Abe fumed.

"Only that we should possibly move the girl and child away from here, where they cannot be found." Michael added.

Abe had a meeting at Arbatel, which Merlin attended. After the meeting it was just Abe and Merlin. "Do you have any idea where Carrie and Albert are?" Abe asked. Merlin shook his head but looked shifty.

"No" Merlin replied.

"Don't give me that Merlin, you have a vested interest, of course you know where they are!" Abe said raising his voice. Merlin sighed.

"My friend, she will absolutely refuse to see you, I guarantee it!" Merlin sighed.

"So you do know where she is." Abe replied. Merlin reluctantly nodded.

"She lives in Scotland. She purchased a cottage from a farmer."

Merlin mumbled. Abe smiled.

"Where exactly?" He asked.

"I'll take you there." Merlin said, they both shifted and flew high up in the sky towards the Scottish borders.

Once they had both landed and spun Merlin looked at Abe. "Maybe I should speak to her first." He whispered. Abe shook his head and walked proudly up the path. He knocked on the door. A woman whom he did not recognise answered the door, Abe stepped back.

"Can I help you?" The woman asked in an Irish accent.

"Er.. yes, I was er… looking for Carrie." He asked awkwardly. The woman smiled.

"Why she's at work, who is asking?" She asked. Abe scratched his chin, looking all around. He saw nurses uniforms hanging on the washing line.

"Er it doesn't matter, I er wanted to surprise her." He said, turned and walked towards the gate.

"She finishes in an hour." The woman called out. Abe put his hand up and smiled. He needed to get to the closest hospital!

Merlin returned to his wild places, Abe went to the local hospital and waited outside. He checked his watch, if the woman was right, Carrie should be walking out of the doors anytime now. A young man stood beside the doors on the opposite side. The door opened and a nurse walked out. She joined the young man and walked away. Still Abe waited, his stomach was turning somersaults, every part of him was trembling as nerves got the better of him. Five minutes later the door opened again. There she was as beautiful as ever! She tied her scarf around her head to shelter from the rain and walked away.

"Carrie" Abe called out. She turned and stopped when she saw him. He walked over to her.

"What do you want?" She asked abruptly.

"Just five minutes of your time, just to explain." He asked.

"There is nothing to explain. I am well aware of the situation, now if you don't mind I have a bus to catch." She said stony faced, turned and walked away. He chased after her and grabbed her arm.

"Carrie please?" He pleaded.

Chapter 25

Peggy could hear coughing coming from Carrie's room, so she hurried to check on her. She ran over to the bed and helped Carrie to sit a little more upright. She then passed her a hanky. Carrie wiped her mouth and handed the hanky back to Peggy, as Peggy passed her a glass of water. Molly had now entered the room and stood gazing at Carrie with a pitiful look on her face.

"What would you like from the chippy?" Peggy asked as she looked at the blood-stained hanky and placed it in the pocket of her pinny. Carrie frowned and shook her head.

"I have no appetite Peggy, but will you eat yours in here?" She asked weakly. Peggy smiled a sad smile and nodded.

"You might feel hungry later. Why don't we order something that Peggy can warm in the oven for you?" Molly suggested. Carrie frowned.

"Molly, I am NOT five! And stop looking at me so pitifully, we were all aware that this was going to happen. If you don't mind, I would like to spend some time with my granddaughter." Carrie tried to raise her voice but was physically unable to do so. Molly winced then left the room. She contacted Abe to make him aware that Carrie's health was deteriorating, he said that he was on his way. Molly picked up her belongings and walked out of the cottage. She walked up the path and looked back at the pretty roses climbing up the wall. Tears stung her eyes as she climbed into her car and drove away.

Peggy walked into Carrie's room carrying a tray, with a teapot, cups, and biscuits. She placed it on the table and poured them both a cup of tea. Peggy passed Carrie's to her, her hand was trembling, forcing the tea to spill in the saucer. Carrie frowned and passed it back to Peggy.

"Where is your supper?" Carrie asked. Peggy screwed her nose up.

"I didnee really fancy anything. I am happy with a couple of biccies." She said and forced a smile.

"You need to eat child. You have only just started to gain weight, you don't want to become a waif again do you?" Carrie scowled. Peggy chuckled, she was so weak, yet still able to insult so well! Peggy thought to herself.

"Aye, anyway, was there something that you wanted to tell me?" Peggy asked as she sipped her tea.

"Yes, yes there is!" Carrie began…..

Carrie and Florence got on so well, as too did Albert, he adored her, so it was decided that Florence would stay, which was just as well, when Katarina and the others launched their never-ending assault on Carrie and Albert. Things were getting worse.

One rainy afternoon, Carrie was watching out of the window for Albert to return from school. The rain was pouring down the window, Carrie knew that Albert would be soaked to the skin, he should have taken his coat, she was thinking to herself when Florence walked into the room, breaking her chain of thought. Florence looked at the clock.

“Albert’s late isn’t he?” She said as she too looked out of the window. Carrie sighed.

“I’m sure he’s just larking about with his friends.” Carrie said unconvincingly. Florence frowned.

“Really! Should we take his coat, see if we can find him. The wee man will be soaked, will he not?” Florence said as she walked out to the hallway, then returned with Carrie’s coat and threw it at her. Carrie smiled and nodded.

They got to the small school house, it was empty. Alberts teacher walked out of the door and fastened her scarf around her head. She smiled at Carrie.

“Everything ok?” She asked.

“Albert isn’t home yet, we wondered if he was still here with his friends.” The teacher frowned and shook her head.

“His brother George collected him early, said that he had an appointment.” The teacher replied. Carrie looked at Florence and they both scowled.

“Did he? Ok well not to worry then.” Carrie smiled as her and Florence walked away from the teacher.

"SHIT! How are we ever going to find him?" Carrie shouted out. Florence put her hand on Carrie's arm.

"Let's go back to the house, maybe he is there now. If not I know a way of finding him." She replied reassuringly.

They got back to the house and Carrie's heart sunk when she realised that there was no sign of Albert anywhere.

"Right go to the kitchen and put the kettle on, I need to pop up the stairs" Florence said as she hung up her dripping wet coat.

"I'm not being funny Florence, but this isn't really the time for tea is it. THE FUCKERS HAVE MY SON!" Carrie screamed as she was becoming hysterical. Florence ran up the stairs and then returned within seconds. She grabbed Carrie's hand and pulled her into the kitchen. She pushed Carrie onto one of the kitchen chairs and sat down opposite her, placing something on the table. It was a black disc. Carrie frowned as Florence held it up towards the light.

"Please show me Albert's location." She asked loudly. She looked intently into the disc. She gasped and showed Carrie. "Have you seen this place before?" Florence asked as they both looked at the grand house being displayed in the disc. Carrie nodded frantically.

"It's a five-minute walk. I pass it every day on my way to work." Carrie said as she stood. She grabbed her wet coat and walked towards the door.

"Carrie, what are you doing? You can't go there alone." Florence shouted.

"Watch me! You need to stay here, in case it is a trap, protect the Grimoire." Carrie called out as she closed the door behind her. She ran as fast as her legs could carry her until she reached the huge wrought iron gates that protected the property. Carrie could feel the rage bubbling inside of her as she hit the gates which collapsed on impact. She marched up to the giant door and hammered on it. No reply. Again she hammered on it hoping to knock it off its hinges, but unfortunately that did not happen. She ran around the back and tried what she believed to be the back entrance into the kitchen. The door was locked. She screamed out in frustration and hit the door full force, but it did nothing.

"*Shapeshift*" she heard. The only time that she had, was when she caught Abe with a woman at his Army base. She closed her eyes, and clearly remembering Ceridwen's instructions from all those years before, the transformation took place. She flew into the sky circling the huge house. She spied an open window, the opening was just big enough for her to hop into. She landed and hopped inside. It was a beautiful bedroom, just like the one in Katarina's apartment all those years ago. Then she heard voices, so she hid behind the huge drapes. Katarina stormed into the room screaming in a fit of rage. Clara followed.

"Where is the book?" Katarina screamed into Clara's face.

"Look he got the brat didn't he? You are never happy!" Clara screamed back. Katarina turned and grabbed Clara's face in a tight grip.

"I told him to get the book. Abraham has disappeared, who knows what is being hatched against us. I MUST STOP THEM!" she screamed, and as she did electricity flowed through her fingers electrocuting Clara's face. She dropped Clara to the floor and stepped on her. "I will kill them both right now. That way, I will be absolutely sure that there is no pro-creation!" She sneered. As she left the room, Carrie quickly spun and set chase. She quietly followed Katarina down the stairs, then more stairs that led to what appeared to be a basement. All those years of living on the street had taught Carrie to be quick and nimble as a matter of survival.

Katarina stopped at a door and using a large key unlocked it then walked inside, slamming the door behind her. Carrie could hear Albert's sobs, lost all control, and took the door clean off of its hinges as she stormed into the room and roared into Katarina's face, grabbing hold of Albert as she did. She watched as electricity flowed down her slender fingers and readied herself for the pain. Instead Katarina sent the lightning to George ,who screamed out in agony, as the electricity ran through his body. Carrie screamed out and charged at Katarina, whose hair was no longer flaming red, but a dull grey colour.

Katarina flew across the room from the force of Carrie and landed in the corner. Again Carrie walked over and hit her as hard as she possibly could. She vanished into black dust.

Carrie turned, grabbed Albert's hand, and ran back the way they had come. As they approached the front door, a huge guard stepped out, blocking their way. Carrie could see lightning coming from one of the hallways. She punched the guard who landed down the hallway. As Katarina appeared, grey and lifeless, she took out a knife, cut the guards arm and began to drink the blood spilling from the wound. Carrie began to gag, then frantically tried to get out of the door. She was so frustrated, constantly hammering on the door, trying to escape. Then the lightning hit her, the pain was intense.
Darkness.......

She opened her eyes, but wherever she was, it was complete darkness. It was damp and smelly, so Carrie guessed that she was back in the basement. She attempted to move but soon realised that she was tied down. She attempted to break whatever was holding her, then realised that she was being held by iron shackles. She screamed out, all the anger, pain, and frustration. It was useless, she was alone.

A while later, she heard the sound of footsteps walking on the stone floor. The door opened and light appeared, making Carrie wince as her eyes adjusted to the light of the candle. "Oh good! You are awake now." Katarina sneered as she approached Carrie, who was shackled down to a stone slab.

"I was going to devour your sons first, but as I had quite a hearty meal earlier, I am still rather full!" She screeched. Carrie did not react. She did not make eye contact, just stared up at the ceiling, infuriating Katarina.

"So instead I thought to myself, I know what, I'll take the life force from the dirty little beggar that's shackled down in my basement. You see I was enlightened earlier. I got to thinking, if I take your lifeforce, I also take your power, thus killing two birds with one stone!" She shrieked.

"Take it. I have nothing left to live for." Carrie muttered under her breath.

"Very well!" She took out a long sharp knife and made a deep cut in Carrie's arm. As hard as it was Carrie forced herself not to flinch, she would not give her the satisfaction. Katarina placed her mouth over the wound and began to drink the blood, as she did she began to choke. She screamed out. She stood up as her hair began to fall out in clumps. Then she took to her heels and ran.

"*Your power is too pure. It burns her. Now Carrie shapeshift again and save your son*!" Carrie heard. She did as was advised and flew up and out of the door. She spun into a mouse and ran underneath the many doors which were in the basement. They were nowhere. She scurried under the final door, spun and was relieved to see Albert tied up in the corner. She ran over to him and began to pull at the rope. She felt a thud deep in her back. She quickly turned to see George, holding a large iron bar. He lifted it high, about to strike her again when she grabbed it, George still holding onto it and threw it across the room.

So enraged was she, that she grabbed the rope and ripped it apart, freeing Albert, who flung his arms around Carrie's neck. She could hear footsteps, quickly she wrapped her arms around Albert and shapeshifted, praying that it would work. It did! She flew out of the house and once a safe distance away she found a deserted alley and shifted back.

Once back at the house, Florence poured water into the big tin bath for Albert, he was covered in cuts and bruises from the beatings that George had given him, then she made Carrie a strong cup of tea. Carrie smiled as she watched Florence dry Albert's hair on the towel, once he had bathed and dressed in clean clothes. "We have to get away from here." Carrie sighed. She loved the house that Doris had left to her, but it was too close. She wanted Albert to have the freedom of every other ten-year-old boy, not be chaperoned everywhere by his mum and auntie! Albert went into the lounge to read his book, Florence looked at her and smiled.

"I have a friend in Scotland, he deals in property. Would you like me to write to him?" She asked as she grinned. Carrie smiled and nodded.

Within six months the house had been sold, Carrie, Albert and Florence began their new lives in Melrose, a small town on the border of England and Scotland. They had a beautiful cottage on a farm, and for the first time ever, Carrie felt as though she truly belonged.

As the years flew by Albert left school when he was fourteen and took a job on the farm next to the cottage. Carrie got herself a job at the local hospital and Florence was happy to stay at home.

Carrie had finished her shift, she looked out of the large hospital window and watched as the rain dropped from the sky. She walked through the big doors and once outside tied her scarf around her head. She began to walk when she heard her name being called. She quickly turned and her heart jumped when she saw Abe standing smiling at her. She walked towards him.

"What do you want?" She asked.

"Just five minutes of your time, I want to explain. He replied.

She walked away, he followed pleading with her. Again she stopped. She turned and looked at him. He was still as handsome and charming as ever, and it infuriated Carrie how he did not age!

"There is a café around the corner. One cup of tea and that's your lot!" She sighed. He grinned like a Cheshire cat as they walked around the corner. Abe spent the next fifteen minutes trying to explain to Carrie what had happened, all those years ago.

"That still doesn't excuse you, for allowing them to one, curse our son and take him, two, murder our beautiful daughter, three, make your other son and my life a living hell, and four, you pretending to love me all in the name of fate and destiny. Does it?" Carrie said as her eyes filled with tears. Abe looked down in shame. "DOES IT?" she raised her voice forcing all of the other customers to look in their direction. Abe shook his head.

"So if you don't mind, I need to leave here now. Take good care of yourself Abe." Carrie said, fighting back the tears as she pushed her chair in and left the café. She ran, sobbing as she did. She couldn't get the bus, so she continued to run. By the time she reached the cottage she was completely breathless, soaked, heartbroken and exhausted.

She walked in through the back door and jumped when she saw Abe sitting at the kitchen table drinking a cup of tea that Florence had made him. She hung up her dripping coat and threw Florence a look as she passed her a steaming cup of tea.

"Well, I have jobs to be getting on with, so I'll leave you two to catch up!" Florence said and winked as she closed the kitchen door.

Abe tapped the chair beside him, beckoning Carrie to sit. Her feet were killing her, and she had no energy to fight so she caved and sat down.

"All those things that you said were true, except one. The moment that I laid eyes on you, I knew that I would become emotionally attached. That affair I had at the base was me trying to distance myself from you, I had been told not to fall in love with you, that we would have to separate once the children were born, that you would not agree to join the guardianship, therefore, you would age normally, I would not. I was told all of that, but Carrie the simple truth is, I have always loved you." He said as tears ran down his cheeks. She placed her hand on his cheek, as much as her head was telling her that it was all lies and that he just needed someone at that moment, her heart was telling her that every word was true, that he did love her, she always knew that he did!

The kitchen door opened, and a very dirty Albert walked in. He took one look at Abe and turned around. Carrie jumped up and grabbed his arm.

"He just wants to explain." Carrie said gently. Albert's face filled with rage. He turned around, looked at Carrie then at Abe.

"Ok then explain this. Why did you hook up with that evil tart? Why did you allow them to kill my little sister? Why did you allow them to curse my brother? AND WHY DID YOU ALLOW THEM TO MAKE MY MUMS AMD MY LIFE A FUCKING MISERY?" He screamed in Abe's face. Carrie grabbed his arm.

"Albert, calm down, please" Carrie begged. He pulled away from her.

"No mum, he can't just waltz in here like nothing has happened and expect to be forgiven!" He yelled and stormed out of the cottage.

Chapter 26

Peggy heard the back door close and looked at Carrie, who was overcome with emotion and exhaustion. "I think that you should rest now. You look exhausted." Peggy said quietly. Carrie grimaced from the pain as she attempted to push herself up.

"Nonsense! If I sleep, I fear I will not wake. There is still so much to tell. Peggy you must hear me out tonight." Carrie said, her voice croaky from all the speaking that she had already done. Peggy sighed, smiled, and nodded.

"Well I don't know about you, but I could do with a coffee. Would you like one?" Peggy asked. Carrie frowned.

"I would love one, but I'm not sure if I can hold it still enough to drink it." Carrie replied sadly.

"Well we could give it a try eh." Peggy said as she picked up the tea tray. "I won't be long!" She added as she walked out of the door. She walked into the kitchen and jumped when she saw William and Abe sitting at the kitchen table.

"What are you two doing here at this time of night?" Peggy asked as she filled the kettle. Abe looked at Peggy as tears filled his eyes, William sighed.

"We came because we heard." William whispered.

"From whom?" Peggy asked.

"Molly" Abe replied. Peggy nodded. "How is she doing?" He added.

"Why don't you go and see for yourself." Peggy suggested. Abe inhaled deeply, stood up and walked towards Carrie's room. He was taken aback when he saw her, it took all of his strength not to react.

"Hello beautiful." He said quietly as he sat in the chair beside her bed, grabbing hold of her cold hand. She turned and smiled, the sweetest smile.

"Hello handsome. What are you doing here?" She asked.

"Well a little birdie told me that there was this incredibly beautiful woman in this area, who might want to spend a little time with me. I don't suppose you have heard of her have you?" Abe said and winked. Carrie chuckled and tapped his hand. There was a tap on the door. William poked his head around. "Hello, I was in the area, so I thought that I would come and say hello." William said awkwardly. Carrie and Abe looked at one another and laughed. Abe stood up, kissed Carrie on the head and walked towards the door.

"I'll be back when you have finished chatting to Peggy." He said and left. He walked along the hallway and began to sob. From the very first day that he met her, the dread began for this time, which was now closer than he had ever imagined, and the pain was intense!

Peggy walked along and put her arm around him. He put his arms around her, burying his face in her shoulder and sobbed uncontrollably.

"So sweet William, I am glad that you randomly decided to pop in, there are things that I have been meaning to say." Carrie said as William sat on the chair. William blushed and smiled. "Firstly I want to thank you. Thank you for taking good care of my Peggy, she is very precious you know." Carrie began. William smiled as he thought about Peggy.

"Sure you never have to thank me for that, I love that Lassie with all of my heart." He said. Carrie smiled and nodded.

"I want you to promise me that you will help her find her brother Robert and watch over them all." She continued. Again William smiled.

"Aye of course I will." He replied. Carrie sighed and nodded.

"Well all I have left to say sweet William is…. That I couldn't be happier that Peggy met such an adorable hard-working chap, and in the short time that I have known you, you have made such a difference to a dying woman's final days. Thank you sweet William!" Carrie said as tears formed in her eyes. William wiped his own tears away.

"I would just like to say that it has been a great honour to spend time with such an interesting, amazing woman, and I hope that me and Peggy always make you proud!" He said as he wept. He stood, took Carrie's hand, kissed it, and left the room, sobbing as he walked up the hallway. Peggy grabbed hold of him and held him tight. Then she sighed, picked up the tray of coffees and walked to Carrie's room.

Peggy held the cup to Carrie's lips, and she took a long sip. "Mmm, lovely!" She said smiling. "Now then, where was I?" She continued.

"Albert had just left the house." Peggy said. Carrie nodded.

"Yes, your father had just left the house." Carrie said as she slipped into deep thought.

Carrie ran after Albert, she caught him up and grabbed his arm. "Albert please, just give him a few minutes." Carrie pleaded.

"Mum, I know how much you love him, but I cannot forgive him for what he has allowed to happen to all of us, especially you. We made a pact remember, I can't sit by and watch him hurt you again Mum, I just can't!" He replied.

"I'll tell him to leave. I'll go back now and tell him to sling his hook." Carrie said frantically.

"No Mum, there is no need. I was going to tell you today, I am moving into the farmhouse with Tilly, we plan to get married." He replied. Carrie gasped. She was aware that he was dating Tilly, and Carrie really liked the girl, but she didn't realise how serious they actually were! "Now go back inside, you are soaking wet and will catch a death." He said, kissed her on the cheek and ran in the direction of the farmhouse.

Carrie walked back to the cottage, tears running down her face. she opened the door, stepped inside, and sobbed. Abe caught her and put his arms around her.

Carrie had changed out of her wet clothes, Florence had lit the fires, so Carrie sat in front of the roaring fire, trying to warm up.

"I've done it again haven't I?" Abe sighed. Carrie looked up from the flames of the fire.

"What do you mean?" She asked.

"I have walked back into your life and again messed everything up for you." He said angrily. Carrie grinned.

"I would love to blame you, to scream and shout at you, tell you that it's all your fault, but that would be wrong. He was going to tell me today that he was moving into the farmhouse, he, and Tilly plan to be married." Carrie said and looked back into the flames.

"Surely he can't be old enough" Abe said. Carrie chuckled.

"Abe he is seventeen!" She replied. Abe hung his head in shame, he couldn't even remember the age of his own son!

A little later the back door closed. Albert opened the door and popped his head around. "I am just going to pack my things." He said and smiled at Carrie. She stood up and walked to the door.

"So soon, I thought that you would wait until you were married?" She asked sadly.

"Mr D offered me the spare room, makes it easier for work, you know milking and that." He replied, touched Carrie's face, and ran up the stairs. Carrie walked back into the lounge.

"Is he not having supper then?" Florence asked. Carrie shook her head.

"No, I don't think that he is." She sighed.

"That means that Abe can join us then!" Florence exclaimed as she walked into the kitchen, whistling as she did.

"You are very alike." Abe said as he chuckled. Carrie nodded. "I like her, she's lovely!" he added. Carrie scowled at him.

"Like… how much do you like her?" Carrie asked suspiciously. Abe burst out laughing.

"Not like that!" He said through the laughter, grabbed Carrie's hand and held it to his face.

"Sorry to interrupt, but I'm going now." Albert said.

Carrie jumped up and followed him to the door. "Do you need a hand, you seem to be struggling?" She said as she tried to take things from him.

"Mum! Don't fuss!" he replied as he pulled things from her, the back door opened, and Tilly walked in. "Tilly is going to help me!" he said as his face reddened with embarrassment.

As they were eating the delicious meal that Florence had cooked, she looked up from her plate and looked at Abe, who was looking at Carrie, who was looking at her food!

"Where are you staying then Abe?" Florence asked. Abe looked at his watch.

"That's a point, I had better get going, I haven't booked anywhere to stay." He said as she reluctantly pushed the plateful of delicious food away.

"Sure he could stay here tonight couldn't he Carrie, now that we have a spare room." Florence said and looked at Carrie. She looked up from her food and scowled at Florence. "Well?" Florence said waiting for Carrie's response. Carrie sighed.

"I suppose so." She sighed.

"That's very kind, I don't want to cause any bother though." Abe said and smiled. Carrie laughed out loud.

"Well that would be a first!" She laughed.

The following morning, Carrie opened her curtains to bright beautiful sunshine. She smiled, it was her day off and for once the sun was shining! She walked down the stairs with a spring in her step, into a bad atmosphere in the kitchen. Abe and Albert were in there alone.

"I am warning you, nothing bad better happen to her, because I'm telling you if it does I will finish you!" Albert sneered, nose to nose with Abe.

"Ahem!" Carrie said loudly as she walked into the room. Albert stepped back.

"Alright Mum, I just popped in to tell you that me and Tilly are getting wed next Thursday." Albert beamed. Carrie frowned.

"So soon! Why so soon?" She asked. Albert grabbed some toast from the plate and took a mouthful as he shrugged.

"Why not?" he said and walked back out of the kitchen door. She looked at Abe and shook her head.

"Kids these days. They are always in such a hurry aren't they!" She sighed. Abe chuckled.

"Carrie, there is something that we need to discuss. Well I need your advice really." Abe said awkwardly. Carrie raised her eyebrow.

"Go on" She replied reluctantly.

"It concerns George." Abe said and winced.

"If you have come here to try and convince me to forgive him, you can forget it Abe, me and that boy were finished a long time ago!" Carrie fumed. Just hearing his name, sent her into a tangent!

"No, no, nothing like that. He is married to a lovely Yorkshire lass called Alice. They have a daughter." Abe began.

"Right, what's that got to do with me?" Carrie asked.

"Well as you can imagine, he is not very nice to either of them, in fact Michael is concerned that he is going to kill them, on Katarina's orders." Abe sighed.

"Again Abe, what has all this got to do with me?"

"She needs a safe place, and I wondered if you could suggest anywhere?" He said squirming as he waited for Carrie's reaction.

"Well sure she could come here. She is the mother of your granddaughter isn't she." Florence said as she put the empty washing basket on the table. Carrie looked at her in disbelief.

"Are you winding me up Florence. We moved here for a peaceful life, not to invite the fuckers up here!" Carrie scowled. Florence laughed.

"Well they haven't found us yet have they?" She replied. Carrie looked straight at Abe then looked at Florence.

"He did!" She replied.

"Ah, but it was Merlin, who showed me where to look." Abe said and smiled.

"No, no, no. they are not staying here! Absolutely not!" Carrie said adamantly.

"But surely you haven't forgotten, how people took you in, when you had no place to go and no-one to look out for you!" Florence said, pricking Carrie's conscience. "If we don't do something, he will kill them both, that's what you said isn't it Abe?" Florence continued. Abe nodded. Carrie thought about it for a few minutes.

"They can stay for a while, until you can find them something more permanent. Why can't they stay at one of the lodges?" Carrie asked. Abe shook his head.

"They are full." He replied. Carrie scoffed.

"What all of them? Has there been an invasion or something?" She laughed. Abe frowned and shook his head.

"No not yet, it won't be long though." He replied. Carrie looked at Abe in bewilderment, she didn't have a clue what he was talking about. There was a tap on the back door.

"Look, bring them here." She turned and said to Abe as she answered the back door. Tilly was standing there. "Hello Tilly, come in." Carrie said cheerfully. Tilly followed her into the kitchen. "Cup of tea?" Carrie asked as she poured the boiling water into the teapot. Tilly smiled and nodded.

Carrie sat at the table with Tilly, Abe had gone to make the arrangements to move Alice and her little girl, and Florence had gone to the shop.

"I have something I need to tell you." Tilly said shyly. Carrie smiled and gestured for her to continue. "The reason that Albie and I are getting married so quickly is because…. I am pregnant." She said and looked down at the floor. "I'm sorry." She said as she began to cry. Carrie put her arms around her.

"Are you happy, you know with the wedding and the baby?" Carrie asked.

"Aye, I adore Albie." She sniffed.

"Well, there is no need to be sorry is there. So long as you are both happy, nothing else matters, does it?" Carrie said and handed her a hanky.

"Thank you." Tilly replied as she wiped her eyes.

"Now then, let me place my hands on your tummy, see if there is anything to tell yet." Carrie said excitedly. She placed her hands over Tilly's abdomen and as she did a clothes peg flew out of the basket and landed on the table. Carrie looked at Tilly and smiled.

"It's a baby girl!" Carrie beamed. Tilly wore the biggest smile.

"Well in that case, I will call her Peggy!" She said and they both howled with laughter.

Later that evening Abe returned with two very weary looking guests. The little girl was about four and hid behind her mother's legs. Alice was so thin, her face was covered in bruises, and she looked absolutely terrified. Carrie got up from the sofa and walked over to them. She placed her hand on Alice's cheek, as she did Alice flinched.

"Did he do this to you?" Carrie asked. Alice nodded nervously.

"Bastard!" Carrie said, making both Alice and her little girl jump. "Sorry" Carrie whispered. She knelt down and looked at the frightened child.

"And what's your name?" Carrie whispered.

"Iris" The tiny voice replied. Carrie smiled.

"That's a beautiful name!" Carrie said and touched the tiny girl's face. Florence walked into the lounge carrying a tray full of biscuits and cakes. "Are you hungry Iris?" Carrie asked. The little girl nodded frantically. "Help yourself, have as much as you want." She continued. Iris looked at her mother for approval. Alice smiled and nodded, and she grabbed the biggest slice of cake!

It was the day of Albert's wedding, and he had stayed at the cottage the night before. He was a bag of nerves. The cottage was busy, with everyone getting ready. Carrie helped Alice to get Iris ready then she went up the stairs to get herself ready. Abe was sitting on the bed.

"About last night…" he began to say. Carrie walked over to him and put her finger over his lips.

"We don't have to do this, not today. What happened, happened and that's all it is." She said and smiled. Abe smiled.

The wedding was a very small do, with a small group of local farmers in attendance, after the church ceremony they went back to the farm for a garden party. Albert and Tilly looked so happy! Everyone had eaten, all the toasts had been said and now they were dancing to the music that a local band were playing. Florence was in her element. She was dancing with Tilly, Alice, and Iris, while Carrie and Abe were talking to Tilly's parents, Mr, and Mrs D.

It was such a beautifully warm, sunny day, until suddenly a dark ominous cloud appeared. It seemed to hover over the garden. Carrie looked up as she felt the cold air surround her. Then the screaming began. Carrie and Abe looked in horror as George had hold of Iris. He was yielding a knife. Florence took a run at him, forcing him to drop the little girl, but then he lunged at Florence with the knife, stabbing her in the chest. She dropped to the ground, Carrie screamed and ran over to her. She was not breathing. The farmers then surrounded George as he lunged at them all with the knife.

Out of nowhere, Albert leapt through the air, landing on top of his brother. The knife flew out of George's hand and Albert began to beat him. All those years that he had been bullied and tormented by him had now come to the surface and Albert could not stop himself.

As George lay motionless on the ground, Mr D grabbed Albert and led him inside.

Abe had called for help and now guardians surrounded the farm. They took George's body, and also took Alice and Iris to another location. Abe walked over to Carrie who was sitting beside her beloved Florence. She was still, lifeless and no breath was coming from her. Abe placed his hand on Carrie's shoulder as she wept. The guardians took Florence's body.

Chapter 27

Carrie slowly walked towards the farmhouse. She walked in through the kitchen to find Albert trembling. He was obviously in shock. She knelt in front of him and held his hands. "You did what you had to do Albert." She said. He began to sob. He wiped his face on his sleeve and held Carrie's hand tight.

"Tomorrow, Tilly, and I are going Mum. I can't tell you where. I don't want my family to have to go through this shit, this is where we say goodbye Mum, because it doesn't matter how hard you try to avoid it, trouble always finds you. I love you with all my heart and I can't thank you enough for always trying to keep me safe, but now my family has to come first." He sobbed. Carrie placed her hand on his cheek and nodded.

"Yes it does son. Promise me that you will be happy. Take good care of yourself, Tilly and young Peggy. I love you son." She said as she ran out of the farmhouse, her heart once again shattered.

A few days later Carrie was looking out of the cottage window. "I must leave. Germany has just invaded Belgium and I have been called to base." Abe said from behind her. She nodded her head, turned, and smiled.

"Stay safe Abe. Enjoy your long life and be happy." Carrie said as she got up to answer the door that was now banging. Mr D was standing at the back door. "Dreadful thing that." He said awkwardly. Carrie nodded. "I hope you don't mind but Sally our prize Collie has just had a litter of pups. Mrs D thought that you might like one, you know to keep you company." He continued. A small black and white fluffball appeared from behind Mr D's legs and looked at Carrie, he was adorable. Carrie bent down and the puppy ran to her. She scooped him up into her arms and grinned at Mr D.

"Thank you so much!" She beamed as the dog licked her face.

"Our pleasure!" Mr D replied as he walked away. She walked into the lounge. It was empty, in fact the entire cottage was empty, except for a note that Abe had left on the mantlepiece.

"Could you fetch me the chest?" Carrie asked Peggy. Peggy nodded and did as she asked. "Look inside. There should be three envelopes. One is for you, one is for Michael, and one is for Abe." Carrie said gasping for breath. Peggy hurriedly looked and found all three. She handed them to Carrie. Carrie handed Peggy hers. "Open it" Carrie barely whispered. Peggy opened the envelope her hands trembling, she knew that it was close. She took out photos and some paperwork.

"The photos are of you and Robert. Tilly used to send them to me." Carrie smiled. Peggy was a mess as the tears poured down her face. The paperwork that was inside were the deeds to the cottage that

Carrie had changed from hers to Peggy's name. "Enjoy this cottage, enjoy your life with sweet William. Promise me that you will find Robert. His third child will be the one who needs to be guided, and it will be a daughter. Take good care of them Peggy and make sure that Robert has the chest. I am so proud of you and cannot thank you enough for making my final days the happiest days. Could you fetch Abe for me?" She asked. Peggy nodded as she wept and left the room.

Abe walked in and before Carrie had even spoken a single word the tears were flowing. He sat down and grabbed her hand. She passed him the envelope. He looked at her with a puzzled expression, then opened it. It was the letter he had written the day he left for war.

"I never read it. Will you read it to me?" She asked.

'Carrie, I want you to know that I love you deeply. It pains me as we will never have the opportunity for our lives to be beautiful together as they should be. I fell in love with you the moment I first laid eyes on you and that has never changed. I feel responsible for a lot of the pain and suffering that you have had to go through and for that I am truly sorry. You are the most wonderful person that I have ever had the pleasure to meet, and you deserve so much more, than the cards that you have been dealt.

I cannot wait to meet our great granddaughter, to tell her what a wonderful person you are, and to assist her in her quest to ensure that everything that you have had to sacrifice has not been in vain. I love you Carrie, more than words can say.

Yours forever

Abe.'

He was now weeping as Carrie's life force was leaving her body. "In answer to your question Carrie. Yes I love you. In fact a part of me will always love you." He sobbed. She took her final breath……..

She was in the meadow, there were people in the distance. She could see Abagail, she knew that she had crossed realms. As she stood in front of Abagail, Polly stood out, she jumped up at Carrie throwing her arms around her. She heard a dog bark and she cried as she saw Merlin, her beloved Collie running towards her. She felt a hand on her shoulder. She turned and gasped as Albert placed his arms around her and held her so tight. She sighed deeply…. She was home….

ABOUT THE AUTHOR

Louise lives in Devon with her husband and five children. When they are not teaching, they love nothing more than walking the moors and coastal paths. They love to explore this beautiful country, always searching for inspiration!

Printed in Great Britain
by Amazon

37899405R00175